CLASSIC
MONSTER
NOVELS
CONDENSED

Books by Joseph Lanzara

Classic Monster Novels Condensed
Frankenstein, Dracula, The Invisible Man

Dante's Inferno: The Graphic Novel

William Shakespeare's Romeo and Juliet Uncensored

John Milton's Paradise Lost In Plain English
A Simple, Line by Line, Paraphrase
of the Complicated Masterpiece

Paradise Lost: The Novel
Based Upon the Epic Poem by John Milton

CLASSIC MONSTER NOVELS CONDENSED

Mary Shelley's
FRANKENSTEIN

Bram Stoker's
DRACULA

H. G. Wells'
THE INVISIBLE MAN

Joseph Lanzara

Published by New Arts Library
P.O. Box 319, Belleville, New Jersey 07109

Printed in the United States of America.

Publisher's Cataloging-In-Publication Data

Lanzara, Joseph.
  Classic monster novels condensed / Joseph Lanzara.

  p. ; cm.

  Three classic (public domain) horror novels - Frankenstein, Dracula, and
The Invisible Man - are condensed into the form of novellas. Using the
original author's words as much as possible, carefully edited, a simplified
narrative has been constructed, preserving all the major plot elements and
important characters.--Provided by publisher.
  Contents: Mary Shelley's Frankenstein -- Bram Stoker's Dracula -- H. G.
Wells' The invisible man.
  ISBN: 978-1-4791-9322-6 (pbk.)

  1. Monsters--Fiction. 2. Frankenstein, Victor (Fictitious character)--
Fiction. 3. Frankenstein's monster (Fictitious character)--Fiction. 4.
Dracula, Count (Fictitious character)--Fiction. 5. Horror fiction. I.
Shelley, Mary Wollstonecraft, 1797-1851. Frankenstein II. Stoker, Bram,
1847-1912. Dracula   III. Wells, H. G. (Herbert George), 1866-1946.
Invisible man IV. Title.

PS3562.A578 C53 2012
813/.54   2012948530

CONTENTS

PREFACE

Somewhere among the 75,000 words or so that make up Mary Shelley's famous novel, Dr. Frankenstein decides he needs a break from his monster-making activities. So he and his best friend go on vacation. And we are treated to a 4,000-word travelogue through Western Europe. *Frankenstein*, it should be noted, was originally intended to be a short story, and there are those who believe Shelley should have stuck to her original plan. The first in this collection of condensed classics is based upon that notion.

Over a hundred years ago three lengthy novels introduced to the world three of the best-loved monsters of all time. You may get around to reading all of them one day. Meanwhile, for fans of immediate gratification, we offer these expertly abridged versions of all three, in one convenient package.

There are plenty of chills in our second entry, *Dracula* by Bram Stoker. But in its original format you'd have to hunt for them among a massive collection of letters, diaries, news articles and other documents that make up his 160,000-word novel. An extensive streamlining operation produced the simple third person narrative that is available here.

Rounding out the trio, and edited down to half its original length, *The Invisible Man* by H.G. Wells cuts to the chase, moving swiftly from its intitial comic tone to the harrowing unexpected consequences of invisibility.

A century after these classic monsters first appeared in print, authors and filmmakers continue to draw inspiration from them. You'll understand why in the exciting tales that follow.

FRANKENSTEIN

Adapted from the novel by
MARY SHELLEY

1.

Is it curiosity that leads you to hear my strange and harrowing narrative? Perhaps you seek knowledge and wisdom, as I once did. Then I ardently hope that the gratification of your wishes may not be a serpent to sting you, as mine has been. For I have suffered great and unparalleled misfortunes. I had determined, at one time, that the memory of these evils should die with me—that I could not endure to renew the grief a recital of these misfortunes would bring. But it is useless, my fate is nearly fulfilled. I wait but for one event, and then I shall repose in peace. Nothing can alter my destiny. Listen to my history, and you will see how irrevocably it is determined. I might fear to encounter your unbelief, perhaps your ridicule. I do not know that the relation of my disasters will be useful to you. I hope that you may deduce an apt moral from my tale, one that may direct you if you succeed in your undertaking, whatever it may be, and console you in case of failure.

I feel exquisite pleasure in dwelling on the recollections of childhood, before misfortune had tainted my mind and changed its bright visions into gloomy and narrow reflections. But, in drawing the picture of my early days, I must not omit those events which led, by insensible steps, to my after tale of misery. When I recount to myself the birth of that passion which afterwards ruled my destiny, I recall how it arose like a mountain river, from ignoble and almost forgotten sources, and swelling as it proceeded, became the torrent which swept away all my hopes and joys.

I am by birth a Genevese. My family is one of the most distinguished of that republic. No human being could have passed a happier childhood than myself. My parents were possessed by the very spirit of kindness and indulgence. My brother Ernest, my junior by six years, was of gentle disposition. And the youngest of our family, William, was the most beautiful little fellow in the world, with lively blue eyes, dimpled cheeks and endearing manners. When I mingled with other families, I distinctly discerned how peculiarly fortunate my lot was.

As a child my temper was sometimes violent, and my passions vehement, but by some law in my nature they were turned, not towards childish pursuits, but to an eager desire to learn, and not to learn all things indiscriminately. I confess that neither the structure of languages, nor the code of governments, nor the politics of various states, possessed attractions for me. It was the secrets of heaven and earth that I desired to learn. Whether it was the outward substance of things, or the inner spirit of nature and the mysterious soul of man that occupied me, my inquiries were directed to the metaphysical, or, in its highest sense, the physical secrets of the world.

When I was thirteen years of age, our parents took my brother, Ernest, my cousin Elizabeth Lavenza, and myself on a party of pleasure to the baths near Thonon. While we were there, two incidents combined to determine my destiny.

We witnessed a most violent thunderstorm. It advanced from behind the mountains of Jura and the thunder burst at once with frightful loudness from various quarters of the heavens. I watched its progress with curiosity and delight. As I stood at the door, on a sudden I beheld a stream of fire issue from an old and beautiful oak which stood about twenty yards from our house, and so soon as the dazzling light vanished the oak had disappeared. When we visited it the next morning we found the tree entirely reduced to thin ribands of wood. I never beheld anything so utterly destroyed.

The inclemency of the weather obliged us to remain a day confined to the inn. In this house I chanced to find a volume of the works of Cornelius Agrippa. I opened it with apathy. The scientific theory which he attempts to demonstrate and the wonderful facts which he relates soon changed this feeling into enthusiasm. A new light seemed to dawn upon my mind, and bounding with joy I communicated my discovery to my father. My father looked carelessly at the title page of my book and said, "Ah! Cornelius Agrippa! My dear Victor, do not waste your time upon this. It is sad trash."

If, instead of this remark, my father had taken the pains to explain to me that the principles of Agrippa had been entirely exploded, and that a modern system of science had been introduced which was real and practical, under such circumstances, I should certainly have thrown Agrippa aside and have contented my imagination, warmed as it was, by returning to my former studies. It is even possible that the train of my ideas would never have received the fatal impulse that led to my ruin. But the cursory glance my father had taken of my volume by no means assured me that he was acquainted with its contents, and I continued to read the ancient philosophy with the greatest avidity.

When I returned home my first care was to procure the whole works of this author, and afterwards of Paracelsus and Albertus Magnus. I read and studied the wild fancies of these writers with delight. They appeared to me treasures known to few beside myself. I took the word of these men for all that they asserted and I became their disciple. While I followed the routine of education in the schools of Geneva, I was to a great degree self taught under the guidance of my new preceptors. I entered with the greatest diligence into the search of the philosopher's stone and the elixir of life. But the latter soon obtained my undivided attention. What glory would attend the discovery if I could banish disease from the human frame and render man invulnerable to any but a violent death!

If my experiments were unsuccessful, I attributed the failure rather to my own inexperience than to a want of skill or fidelity in my instructors. And thus for a time I was occupied by exploded systems, mingling a thousand contradictory theories and floundering desperately in a very slough of multifarious knowledge, guided by an ardent imagination and childish reasoning.

When I had attained the age of seventeen, my parents resolved that I should become a student at the university of Ingolstadt. I had hitherto attended the schools of Geneva, but my father thought it necessary that I should be made acquainted with other customs than those of my native country. My departure was therefore fixed at an early date, but before the day resolved upon could arrive, the first misfortune of my life occurred—an omen, as it were, of my future misery.

My cousin Elizabeth Lavenza had caught the scarlet fever. Her illness was severe and she was in the greatest danger. Everyone loved Elizabeth. We had been brought up together. There was not quite a year difference in our ages. Though several times removed by blood, we called each other familiarly by the name of cousin. No word, no expression can describe the kind of relation in which she stood to me—my more than sister. Harmony was the soul of our companionship and the diversity and contrast that subsisted in our characters only drew us nearer together.

During her illness, many arguments had been urged, in vain, to persuade my mother to refrain from attending the sick bed. With disregard for our entreaties, her watchful attentions triumphed over the malignity and Elizabeth was saved—but the consequences were fatal to her savior. On her death-bed the fortitude and benignity of this best of women did not desert her. She joined the hands of Elizabeth and myself: "My children," she said, "my firmest hopes of future happiness are placed on the prospect of your union."

I was new to sorrow, but it did not the less alarm me. I was unwilling to quit the sight of those that remained to me. Above all I desired to see my sweet Elizabeth consoled. She veiled her grief and strove to act the comforter to us all. She devoted herself to those whom she had been taught to call her uncle and cousins. Never was she so enchanting as at this time when she summoned the sunshine of her smiles in her endeavors to make us forget.

The day of my departure for Ingolstadt, which had been deferred by these events, at length arrived. Henry Clerval, my dearest friend, spent the last evening with us. We sat late. We could not tear ourselves away from each other, nor persuade ourselves to say the word "Farewell!" We retired under the pretence of seeking repose. When at morning's dawn I descended to the carriage which was to convey me away, they were all there—my father again to bless me, Clerval to press my hand once more, and my Elizabeth to renew her entreaties to her playmate and friend that I would write often. I threw myself into the chaise that was to convey me away and indulged in the most melancholy reflections. I loved my brothers, Elizabeth, and Clerval. These were old familiar faces, but I believed myself totally unfitted for the company of strangers.

My journey to Ingolstadt was long and fatiguing. At length the high white steeple of the town met my eyes. I alighted, and was conducted to my solitary apartment, to spend the evening as I pleased.

The next morning I delivered my letters of introduction and paid a visit to some of the principal professors. Chance led me first to M. Krempe, professor of natural philosophy. He was an uncouth man, but deeply imbued in the secrets of his science. He wrote down a list of several books which he desired me to procure, and dismissed me, after mentioning that in the beginning of the following week he intended to commence a course of lectures upon natural philosophy in its general relations, and that on alternate days fellow-professor M. Waldman would lecture upon chemistry.

M. Krempe was a little squat man with a gruff voice and a repulsive countenance. The teacher, therefore, did not prepossess me in favor of his pursuits. I could not consent to go and hear that little conceited fellow deliver sentences out of a pulpit. But as the ensuing week commenced, I recollected what he had said of M. Waldman, whom I had never seen, as he had hitherto been out of town.

Partly from curiosity and partly from idleness I went into the lecturing room, which M. Waldman entered shortly after. This professor was very unlike his colleague. He appeared about fifty years of age, but with an aspect expressive of the greatest benevolence. A few grey hairs covered his temples. His person was short but remarkably erect, and his voice the sweetest I had ever heard. He began his lecture by a recapitulation of the history of chemistry and the various improvements made by different men of learning, pronouncing with fervor the names of the most distinguished discoverers. He then took a cursory view of the present state of the science and explained many of its elementary terms. He concluded by provoking an appreciation of modern chemistry in terms I shall never forget:

"The ancient teachers of this science," said he, "promised impossibilities, and performed nothing. The modern masters promise very little. They know that metals cannot be transmuted and that the elixir of life is a fantasy. But these philosophers whose hands seem only made to dabble in dirt and their eyes to pore over the microscope or crucible, have indeed performed miracles. They penetrate into the recesses of nature and show how she works in her hiding places. They ascend into the heavens. They have discovered how the blood circulates and the nature of the air we breathe. They have acquired new and almost unlimited powers. They can command the thunders of heaven, mimic the earthquake, and even mock the invisible world with its own shadows."

Such were the professor's words—rather let me say such the words of fate, enounced to destroy me. As he went on I felt as if my soul were grappling with a palpable enemy. One by one the various keys were touched which formed the mechanism of my being. Chord after chord was sounded, and soon my mind was filled with one thought, one conception, one purpose. So much has been done, exclaimed the soul of Victor Frankenstein—more, far more, will I achieve. Treading in the steps already marked, I will pioneer a new way, explore unknown powers, and unfold to the world the deepest mysteries of creation.

From this day natural philosophy, and particularly chemistry, in the most comprehensive sense of the term, became nearly my sole occupation. I read with ardor those works so full of genius and discrimination which modern inquirers have written on these subjects. I attended the lectures and cultivated the acquaintance of the men of science of the university, and I found even in M. Krempe a great deal of sound sense and real information.

My progress was rapid. My zeal was indeed the wonder of the students and my proficiency that of the masters. Two years passed in this manner during which I paid no visit to Geneva, but was engaged heart and soul in the pursuit of some discoveries which I hoped to make. None but those who have experienced them can conceive of the enticements of science. In other studies you go as far as others have gone before you and there is nothing more to know, but in a scientific pursuit there is continual food for discovery and wonder.

One of the phenomena which had peculiarly attracted my attention was the structure of the human frame, and indeed any animal endued with life. From where, I often asked myself, did the principle of life proceed? I determined thenceforth to apply myself more particularly to those branches of natural philosophy which relate to physiology. To examine the causes of life, we must first have recourse to death. I became acquainted with the science of anatomy, but this was not sufficient. I must also observe the natural decay and corruption of the human body. In my education my father had taken the greatest precautions that my mind should be impressed with no supernatural horrors. I do not ever remember to have trembled at a tale of superstition, or to have feared the apparition of a spirit. Darkness had no effect upon my fancy, and a churchyard was to me merely the receptacle of bodies deprived of life. Now I was led to examine the cause and progress of this decay, and forced to spend days and nights in vaults and charnel houses. My attention was fixed upon every object that was the most offensive to the delicacy of the human feelings. I saw how the fine form of man was degraded and wasted. I beheld the corruption of death consume the blooming cheek of life. I saw how the worm inherited the wonders of the eye and brain. I paused, examining and analyzing all the minutia of causation as exemplified in the change from life to death and death to life, until from the midst of this darkness a sudden light broke in upon me—a light so brilliant and wondrous, yet so simple, that while I became dizzy with the immensity of the prospect which it illustrated, I was surprised that among so many men of genius who had directed their inquiries towards the same science, I alone should discover so astonishing a secret.

Though may it appear so, I am not recording the vision of a madman. The sun does not more certainly shine in the heavens than that which I now affirm is true. Some miracle might have produced it, yet the stages of the discovery were distinct and probable. After days and nights of incredible labor and fatigue I succeeded in discovering the cause of generation and life—nay, more, I became myself capable of bestowing animation upon lifeless matter.

The astonishment which I had at first experienced on this discovery soon gave place to delight and rapture. After so much time spent in painful labor, to arrive at once at the summit of my desires was the most gratifying consummation of my toils. What had been the study and desires of the wisest men since the creation of the world was now within my grasp.

I see by your eagerness, and the wonder and hope which your eyes express, my friend, that you expect to be informed of the secret with which I am acquainted. That cannot be. Listen patiently until the end of my story and you will easily perceive why I am reserved upon that subject. I will not lead you on, unguarded and ardent as I then was, to your destruction and infallible misery. Learn from me, if not by my precepts, at least by my example, how dangerous is the acquirement of knowledge, and how much happier that man is who believes his native town to be the world, than he who aspires to become greater than his nature will allow.

When I found so astonishing a power placed within my hands I hesitated a long time concerning the manner in which I should employ it. Although I possessed the capacity of bestowing animation, yet to prepare a frame for the reception of it, with all its intricacies of fibers, muscles, and veins, still remained a work of inconceivable difficulty and labor. I doubted at first whether I should attempt the creation of a being like myself, or one of simpler organization, but my imagination was too much exalted by my first success to permit me to doubt of my ability to give life to an animal as complex and wonderful as man.

It was with these feelings that I began the creation of a human being. As the minuteness of the parts formed a great hindrance to my speed, I resolved, contrary to my first intention, to make the being of a gigantic stature, that is to say, about eight feet in height and proportionably large. After having formed this determination and having spent some months in successfully collecting and arranging my materials, I began.

No one can conceive the variety of feelings which bore me onwards in the first enthusiasm of success. Life and death appeared to me infinite bounds which I should break through and pour a torrent of light into our dark world. A new species would bless me as its creator and source. Many happy and excellent natures would owe their being to me. No father could claim the gratitude of his child so completely as I should deserve theirs. Pursuing these reflections, I thought that if I could bestow animation upon lifeless matter, I might in process of time renew life where death had apparently devoted the body to corruption.

These thoughts supported my spirits. But while I pursued my undertaking with unremitting ardor, my cheek grew pale with study and my person became emaciated with confinement. Sometimes, on the very brink of certainty, I failed, yet still I clung to the hope which the next day or the next hour might realize. The moon gazed on my midnight labors while with breathless eagerness I pursued nature to her hiding places. Who shall conceive the horrors of my secret toil as I dabbled among the unhallowed damps of the grave or tortured the living animal to animate the lifeless clay? My limbs now tremble and my eyes swim with the remembrance, but then a resistless, almost frantic impulse urged me forward. I seemed to have lost all soul or sensation but for this one pursuit. I collected bones from charnel houses, and disturbed with profane fingers the tremendous secrets of the human frame. In a solitary chamber, or rather cell, at the top of the house and separated from all the other apartments by a gallery and staircase I kept my workshop of filthy creation. My eyeballs were starting from their sockets in attending to the details of my employment. The dissecting room and the slaughterhouse furnished many of my materials and often did my human nature turn with loathing from my occupation.

My father would not have been unjust to reproach my silence in his letters, but he only made note of his concern by inquiring into my occupations more particularly than before. But I could not tear my thoughts from my employment, which had taken an irresistible hold of my imagination and caused me even to forget those friends who were so many miles absent. Winter, spring, and summer passed away during my labors, but I did not watch the blossom or the expanding leaves. I appeared rather like one doomed by slavery to toil in the mines, or any other unwholesome trade, than an artist occupied by his favorite employment. Every night I was oppressed by a slow fever, and I became nervous to a most painful degree. The fall of a leaf startled me, and I shunned my fellow-creatures as if I had been guilty of a crime.

It was on a dreary night of November that I beheld the accomplishment of my toils. With an anxiety that almost amounted to agony, I collected the instruments of life around me, that I might infuse a spark of being into the lifeless thing that lay at my feet. It was already one in the morning. The rain pattered dismally against the panes and my candle was nearly burnt out, when, by the glimmer of the half-extinguished light I saw the dull yellow eye of the creature open. It breathed hard and a convulsive motion agitated its limbs.

How can I describe my emotions at this catastrophe, or how delineate the wretch whom with such infinite pains and care I had endeavored to form? His limbs were in proportion and I had selected his features as beautiful. Beautiful!—Great God! His yellow skin scarcely covered the work of muscles and arteries beneath. His hair was of a lustrous black and flowing, his teeth of a pearly whiteness. But these luxuriances only formed a more horrid contrast with his shriveled complexion, his straight black lips and watery eyes that seemed almost of the same dull color as the sockets in which they were set.

I had worked hard for nearly two years for the sole purpose of infusing life into an inanimate body. For this I had deprived myself of rest and health. I had desired it with an ardor that far exceeded moderation, but now that I had finished, the beauty of the dream vanished and breathless horror and disgust filled my heart. Unable to endure the aspect of the being I had created, I rushed out of the room. I continued a long time traversing my bedchamber, unable to compose my mind to sleep. At length nervous exhaustion triumphed and I threw myself on the bed in my clothes, craving a few moments of forgetfulness. But it was in vain. I slept, indeed, but I was disturbed by the wildest dreams. I thought I saw Elizabeth in the bloom of health walking in the streets of Ingolstadt. Delighted and surprised, I embraced her, but as I imprinted the first kiss on her lips they became livid with the hue of death, her features appeared to change and I thought that I held the corpse of my dead mother in my arms. A shroud enveloped her form and I saw the grave-worms crawling in the folds of the flannel. I started from my sleep with horror. A cold dew covered my forehead, my teeth chattered and every limb became convulsed. Then, by the dim and yellow light of the moon as it forced its way through the window shutters, I beheld the wretch—the miserable monster whom I had created. He held up the curtain of the bed.

His eyes, if eyes they may be called, were fixed on me. His jaws opened and he muttered some inarticulate sounds while a grin wrinkled his cheeks. He might have spoken but I did not hear. One hand was stretched out, seemingly to detain me, but I escaped and rushed downstairs. I took refuge in the courtyard belonging to the house which I inhabited, where I remained during the rest of the night, walking up and down in the greatest agitation, listening attentively, catching and fearing each sound as if it were to announce the approach of the demoniacal corpse to which I had so miserably given life.

Oh, no mortal could support the horror of that countenance! A mummy again endued with animation could not be so hideous as that wretch. I had gazed on him while unfinished. He was ugly then, but when those muscles and joints were rendered capable of motion, it became a thing such as even Dante could not have conceived.

I passed the night wretchedly. Sometimes my pulse beat so heavily that I felt the palpitation of every artery. At others, I nearly sank to the ground through languor and extreme weakness. Mingled with this horror, I felt the bitterness of disappointment. Dreams that had been my food and pleasant rest for so long a space were now become a hell to me. And the change was so rapid, the overthrow so complete!

Morning, dismal and wet, at length dawned, and my sleepless and aching eyes discovered the church of Ingolstadt, its white steeple and clock, which indicated the sixth hour. The porter opened the gates of the court which had that night been my asylum, and I went into the streets with quick steps, as if I sought to avoid the wretch whose encounter I feared at every turn. I did not dare return to the apartment, but felt impelled to hurry on, chilled by the drizzle which fell from a black and comfortless sky.

I continued walking in this manner for some time, and came at length opposite to the inn where various carriages usually stopped. I paused, I knew not why, but I remained some minutes with my eyes fixed on a coach that was coming towards me from the other end of the street. As it drew nearer, I observed that it was the Swiss coach. It stopped just where I was standing, and as the door opened I perceived Henry Clerval, who, on seeing me, instantly sprung out.

"My dear Frankenstein," he exclaimed, "how glad I am to see you! How fortunate that you should be here at the very moment of my arrival!"

Nothing could equal my delight on seeing Clerval. We had both long hoped that he would have success in persuading his father to permit him to come to Ingolstadt. His presence brought back to my thoughts my father, Elizabeth, my brothers, and all those scenes of home so dear to my recollection. I grasped his hand, and in a moment forgot my horror and misfortune.

"It gives me the greatest delight to see you," I said as we walked towards the college, "but tell me how you left my father, brothers, and Elizabeth."

"Very well, and very happy, only a little uneasy that they hear from you so seldom. Of Elizabeth and your father, by the by, I mean to lecture you a little upon their behalf. You should know that Ernest, now that he is sixteen, is desirous to enter into foreign service. Your father is not pleased with the idea of a military career in a distant country, but Ernest never had your powers of application. He looks upon study as an odious fetter. His time is spent in the open air, climbing the hills or rowing on the lake. It is feared that he will become an idler, unless we yield the point, and permit him to enter on the profession which he has selected.

"As for little darling William, he has already had one or two little 'wives,' but Louisa Biron is his favorite, a pretty little girl of five years of age. I wish you could see him. He is very tall of his age. When he smiles, two little dimples appear on each cheek, which are rosy with health.—But, my dear Frankenstein," he continued, stopping short and gazing full in my face, "I did not note until now how very ill you appear, so thin and pale. You look as if you have not slept for several nights."

I made my excuses and brushed aside his concern. I trembled excessively. I could not endure to think of, and far less to allude to the occurrences of the preceding night. I walked with a quick pace and we soon arrived at my college. I then reflected, and the thought made me shiver, that the creature whom I had left in my apartment might still be there, alive, and walking about. I dreaded to behold this monster, but I feared still more that Henry should see him. I had him remain a few minutes at the bottom of the stairs as I darted up towards my own room. My hand was already on the lock of the door before I recollected myself. I then paused, and a cold shivering came over me. I threw the door forcibly open, as children are accustomed to do when they expect a spectre to stand waiting for them on the other side, but nothing appeared. I stepped fearfully in. The apartment was empty. My bedroom was freed from its hideous guest, and when I became assured that my enemy had indeed fled, I ran down to fetch Clerval.

We ascended into my room, and the servant presently brought breakfast, but I was unable to contain myself. It was not joy only that possessed me. I felt my flesh tingle with excess of sensitiveness, and my pulse beat rapidly. I was unable to remain for a single instant in the same place. I talked incessantly, and laughed aloud. Clerval at first attributed my unusual spirits to joy on his arrival, but when he observed me more closely he saw a wildness in my eyes, and my loud unrestrained laughter frightened and astonished him.

"My dear Victor," cried he, "for God's sake, what is the matter? Do not laugh in that manner. How ill you are! What is the cause of all this?"

"Do not ask me," cried I, putting my hands before my eyes. "Oh, help me! help me!" For I thought I saw the dreaded spectre glide into the room. I imagined that the monster seized me. I struggled furiously and fell down in a fit.

Poor Clerval! What must have been his feelings? A meeting, which he anticipated with such joy, so strangely turned to alarm. But I was not the witness of his grief, for I was lifeless, and did not recover my senses for a long, long time. A nervous fever confined me for several months. During all that time Henry was my only nurse. I afterwards learned that, knowing my father's advanced age and unfitness for so long a journey, and how wretched my sickness would make Elizabeth, he spared them this grief by concealing the extent of my disorder.

I could not have a more kind and attentive nurse than my friend. But I was in reality very ill. I raved incessantly of the monster on whom I had bestowed existence and which was forever before my eyes. At first Henry believed my words to be the wanderings of my disturbed imagination, but the persistence with which I returned to the same subject, persuaded him that my disorder indeed owed its origin to some uncommon and terrible event.

By very slow degrees I recovered. The fallen leaves had disappeared, and the young buds were shooting forth from the trees that shaded my window. It was a divine spring and the season contributed greatly to my convalescence. My gloom disappeared and I felt sentiments of joy and affection revive in my bosom.

I thanked my friend and expressed remorse and begged forgiveness for the disappointment I had caused him.

"You will repay me entirely," he responded, "if you do not discompose yourself, but get well as fast as you can. And since you appear in such good spirits, may I speak to you on one subject of concern?"

I trembled. One subject! What could it be? Could he allude to an object on whom I dared not even think?

"Compose yourself," said Clerval, who observed my change of color. "I will not mention it if it agitates you, but your father and cousin would be very happy if they received a letter from you in your own handwriting. They hardly know how ill you have been and are uneasy at your long silence."

"Is that all, my dear Henry? How could you suppose that my first thoughts would not fly towards those dear friends whom I love and who are so deserving of my love.

"Dear, dear Elizabeth!" I exclaimed, "I will write instantly, and relieve them from the anxiety they must feel." I wrote, and this exertion greatly fatigued me. But my convalescence had commenced, and proceeded regularly. In another fortnight I was able to leave my chamber.

Summer passed, and my return to Geneva was fixed for the latter end of autumn, but winter and snow arrived, the roads were deemed impassable, and my journey was retarded until the ensuing spring. I felt this delay very bitterly, for I longed to see my native town and my beloved friends. The month of May had already commenced, and I expected the letter daily which was to fix the date of my departure, when Henry proposed a pedestrian tour in the environs of Ingolstadt, that I might bid a personal farewell to the country I had so long inhabited. I acceded with pleasure to this proposition. I was fond of exercise, and Clerval had always been my favorite companion in the rambles of this nature that I had taken among the scenes of my native country.

We passed a fortnight in these perambulations. My health and spirits had long been restored, and they gained additional strength from the salubrious air I breathed and the conversation of my friend. Clerval called forth the better feelings of my heart. He again taught me to love the aspect of nature and the cheerful faces of children. A serene sky and verdant fields filled me with ecstasy.

We returned to our college on a Sunday afternoon, where I found the following letter from my father:

"My Dear Victor,

"You have probably waited impatiently for a letter to fix the date of your return to us, and I was at first tempted to write only a few lines, merely mentioning the day on which I should expect you. But that would be a cruel kindness, and I dare not do it. What would be your surprise, my son, when you expected a happy and glad welcome, to behold, on the contrary, tears and wretchedness? How, Victor, can I relate our misfortune? I wish to prepare you for the woeful news, but I know it is impossible. Even now your eye skims over the page, to seek the words which are to convey to you the horrible tidings.

"William is dead!—that sweet child, whose smiles delighted and warmed my heart, who was so gentle, yet so gay! Victor, he is murdered!

"I will not attempt to console you, but will simply relate the circumstances of the tragedy.

"Last Thursday (May 7th), I, my niece, and your two brothers, went to walk in Plainpalais. The evening was warm and serene, and we prolonged our walk farther than usual. It was already dusk before we thought of returning, and then we discovered that William and Ernest, who had gone on before, were not to be found. We accordingly rested on a seat until they should return. Presently Ernest came, and inquired if we had seen his brother. He said that they had been playing together, that William had run away to hide himself, and that he vainly sought for him, and afterwards waited for him a long time, but that he did not return.

"This account rather alarmed us, and we continued to search for him until night fell, when Elizabeth conjectured that he might have returned to the house. He was not there. We returned again, with torches, for I could not rest when I thought that my sweet boy had lost himself and was exposed to all the damps and dews of night. Elizabeth also suffered extreme anguish. About five in the morning I discovered my lovely boy, whom the night before I had seen blooming and active in health, stretched on the grass livid and motionless, the print of the murderer's finger on his neck.

"He was conveyed home, and the anguish that was visible in my countenance betrayed the secret to Elizabeth. She was very earnest to see the corpse. At first I attempted to prevent her, but she persisted, and entering the room where it lay, hastily examined the neck of the victim, and exclaimed, 'O God! I have murdered my darling infant!'

"She fainted, and was restored with extreme difficulty. When she again lived, it was only to weep and sigh. She told me that that same evening William had teased her to let him wear a very valuable miniature that she possessed of your mother. This picture is gone, and was doubtless the temptation which urged the murderer to the deed. We have no trace of him at present, although our exertions to discover him are unremitted. But they will not restore my beloved William!"

Clerval, who had watched my countenance as I read this letter, was surprised to observe the despair that succeeded to the joy I at first expressed on receiving news from my friends. I threw the letter on the table, and covered my face with my hands.

"My dear Frankenstein," exclaimed Henry, when he perceived me weep with bitterness, "are you always to be unhappy? My dear friend, what has happened?"

I motioned to him to take up the letter, while I walked up and down the room in the extremest agitation. Tears also gushed from the eyes of Clerval, as he read the account of my misfortune.

"I can offer you no consolation, my friend," said he. "Your disaster is irreparable. What do you intend to do?"

"To go instantly to Geneva. Come with me, Henry, to order the horses."

As soon as the horses arrived, I hurried into a cabriolet, and bade farewell to my friend.

It was completely dark when I arrived in the environs of Geneva. As I drew nearer home, grief and fear again overcame me. The darkened mountains appeared a vast and dim scene of evil, and I foresaw obscurely that I was destined to become the most wretched of human beings. Alas! I prophesied truly, and failed only in that in all the misery I imagined and dreaded, I did not conceive the hundredth part of the anguish I was destined to endure.

The gates of the town were already shut, and I was obliged to cross the lake in a boat to arrive at Plainpalais. During this short voyage I saw the lightnings playing on the summit of Mont Blanc in the most beautiful figures. The storm appeared to approach rapidly and on landing I ascended a low hill, that I might observe its progress. The heavens were clouded and I soon felt the rain coming slowly in large drops, but its violence quickly increased.

I quitted my seat and walked on, although the darkness and storm increased every minute and the thunder burst with a terrific crash over my head. Vivid flashes of lightning dazzled my eyes, illuminating the lake, making it appear like a vast sheet of fire. While I watched the tempest, so beautiful yet terrific, I wandered on with a hasty step. This noble war in the sky elevated my spirits, I clasped my hands and exclaimed aloud, "William, dear angel this is thy funeral, this thy dirge!" As I said these words I perceived in the gloom a figure which stole from behind a clump of trees near me. I stood fixed, gazing intently. I could not be mistaken. A flash of lightning illuminated the object, and discovered its shape plainly to me. Its gigantic stature and the deformity of its aspect, more hideous than belongs to humanity, instantly informed me that it was the wretch, the filthy demon to whom I had given life. What did he there? Could he be (I shuddered at the conception) the murderer of my brother? No sooner did that idea cross my imagination than I became convinced of its truth. My teeth chattered and I was forced to lean against a tree for support. The figure passed me quickly and I lost it in the gloom. Nothing in human shape could have destroyed that fair child. *He* was the murderer! I could not doubt it. The mere presence of the idea was irresistible proof of the fact. I thought of pursuing the devil but it would have been in vain, for another flash discovered him to me hanging among the rocks of the nearly perpendicular ascent of Mont Saleve, a hill that bounds Plainpalais on the south. He soon reached the summit and disappeared.

I remained motionless. The thunder ceased, but the rain still continued, and the scene was enveloped in an impenetrable darkness. I revolved in my mind the events which I had until now sought to forget: the whole train of my progress towards the creation; the appearance of the work of my own hands alive at my bedside; its departure. Two years had now nearly elapsed since the night on which he first received life, and was this his first crime? Alas! Had I turned loose into the world a depraved wretch whose delight was in carnage and misery?

It was about five in the morning when I entered my father's house. I told the servants not to disturb the family, and went into the library to attend their usual hour of rising.

I stood in the same place where I had last embraced my father before my departure for Ingolstadt four years ago. I gazed on the picture of my sweet mother, which stood over the mantelpiece. Below this was a miniature of William. My tears flowed when I looked upon it. While I was thus engaged, Ernest entered. He expressed a sorrowful delight to see me: "Welcome, my dearest Victor," said he. "Ah! I wish you had come three months ago, and then you would have found us all joyous and delighted! You come to us now to share a misery which nothing can alleviate, yet your presence will, I hope, revive our father, who seems sinking under his misfortune, and you will induce poor Elizabeth to cease her vain and tormenting self-accusations. Poor William! He was our darling and our pride!"

Tears unrestrained fell from my brother's eyes. Before, I had only imagined the wretchedness of my desolated home. The reality came on me as a new, and a not less terrible disaster. I tried to calm Ernest. I inquired more minutely concerning my father and her I named my cousin.

"She most of all," said Ernest, "requires consolation. She accused herself of having caused the death of my brother, and that made her very wretched. But since the murderer has been discovered—"

"The murderer discovered! Good God! How can that be? Who could attempt to pursue him? One might as well try to overtake the winds."

"I do not know what you mean," replied my brother, in accents of wonder, "but to us her discovery completes our misery. No one would believe it at first, and even now Elizabeth will not be convinced, notwithstanding all the evidence. Indeed, who would credit that Justine Moritz, who was so amiable and fond of all the family, could suddenly become capable of so frightful, so appalling a crime?"

"Justine Moritz! Poor girl, is she the accused? But it is wrongfully—every one knows that. No one believes it, surely, Ernest?"

"No one did at first, but several circumstances came out that have almost forced conviction upon us, and her own behavior has been so confused as to add to the evidence against her. But she will be tried today, and you will then hear all."

Gentle, unfortunate, orphaned Justine, who my mother brought into our family when she was twelve years of age, there to learn the duties of a servant, a condition which, in our fortunate country, does not include the idea of ignorance, and a sacrifice of the dignity of a human being—she, who, in seven years of faithful service, induced such great attachment from our family, and was the most grateful little creature in the world—she was now accused of the murder of the youngest in that family which she had so lovingly attended to.

Ernest related that the morning on which the murder of poor William had been discovered Justine had been taken ill and confined to her bed for several days. During this interval one of the servants, happening to examine the apparel she had worn on the night of the murder, had discovered in her pocket the picture of my mother, which had been judged to be the temptation of the murderer. The servant instantly showed it to one of the others, who, without saying a word to any of the family, went to a magistrate, and, upon their deposition, Justine was apprehended. On being charged with the fact, the poor girl confirmed the suspicion in a great measure by her extreme confusion of manner.

This was a strange tale, but it did not shake my faith, and I replied earnestly, "You are all mistaken. I know the murderer. Justine, poor, good Justine, is innocent."

My father and the rest of the family being obliged to attend as witnesses, I accompanied them to the court. During the whole of this wretched mockery of justice I suffered living torture. It was to be decided, whether the result of my curiosity and lawless devices would cause the death of two of my fellow-beings: one a smiling babe, full of innocence and joy, the other gazed on and unjustly execrated by thousands.

The trial began, and after the advocate against her had stated the charge, several witnesses were called. Several strange facts combined against her, which might have staggered any one who had not such proof of her innocence as I had.

Justine was called on for her defense. Sometimes she struggled with her tears, but when she was desired to plead she collected her powers and spoke in an audible, although variable voice.

Concerning the picture she could give no account:

"Did the murderer place it there? I know of no opportunity afforded him for so doing. I believe that I have no enemy on earth, surely none who would have been so wicked as to destroy me wantonly."

Several witnesses were called who had known her for many years, but fear and hatred of the crime of which they supposed her guilty rendered them timorous and unwilling to come forward. When Elizabeth saw even this last resource about to fail the accused, although violently agitated, she desired permission to address the court.

After berating the cowardice of Justine's pretended friends, she recounted the great affection and care with which Justine had nursed my mother in her last illness, and how warmly she was attached to the child who was now dead, and acted towards him like a most affectionate mother. As to the bauble on which the chief proof rested, if Justine had earnestly desired it, asserted Elizabeth, she should have willingly given it to her, so much did she esteem and value her. A murmur of approbation followed Elizabeth's simple and powerful appeal, but it was not to the favor of poor Justine. The public indignation was turned upon her with renewed violence, charging her with the blackest ingratitude.

My own agitation and anguish was extreme during the whole trial. I alone possessed absolute certainty of her innocence. I did not for a minute doubt the identity of the murderer. But what story had I to tell?—a tale so utterly improbable: A being whom I myself had formed had murdered my brother, and in his hellish sport had betrayed the innocent Justine to death and ignominy. If any other had communicated such a relation to me, I should have looked upon it as the ravings of insanity.

When I perceived that the popular voice and the countenances of the judges had already condemned my unhappy victim, I rushed out of the court in agony. The tortures of the accused did not equal mine. She was sustained by innocence, but the fangs of remorse tore my bosom and would not forego their hold.

I passed a night of unmingled wretchedness. In the morning I went to the court. My lips and throat were parched. I dared not ask the fatal question, but I was known, and the officer guessed the cause of my visit. The ballots had been thrown. They were all black, and Justine was condemned and sentenced to hang.

From the tortures of my own heart, I turned to contemplate the deep and voiceless grief of my Elizabeth. This also was my doing! And my father's woe, and the desolation of that late so smiling home—all was the work of my thrice-accursed hands!

Ye weep, unhappy ones, but these are not your last tears! Again shall you raise the funeral wail, and the sound of your lamentations shall again and again be heard! Frankenstein, your son, your kinsman, your early, much-loved friend, he who would spend each vital drop of blood for your sakes—who has no thought nor sense of joy, except as it is mirrored also in your dear countenances—he bids you weep—to shed countless tears brought on by his own hands, creators of abominable life and horrific death!

Thus spoke my prophetic soul, as, torn by remorse, horror, and despair, I beheld those I loved spend vain sorrow upon the graves of William and Justine, the first hapless victims to my unhallowed arts.

It was about the middle of the month of August, nearly two months after the death of Justine, that the whirlwind passions of my soul led me to seek some relief from my intolerable sensations. My wanderings were directed towards the valley of Chamonix. I had visited it frequently during my boyhood. A tingling long-lost sense of pleasure often came across me during this journey. Some turn in the road, some new object suddenly perceived and recognized, reminded me of light-hearted days of boyhood. The weight upon my spirit was sensibly lightened as I plunged yet deeper in the ravine of Arve. As I ascended higher, the valley assumed a more magnificent and astonishing character, rendered sublime by the mighty Alps, whose white and shining pyramids and domes towered above all. I was determined to proceed without a guide, for I was well acquainted with the path, and the presence of another would destroy the solitary grandeur of the scene. The ascent is precipitous, but the path is cut into continual and short windings, which enable you to surmount the perpendicularity of the mountain. It is a scene terrifically desolate.

It was nearly noon when I arrived at the top of the ascent. A mist covered the sea of ice and the surrounding mountains. From the side where I stood Montanvert was exactly opposite at the distance of a league, and above it rose Mont Blanc in awful majesty. For some time I sat in a recess of the rock, gazing on this wonderful and stupendous scene. My heart, which was before sorrowful, now swelled with something like joy. I suddenly beheld the figure of a man at some distance, advancing towards me with superhuman speed. He bounded over the crevices in the ice, among which I had walked with caution. His stature, also, as he approached, seemed to exceed that of man. I was troubled. A mist came over my eyes, and I felt a faintness seize me. I perceived, as the shape came nearer, that it was the wretch whom I had created. Its unearthly ugliness rendered it almost too horrible for human eyes. Rage and hatred at first deprived me of utterance.

"Devil," I suddenly exclaimed, "do you dare approach me? And do not you fear the fierce vengeance of my arm wreaked on your miserable head? Begone, vile insect! or rather, stay, that I may trample you to dust! Oh, that I could, with the extinction of your miserable existence, restore those victims whom you have so diabolically murdered!"

"I expected this reception," said the demon. "All men hate the wretched. How, then, must I be hated, who am miserable beyond all living things! Yet you, my creator, detest and spurn me, your creature, to whom you are bound by ties only dissoluble by the annihilation of one of us. You propose to kill me. How dare you sport thus with life? Do your duty towards me, and I will do mine towards you and the rest of mankind. If you will comply with my conditions, I will leave them and you at peace. But if you refuse, I will glut the maw of death, until it be satiated with the blood of your remaining friends."

"Abhorred monster! Fiend that you are! The tortures of hell are too mild a vengeance for your crimes. Wretched devil! You reproach me with your creation. Come on, then, that I may extinguish the spark which I so negligently bestowed." My rage was without bounds. I sprang on him, impelled by all the feelings which can arm one being against the existence of another.

He easily eluded me, and said, "Be calm! I entreat you to hear me, before you give vent to your hatred on my devoted head. Have I not suffered enough that you seek to increase my misery? Life, although it may only be an accumulation of anguish, is dear to me, and I will defend it. Remember, you have made me more powerful than yourself. But I will not be tempted to set myself in opposition to you. I am your creature, and I will be even mild and docile to my natural lord and king, if you will also perform your part, that which you owe me. Oh, Frankenstein, remember that I am your creature. I ought to be your Adam, but I am rather the fallen angel whom you drive from joy for no misdeed. Everywhere I see bliss from which I alone am excluded. I was benevolent and good. Misery made me a fiend.

"You accuse me of murder, and yet you would, with a satisfied conscience, destroy your own creature. Yet I ask you not to spare me. Listen to me, and then, if you can, and if you will, destroy the work of your hands. My tale is long and strange, and the temperature of this place is not fitting to your fine sensations. Come to the hut upon the mountain. The sun is yet high in the heavens. Before it descends to hide itself behind yon snowy precipices and illuminate another world, you will have heard my story and can decide."

My heart was full. For the first time I felt what the duties of a creator towards his creature were. I weighed the various arguments that he had used, and determined at least to listen to his tale. He led the way across the ice. I followed. The air was cold and as we ascended the opposite rock the rain again began to descend. We entered the hut, the fiend with an air of exultation, I with a heavy heart and depressed spirits. But I consented to listen, and seating myself by the fire which my odious companion had lighted, he thus began:

2.

It is with considerable difficulty that I remember the original era of my being. All the events of that period appear confused and indistinct. A strange multiplicity of sensations seized me, and I saw, felt, heard, and smelt, at the same time, and it was indeed a long time before I learned to distinguish between the operations of my various senses. I walked, and, I believe, descended, and after quitting your apartment, found that I could wander on at liberty. The light became more and more oppressive to me, and the heat wearying me as I walked, I sought a place where I could receive shade. This was the forest near Ingolstadt.

I felt tormented by hunger and thirst. I ate some berries which I found hanging on the trees or lying on the ground and I slaked my thirst at the brook. Before I had quitted your apartment, on a sensation of cold, I had covered myself with some clothes, but these were insufficient to secure me from the dews of night. I found a huge cloak, with which I enclosed myself, and sat down upon the ground. I was a poor, frightened, miserable wretch. Innumerable sounds rung in my ears, and on all sides various scents saluted me. The only object that I could distinguish was the bright moon, and I fixed my eyes on that with pleasure. Then lying down, I was overcome by sleep.

It was morning when I awoke. I was delighted when I first discovered those pleasant sounds which proceeded from the throats of the little winged animals. I tried to imitate them, but was unable. Sometimes I wished to express my sensations in my own mode, but the uncouth and inarticulate sounds which broke from me frightened me into silence again.

I determined to recommence my travels and proceeded across the fields for several hours, until at sunset I arrived at a village. How miraculous did this appear! The huts, the neater cottages, and stately houses, engaged my admiration by turns. The vegetables in the gardens, the milk and cheese that I saw placed at the windows of some of the cottages, allured my appetite. One of the best of these I entered, but I had hardly placed my foot within the door before the children shrieked and one of the women fainted. The whole village was roused. Some fled, some attacked me, until, grievously bruised by stones and many other kinds of missile weapons, I escaped to the open country and fearfully took refuge in a low hovel, quite bare, and making a wretched appearance after the palaces I had beheld in the village. This hovel, however, joined a cottage of a neat and pleasant appearance. But after my late dearly bought experience, I dared not enter it. My place of refuge was constructed of wood, but so low that I could with difficulty sit upright in it. No wood, however, was placed on the earth, which formed the floor, but it was dry and although the wind entered it by innumerable chinks, I found it an agreeable asylum from the snow and rain.

I was about to procure myself a little water, when I heard a step, and looking through a small chink, I beheld a young creature, with a pail on her head, passing before my hovel. The girl was young and of gentle demeanor, unlike what I have since found cottagers and farmhouse servants to be. Yet she was meanly dressed, a coarse blue petticoat and a linen jacket being her only garb. Her fair hair was plaited, but not adorned. Her pail was partly filled with milk. As she walked along, a young man met her whose countenance expressed despondence. Uttering a few sounds with an air of melancholy, he took the pail from her head and bore it to the cottage himself. She followed and they disappeared. Presently I saw the young man again with some tools in his hand cross the field behind the cottage.

On examining my dwelling, I found that one of the windows of the cottage had formerly occupied a part of it, but the panes had been filled up with wood. In one of these was a small and almost imperceptible chink, through which the eye could just penetrate. Through this crevice a small room was visible, whitewashed and clean, but very bare of furniture. In one corner near a small fire sat an old man, leaning his head on his hands in a disconsolate attitude. The young girl was occupied in arranging the cottage, but presently she took something out of a drawer, which employed her hands, and she sat down beside the old man, who, taking up an instrument, began to play, and to produce sounds sweeter than the voice of the thrush or the nightingale. It was a lovely sight, even to me, poor wretch, who had never beheld aught beautiful before. The silver hair and benevolent countenance of the aged cottager won my reverence, while the gentle manners of the girl enticed my love.

Soon the young man returned, bearing on his shoulders a load of wood. The girl met him at the door, helped to relieve him of his burden, and taking some of the fuel into the cottage, placed it on the fire. Then she and the youth went apart into a nook of the cottage and he showed her a large loaf and a piece of cheese. She seemed pleased, and went into the garden for some roots and plants, which she placed in water, and then upon the fire.

The old man had been pensive, but on the appearance of his companions he assumed a more cheerful air, and they sat down to eat. The meal was quickly dispatched. The young woman was again occupied in arranging the cottage, while the old man, whom I perceived to be blind, walked before the cottage in the sun, leaning on the arm of the youth. Nothing could exceed in beauty the contrast between these two excellent creatures. One had silver hairs and a countenance beaming with benevolence and love, the younger was slight and graceful in his figure, and his features were molded with the finest symmetry.

That night I lay on some straw I had gathered, but I could not sleep. I thought of the occurrences of the day. What chiefly struck me was the gentle manners of these people, and I longed to join them. But I remembered too well the treatment I had suffered the night before from the barbarous villagers, and resolved, whatever course of conduct I might hereafter think it right to pursue, that for the present I would remain quietly in my hovel, watching, and endeavoring to discover the motives which influenced their actions.

A considerable period elapsed before I discovered one of the causes of the uneasiness of this amiable family. It was poverty, which they suffered in a very distressing degree. Their nourishment consisted entirely of the vegetables of their garden, and the milk of one cow, which gave very little during the winter when its masters could scarcely procure food to support it. They often, I believe, suffered the pangs of hunger very poignantly, especially the two younger cottagers, for several times they placed food before the old man when they reserved none for themselves.

This trait of kindness moved me sensibly. I had been accustomed during the night to steal a part of their store for my own consumption, but thenceforth I abstained, and satisfied myself with berries, nuts, and roots, which I gathered from a neighboring wood.

I discovered also another means through which I was enabled to assist their labors. I found that the youth spent a great part of each day in collecting wood for the family fire, and during the night I often took his tools, the use of which I quickly discovered, and brought home firing sufficient for the consumption of several days.

I remember the first time that I did this the young woman, when she opened the door in the morning, appeared greatly astonished on seeing a great pile of wood on the outside. She uttered some words in a loud voice, and the youth joined her, who also expressed surprise. I observed, with pleasure, that he did not go to the forest that day, but spent it in repairing the cottage and cultivating the garden.

By degrees I made a discovery of still greater moment. I found that these people possessed a method of communicating their experience and feelings to one another by articulate sounds. This was indeed a godlike science, and I ardently desired to become acquainted with it. By great application, after having remained during the space of several revolutions of the moon in my hovel, I discovered the names that were given to some of the most familiar objects of discourse. I learned and applied the words, *fire*, *milk*, *bread*, and *wood*. I learned also the names of the cottagers themselves. The youth and his companion had each of them several names, but the old man had only one, which was *father*. The girl was called *sister*, or *Agatha*, and the youth *Felix*, *brother*, or *son*. I cannot describe the delight I felt when I learned the ideas appropriated to each of these sounds and was able to pronounce them.

I admired the perfect forms of my cottagers—their grace, beauty and delicate complexions, but how was I terrified when I viewed myself in a transparent pool! At first I started back, unable to believe that it was indeed I who was reflected in the mirror, and when I became fully convinced that I was in reality the monster that I am, I was filled with the bitterest sensations of despondence and mortification. Alas! I did not yet entirely know the fatal effects of this miserable deformity.

My mode of life in my hovel was uniform. During the morning, I attended the motions of the cottagers, and when they were dispersed in various occupations I slept. The remainder of the day was spent in observing my friends. When they had retired to rest, if there was any moon, or the night was star-lit, I went into the woods and collected my own food and fuel for the cottage. When I returned, as often as it was necessary I cleared their path from the snow and performed those offices that I had seen done by Felix. These labors performed by an invisible hand greatly astonished them, and once or twice I heard them utter the words *good spirit* and *wonder.*

I looked upon the venerable blind father, the gentle Agatha, and the excellent Felix as superior beings who would be the arbiters of my future destiny. I formed in my imagination a thousand pictures of presenting myself to them, and their reception of me. I imagined that they would be disgusted, until by my gentle demeanor and conciliating words, I should first win their favor, and afterwards their love.

The pleasant showers and genial warmth of spring greatly altered the aspect of the earth. The birds sang in more cheerful notes, and the leaves began to bud forth on the trees. It surprised me that what before was desert and gloomy should now bloom with the most beautiful flowers and verdure. My senses were gratified and refreshed by a thousand scents of delight and a thousand sights of beauty.

I improved rapidly in the knowledge of language, so that in two months I began to comprehend most of the words uttered by my protectors. Every conversation of the cottagers now opened new wonders to me.

I heard of the difference of sexes and the birth and growth of children; how the father doted on the smiles of the infant; how all the life and cares of the mother were wrapped up in the precious charge; how the mind of youth expanded and gained knowledge; of brother, sister, and all the various bonds between one human being and another.

But where were my friends and relations? No father had watched my infant days, no mother had blessed me with smiles and caresses. From my earliest remembrance I had been as I then was in height and proportion. I had never yet seen a being resembling me. What was I?—a figure hideously deformed and loathsome, not of the same nature as man. I was more agile than they, and could subsist upon coarser diet. I bore the extremes of heat and cold with less injury to my frame. My stature far exceeded theirs. When I looked around, I saw and heard of none like me. Was I then a monster, a blot upon the earth, from which all men fled, and whom all men disowned?

There were nights when, in place of the musical interludes, Felix would read to the others. By now I had improved sufficiently in my comprehension of language to share the unbounded listening pleasure this pastime afforded, and in addition to broadly increase my general education of the world beyond my forest. This reading had puzzled me extremely at first, but by degrees I conjectured that he found on the paper signs for speech which he understood.

At the same time I observed that while Felix was proficient in reading, Agatha was not, and he would often guide her efforts as she attempted to read from a charming collection of children's stories. This proved a great fortune for me whereby I benefited by shared access to these lessons on the art of deciphering letters upon a page.

To practice my skill, in the cottagers' absence I would borrow these little books, always careful to return them to their exact original locations. Later I was drawn to more advanced works, dusty volumes which had perhaps been favorites of the old man before he lost his sight. These books produced in me an infinity of new images that elevated me above the wretched sphere of my own reflections to admire and love the heroes of past ages.

But one narrative, *Paradise Lost*, excited different and far deeper emotions. I read it as a true history. It moved every feeling of wonder and awe that the picture of an omnipotent God warring with his creatures was capable of exciting. I often referred the several situations, as their similarity struck me, to my own. Like Adam, I was apparently united by no link to any other being in existence. But his state was far different from mine in every other respect. He had come forth from the hands of God a perfect creature, happy and prosperous, guarded by the especial care of his Creator. He was allowed to converse with and acquire knowledge from beings of a superior nature. But I was wretched, helpless, and alone. Many times I considered Satan as the fitter emblem of my condition, for often, like him, when I viewed the bliss of my protectors, the bitter gall of envy rose higher within me.

Another circumstance strengthened and confirmed these feelings. Soon after my arrival in the hovel, I discovered some papers in the pocket of the dress which I had taken from your laboratory. At first I had neglected them, but now that I was able to decipher the characters in which they were written, I began to study them with diligence. It was your journal of the four months that preceded my creation. You minutely described in these papers every step you took in the progress of your work. You doubtless recollect these papers. Here they are. Everything is related in them which bears reference to my accursed origin. The minutest description of my odious and loathsome person is given in language which painted your own horrors and rendered mine indelible. I sickened as I read.

"Accursed creator!" I exclaimed in agony. "Why did you form a monster so hideous that even *you* turned from me in disgust? God, in pity, made man beautiful and alluring, after his own image, but my form is a filthy type of yours, more horrid even from the very resemblance. Satan had his companions, fellow-devils, to admire and encourage him, but I am solitary and abhorred. No Eve soothes my sorrows, nor shares my thoughts. I am alone."

These were the reflections of my hours of despondency and solitude. But when I contemplated the virtues of the cottagers and their benevolent and amiable dispositions, my heart yearned to be known and loved by them. I dared not think that they would turn from me with disdain and horror. The poor that stopped at their door were never driven away. Could they turn from one, however monstrous, who solicited their compassion and friendship? I resolved not to despair, but in every way to fit myself for an interview with them which would decide my fate. I revolved many projects, but that on which I finally fixed was to enter the dwelling when the blind old man should be alone. The unnatural hideousness of my person should have no significance to him. My voice, although harsh, had nothing terrible in it. I thought, therefore, that if I could gain the good will and mediation of the old one, I might be tolerated by my younger protectors.

One day, when the sun shone on the red leaves that strewed the ground and diffused cheerfulness, although it denied warmth, Agatha and Felix departed on a long country walk, and the old man at his own desire was left alone in the cottage. When his children had departed, he took up his guitar, and played several mournful but sweet airs, more sweet and mournful than I had ever heard him play before. At length, laying aside the instrument, he sat absorbed in reflection.

My heart beat quick. This was the hour and moment of trial which would decide my hopes or realize my fears. All was silent in and around the cottage. It was an excellent opportunity, yet when I proceeded to execute my plan, my limbs failed me and I sank to the ground. Again I rose and with renewed determination, I approached the door of their cottage.

I knocked. "Who is there?" said the welcoming voice. "Come in."

I entered. "Pardon this intrusion," said I. "I am a traveler in want of a little rest. You would greatly oblige me if you would allow me to remain a few minutes before the fire."

"Enter," said the old man, "and I will try in what manner I can relieve your wants, but, unfortunately my children are from home, and as I am blind, I am afraid I shall find it difficult to procure food for you."

"Do not trouble yourself, my kind host, I have food. It is warmth and rest only that I need."

I sat down, and a silence ensued. I knew that every minute was precious to me, yet I remained irresolute in what manner to commence the interview, when the old man addressed me—

"By your language, stranger, I suppose you are my countryman. Are you French?"

"No, but I was educated by a French family, and understand that language only. I am now going to claim the protection of some friends, whom I sincerely love, and of whose favor I have some hopes."

"Are they Germans?"

"No, they are French. These amiable people to whom I go have never seen me, and know little of me. I am an unfortunate and deserted creature. I have no relation or friend upon earth. I am full of fears, for if I fail there, I am an outcast in the world forever."

"Do not despair. To be friendless is indeed to be unfortunate, but the hearts of men, when unprejudiced by any obvious self interest, are full of brotherly love and charity."

"These people are kind—they are the most excellent creatures in the world. I tenderly love these friends. I have, unknown to them, been for many months in the habits of daily kindness towards them, but they believe that I wish to injure them, and it is that prejudice which I wish to overcome."

"Where do these friends reside?"

"Near this spot."

The old man paused, and then continued, "If you will unreservedly confide to me the particulars of your tale, I perhaps may be of use in undeceiving them. I am blind, and cannot judge of your countenance, but there is something in your words which persuades me that you are sincere. I am poor, but it will afford me true pleasure to be in any way serviceable to a human creature."

"Excellent man! You raise me from the dust by this kindness. I shall be forever grateful, and your present humanity assures me of success with those friends whom I am on the point of meeting."

"May I know the names and residence of those friends?"

I paused. This, I thought, was the moment of decision, which was to rob me of, or bestow happiness on me forever. I struggled vainly for firmness sufficient to answer him, but the effort destroyed all my remaining strength. I sank on the chair, and sobbed aloud. At that moment I heard the steps of my younger protectors. I had not a moment to lose, but, seizing the hand of the old man, I cried, "Now is the time!—save and protect me! You and your family are the friends whom I seek. Do not you desert me in the hour of trial!"

"Great God!" exclaimed the old man, "who are you?"

At that instant the cottage door was opened, and Felix and Agatha entered. Who can describe their horror and consternation on beholding me? Agatha screamed, and Felix darted forward and with supernatural force tore me from his father, to whose knees I clung. In a transport of fury he dashed me to the ground and struck me violently with a stick. I could have torn him limb from limb, as the lion rends the antelope, but my heart sunk within me as with bitter sickness and I refrained. When I saw him on the point of repeating his blow, I quitted the cottage and escaped into the wood.

Cursed, cursed creator! Why did I live? Why, in that instant, did I not extinguish the spark of existence which you had so wantonly bestowed? I know not. Despair had not yet taken possession of me. My feelings were those of rage and revenge. I could with pleasure have destroyed the cottage and its inhabitants and have glutted myself with their shrieks and misery.

Overcome by pain and no longer restrained by the fear of discovery, I gave vent to my anguish in fearful howlings. I was like a wild beast that had broken the toils, destroying the objects that obstructed me, and ranging through the wood with a stag-like swiftness. Oh, what a miserable night I passed! The cold stars shone in mockery, and the bare trees waved their branches above me. Now and then the sweet voice of a bird burst forth amidst the universal stillness. All, save I, were at rest or in enjoyment. Like the arch-fiend, I bore a hell within me, and finding myself excluded from all sympathy, wished to tear up the trees, spread havoc and destruction around me, and then to have sat down and enjoyed the ruin.

Feelings of revenge and hatred filled my bosom, but when I thought of my friends, of the mild voice of the old man, the gentle eyes of Agatha, and even the heroic protectiveness of Felix, these thoughts vanished, and a gush of tears somewhat soothed me. But again, when I reflected that they had spurned and deserted me, anger returned, a rage of anger and fury that burst all bounds of reason and reflection. I resolved to fly far from the scene of my misfortunes. But to me, hated and despised, every country must be equally horrible. At length the thought of you crossed my mind. I learned from your papers that you were my father, my creator, and to whom could I apply with more fitness than to him who had given me life? Among the topics of which Felix had read aloud, geography had not been omitted. I had learned the relative situations of the different countries of the earth. You had mentioned

Geneva as the name of your native town, and towards this place I resolved to proceed. On you only had I any claim for pity and redress, and from you I determined to seek that justice which I vainly attempted to gain from any other being that wore the human form.

It was late in autumn when I quitted the district where I had so long resided. My travels were long, and the sufferings I endured that winter were intense. I travelled only at night, and the sun became heatless; rain and snow poured around me; mighty rivers were frozen; the surface of the earth was hard, and chill, and bare, and I found no shelter. Oh, earth! how often did I imprecate curses on the cause of my being! The nearer I approached to your habitation, the more deeply did I feel the spirit of revenge enkindled in my heart. The labors I endured were not alleviated by the bright sun or the gentle breezes of spring.

It was evening when I reached the environs of Geneva, and I retired to a hiding-place among the fields that surround it to meditate in what manner I should apply to you. I was oppressed by fatigue and hunger, and far too unhappy to enjoy the prospect of the sun setting behind the stupendous mountains of Jura.

At this time a slight sleep relieved me from the pain of reflection, which was disturbed by the approach of a beautiful child who came running into the recess I had chosen, with all the sportiveness of infancy. Suddenly, as I gazed on him, an idea seized me, that this little creature was unprejudiced, and had lived too short a time to have imbibed a horror of deformity. If, therefore, I could take him, and educate him as my companion and friend, I should not be so desolate in this peopled earth.

Urged by this impulse, I seized on the boy as he passed and drew him towards me. As soon as he beheld my form, he placed his hands before his eyes and uttered a shrill scream. I drew his hand forcibly from his face and said, "Child, what is the meaning of this? I do not intend to hurt you. Listen to me."

He struggled violently. "Let me go," he cried, "monster! ugly wretch! You wish to eat me and tear me to pieces— You are an ogre—Let me go, or I will tell my papa."

"Boy, you will never see your father again. You must come with me."

"Hideous monster! Let me go. My papa is Dr. Franken-stein—He will punish you."

"Frankenstein! You belong then to my enemy—to him towards whom I have sworn eternal revenge. You shall be my first victim!"

The child still struggled and loaded me with epithets which carried despair to my heart. I grasped his throat to silence him, and in a moment he lay dead at my feet.

I gazed on my victim, and my heart swelled with exulta-tion and hellish triumph. Clapping my hands, I exclaimed, "I too can create desolation. My enemy is not invulnerable. This death will carry despair to him, and a thousand other miseries shall torment and destroy him."

As I fixed my eyes on the child, I saw something glitter-ing on his breast. I took it. It was a portrait of a most lovely woman. In spite of my malignity, it softened and attracted me. For a few moments I gazed with delight on her dark eyes, fringed by deep lashes, and her lovely lips. But presently my rage returned. I remembered that I was forever deprived of the delights that such beautiful creatures could bestow, and that she whose resemblance I contemplated would, in regarding me, have changed that air of divine benignity to one expressive of disgust and affright. Can you wonder that such thoughts transported me with rage?

I left the spot where I had committed the murder, and seeking a more secluded hiding place, I entered a barn which had appeared to me to be empty. A woman was sleeping on some straw. She was young, not indeed so beautiful as her whose portrait I held, but of an agreeable aspect, and blooming in the loveliness of youth and health. Here, I thought, is one of those whose joy-imparting smiles are bestowed on all but me. I bent over her and whispered, "Awake, fairest, thy lover is near—he who would give his life but to obtain one look of affection from thine eyes."

The sleeper stirred. A thrill of terror ran through me. Thanks to the lessons of Felix and the sanguinary laws of man, I had learned how to work mischief. I placed the portrait securely in one of the folds of her dress. She moved again, and I fled.

For some days I haunted the spot where these scenes had taken place, sometimes wishing to see you, sometimes resolved to quit the world and its miseries forever. At length I wandered towards these mountains, and have ranged through their immense recesses, consumed by a burning passion which you alone can gratify. We may not part until you have promised to comply with my requisition. I am alone and miserable. Man will not associate with me. But one as deformed and horrible as myself would not deny herself to me. My companion must be of the same species and have the same defects.

This being you must create.

3.

The being finished speaking and fixed his looks upon me in expectation of a reply. But I was bewildered, perplexed and unable to arrange my ideas sufficiently to understand the full extent of his proposition. He continued—

"You must create a female for me. This you alone can do, this I demand of you, and you must not refuse."

The latter part of his tale had kindled anew in me the anger that had died away while he narrated his peaceful life among the cottagers, and as he said this, I could no longer suppress the rage that burned within me.

"I do refuse it," I replied, "and no torture shall ever extort a consent from me. Shall I create another like yourself, whose joint wickedness might desolate the world!"

"I will keep no terms with my enemies," replied the fiend. "I am miserable, and they shall share my wretchedness. Yet it is in your power to recompense me, and deliver them from an evil which it only remains for you to make so great that not only you and your family, but thousands of others, shall be swallowed up in the whirlwinds of its rage!"

A fiendish anguish animated him as he said this. His face was wrinkled into contortions too horrible to behold. But presently he calmed himself and proceeded—

"But instead of threatening, I am content to reason with you. If any being felt emotions of benevolence towards me, I should return them an hundredfold. For that one creature's sake, I would make peace with the whole kind. But such dreams of bliss cannot be realized. What I ask of you is reasonable and moderate. I demand a creature of another sex, but as hideous as myself, with whom I can

47

live in the interchange of those sympathies necessary for my being. The gratification is small, but it is all that I can receive, and it shall content me. It is true we shall be monsters, cut off from all the world, but on that account we shall be more attached to one another. Our lives will not be happy, but they will be harmless, and free from the misery I now feel. Oh, my creator, do not deny me my request! Let me feel gratitude towards you for one benefit! Let me see that I excite the sympathy of some existing thing!"

He saw my change of feeling and continued—

"If you consent, neither you nor any other human being shall ever see us again. I will go to the vast wilds of South America. My food is not that of man. I do not destroy the lamb and the kid to glut my appetite. Acorns and berries afford me sufficient nourishment. My companion will be of the same nature as myself and will be content with the same fare. We shall make our bed of dried leaves. The sun will shine on us as on man, and will ripen our food. The picture I present to you is peaceful and human. My evil passions will have fled, and in my dying moments I shall not curse my maker."

When I looked upon him, when I saw the filthy mass that moved and talked, my heart sickened and my feelings were altered to those of horror and hatred. I shuddered at his threats, and the possible consequences should I refuse his demand. Yet I was also moved by the justice in his argument. His tale, and the feelings he now expressed, proved him to be a creature of fine sensations, and did I as his maker not owe him all the portion of happiness that it was in my power to bestow.

After a long pause of reflection, I concluded that the justice due both to him and my fellow-creatures demanded of me that I should comply with his request.

Upon my return to my home in Geneva, my haggard and wild appearance awoke intense alarm to my family, but I answered no question. Scarcely did I speak. I felt as if I were placed under a ban—as if I had no right to claim their sympathies—as if never more might I enjoy companionship with them. Yet I loved them to adoration, and to save them I resolved to dedicate myself to my most abhorred task.

To my father I expressed a wish to visit England, concealing the true reasons of this request. A few months, or at most a year, was the period contemplated. In one kind paternal precaution, my father took to ensure my having a companion. Without previously communicating with me, in concert with Elizabeth, he arranged that Clerval should join me at Strasbourg. I rejoiced that thus I should be saved many hours of lonely, maddening reflection. For myself, there was one reward I promised myself from my detested toils—one consolation for my unparalleled sufferings. It was the prospect of that day when I might claim Elizabeth and forget the past in my union with her.

It was in the latter end of September that I again quitted my native country. I threw myself into the carriage that was to convey me away, hardly knowing whither I was going. I remembered only, and it was with a bitter anguish that I reflected on it, to order that my chemical instruments should be packed to go with me. I arrived at Strasbourg, where I waited two days for Clerval. He came. Alas, how great was the difference between us! He was alive to every new scene, joyful when he saw the beauties of the setting sun, and more happy when he beheld it rise and recommence a new day. By contrast, I was occupied by gloomy thoughts and saw not the descent of the evening star, nor the golden sunrise reflected in the Rhine.

We proceeded by sea to England. It was on a clear morning in the latter days of December that I first saw the white cliffs of Britain, and at length the numerous steeples of London. We determined to remain several months in this wonderful and celebrated city. Clerval desired the intercourse of the men of genius and talent who flourished at this time. I often refused to accompany him, alleging another engagement, that I might remain alone. I now also began to collect the materials necessary for my new creation, and this was to me like the torture of single drops of water continually falling on the head. Every thought that was devoted to it was an extreme anguish, and every word that I spoke in allusion to it caused my lips to quiver and my heart to palpitate.

After passing some months in London, we received an invitation from a person in Scotland who had formerly been our visitor at Geneva. Clerval eagerly desired to accept this invitation, but I was in no mood to laugh and talk with strangers. Accordingly I told Clerval that I wished to make the tour of Scotland alone. "Do you," said I, "enjoy yourself, and let this be our rendezvous. I may be absent a month or two, but do not interfere with my motions, I entreat you, leave me to peace and solitude for a short time, and when I return, I hope it will be with a lighter heart, more congenial to your own temper."

I determined to visit some remote spot of Scotland and commence my work in solitude. I did not doubt but that the monster followed me. With this resolution I traversed the northern highlands, and fixed on one of the remotest of the Orkneys as the scene of my labors. It was a place fitted for such a work, being hardly more than a rock, whose high sides were continually beaten upon by the waves. The soil was barren, scarcely affording pasture for a few miserable cows, and oatmeal for its inhabitants, which consisted of five persons, whose gaunt and scraggy limbs gave tokens of their miserable fare. Vegetables and bread, when they indulged in such luxuries, and even fresh water, was to be procured from the mainland, which was about five miles distant.

On the whole island there were but three miserable huts, and one of these was vacant when I arrived. This I hired. It contained but two rooms, and these exhibited all the squalidness of the most miserable penury. The thatch had fallen in, the walls were unplastered, and the door was off its hinges. I ordered it to be repaired, bought some furniture, and took possession, an incident which would doubtless have occasioned some surprise, had not all the senses of the cottagers been benumbed by want and squalid poverty. As it was, I lived ungazed at and unmolested.

In this retreat I devoted the morning to labor, but in the evening, when the weather permitted, I walked on the stony beach of the sea, to listen to the waves as they roared and dashed at my feet. It was a monotonous yet ever-changing scene. I thought of Switzerland. It was far different from this desolate and appalling landscape. Its hills are covered with vines, and its cottages are scattered thickly in the plains. Its fair lakes reflect a blue and gentle sky, and when troubled by the winds, their tumult is but as the play of a lively infant, when compared to the roarings of the giant ocean.

In this manner I distributed my occupations when I first arrived, but as I proceeded in my labor it became every day more horrible and irksome to me. Sometimes I could not prevail on myself to enter my laboratory for several days, and at other times I toiled day and night in order to complete my work. It was indeed a filthy process in which I was engaged. During my first experiment, a kind of enthusiastic frenzy had blinded me to the horror of my employment. My mind was intently fixed on the consummation of my labor, and my eyes were shut to the horror of my proceedings. But now I went to it in cold blood, and my heart often sickened at the work of my hands.

I sat one evening in my laboratory after the sun had set and the moon was just rising from the sea. Without sufficient light for my employment I remained idle. As I sat, a train of reflection occurred to me which led me to consider the effects of what I was now doing. Three years before I was engaged in the same manner, and had created a fiend whose unparalleled barbarity had desolated my heart and filled it forever with the bitterest remorse. I was now about to form another being of whose dispositions I was alike ignorant. She might become ten thousand times more malignant than her mate and delight, for its own sake, in murder and wretchedness. He had sworn to quit the neighborhood of man and hide himself in deserts, but she had not. She might refuse to comply with a compact made before her creation. They might even hate each other. The creature who already lived loathed his own deformity. Might he not conceive a greater abhorrence for it when it came before his eyes in the female form? She also might turn with disgust from him to the superior beauty of man. She might quit him, and he be again alone, exasperated by the fresh provocation of being deserted by one of his own species.

Even if they were to leave Europe and inhabit the deserts of the new world, yet one of the first results of those sympathies for which the demon thirsted would be children, and a race of devils would be propagated upon the earth who might make the very existence of the species of man a condition precarious and full of terror. Had I right, for my own benefit, to inflict this curse upon everlasting generations? Now, for the first time, the selfishness of my promise burst upon me. I shuddered to think that future ages might curse me as their pest, who had not hesitated to buy its own peace at the price of the existence of the whole human race.

My heart failed within me. I thought with a sensation of madness on my promise of creating another being like to the first. Trembling with passion, I tore to pieces the thing on which I was engaged.

I left the room, and locking the door, made a solemn vow in my own heart never to resume my labors. With trembling steps, I sought my own apartment. Several hours passed, and I remained near my window gazing on the sea. It was almost motionless, for the winds were hushed and all nature reposed under the eye of the quiet moon. A few fishing vessels alone specked the water, and now and then the gentle breeze wafted the sound of voices as the fishermen called to one another. I felt the silence, although I was hardly conscious of its extreme profundity, until my ear was suddenly arrested by the paddling of oars near the shore, and a person landed close to my house.

In a few minutes after, I heard the creaking of my door, and presently I heard the sound of footsteps along the passage. I trembled from head to foot, and was overcome by the sensation of helplessness. The door opened, and the wretch whom I dreaded appeared. His countenance expressed the utmost extent of malice and treachery. Shutting the door, he approached me, and said in a smothered voice, "You have destroyed the work which you began. What is it that you intend? Do you dare to break your promise?"

"Begone!" I cried. "I do break my promise. Never will I create another like yourself, equal in deformity and wickedness. I shall not in cool blood set loose upon the earth a demon whose delight is in death and wretchedness. Begone! I am firm and your words will only exasperate my rage."

The monster let out a howl of devilish despair and gnashed his teeth in the impotence of anger. "Shall each man find a wife for his bosom, and each beast have his mate, and I be alone? Are you to be happy while I grovel in the intensity of my wretchedness? Man, you may hate, but beware. Your hours will pass in dread and misery. You can blast my other passions, but revenge will remain—revenge, henceforth dearer than light or food! I may die, but first you, my tyrant and tormentor, shall curse the sun that gazes on your misery."

"Devil, cease, and do not poison the air with these sounds of malice. I have declared my resolution to you and I am no coward to bend beneath words. Leave me. I am inexorable."

"It is well. I go, but remember, I shall be with you on your wedding-night."

He quitted the house with precipitation. In a few moments I saw him in his boat, which shot across the waters and was soon lost amidst the waves. All was again silent, but his words rung in my ears. I burned with rage. I walked up and down my room hastily and perturbed, while my imagination conjured up a thousand images to torment and sting me. Why had I not followed him, and closed with him in mortal strife? But I had suffered him to depart, and he had directed his course towards the mainland. I shuddered to think who might be next sacrificed to his insatiate revenge. And then I thought again of his words: "*I will be with you on your wedding-night.*" That then was the period fixed for the fulfillment of my destiny. In that hour I should die, and at once satisfy and extinguish his malice.

The night passed away, and the sun rose from the ocean. I walked about the isle like a restless spectre, separated from all it loved, and miserable in the separation. I saw a fishing-boat land close to me, and one of the men brought me a packet. It contained letters from Geneva, and one from Clerval, entreating me to join him. He said that he was wearing away his time fruitlessly where he was. He besought me, therefore, to leave my solitary isle, and to meet him at Perth, that we might proceed southwards together. This letter in a degree recalled me to life, and I determined to quit my island at the expiration of two days.

Yet, before I departed, there was a task to perform, on which I shuddered to reflect. I must pack up my chemical instruments, and for that purpose I must enter the room which had been the scene of my odious work, and I must handle those utensils, the sight of which was sickening to me. The next morning at daybreak I summoned sufficient courage and unlocked the door of my laboratory. The remains of the half-finished creature lay scattered on the floor, and I almost felt as if I had mangled the living flesh of a human being. I paused to collect myself and then entered the chamber. With trembling hand I conveyed the instruments out of the room. The odious relics of my work I put into a basket, with a great quantity of stones, and laying them up, determined to throw them into the sea.

Between two and three in the morning the moon rose, and putting my basket aboard a little skiff, I sailed out about four miles from the shore. The scene was perfectly solitary. A few boats were returning towards land, but I sailed away from them. I felt as if I was about the commission of a dreadful crime. At one time the moon was suddenly overspread by a thick cloud, and I took advantage of the moment of darkness, and cast my basket into the sea. I listened to the gurgling sound as it sunk, and then sailed away from the spot. The sky became clouded, but the air was pure, although chilled by the breeze that was then rising. But it refreshed me, and filled me with such agreeable sensations, that I resolved to prolong my stay on the water, and fixing the rudder in a direct position, stretched myself at the bottom of the boat. Clouds hid the moon, everything was obscure, and I heard only the sound of the boat as its keel cut through the waves. The murmur lulled me and in a short time I slept soundly.

I do not know how long I remained in this situation, but when I awoke the sun had already mounted considerably. The wind was high and the waves continually threatened the safety of my little skiff. I found that the wind was northeast, and must have driven me far from the coast from which I had embarked. Some hours passed thus, but by degrees, as the sun declined towards the horizon, the wind died away into a gentle breeze, and the sea became free from breakers. But these gave place to a heavy swell. I felt sick and hardly able to hold the rudder, when suddenly I saw a line of high land towards the south.

I resolved to sail directly towards the town, as a place where I could most easily procure nourishment. Fortunately I had money with me. As I turned the promontory, I perceived a small neat town and a good harbor, which I entered.

As I was occupied in fixing the boat and arranging the sails, several people crowded towards the spot. They seemed much surprised at my appearance, but instead of offering me any assistance, whispered together with gestures that at any other time might have produced in me a slight sensation of alarm. As it was, I merely remarked that they spoke English, and I therefore addressed them in that language: "My good friends," said I, "will you be so kind as to tell me the name of this town and inform me where I am?"

"You will know that soon enough," replied a man with a hoarse voice. "Maybe you are come to a place that will not prove much to your taste, but you will not be consulted as to your quarters, I promise you."

I was exceedingly surprised on receiving so rude an answer from a stranger, and I was also disconcerted on perceiving the frowning and angry countenances of his companions. "Why do you answer me so roughly?" I replied. "Surely it is not the custom of Englishmen to receive strangers so inhospitably."

"I do not know," said the man, "what the custom of the English may be, but it is the custom of the Irish to hate villains."

While this strange dialogue continued, I perceived the crowd rapidly increase. Their faces expressed a mixture of curiosity and anger, which annoyed and in some degree alarmed me. I inquired the way to the inn, but no one replied. I then moved forward and a murmuring sound arose from the crowd as they followed and surrounded me. An ill-looking man tapped me on the shoulder and said,

"Come, sir, you must follow me to Mr. Kirwin's, to give an account of yourself."

"Who is Mr. Kirwin? Why am I to give an account of myself? Is not this a free country?"

"Ay, sir, free enough for honest folks. Mr. Kirwin is a magistrate, and you are to give an account of the death of a gentleman who was found murdered here last night."

I must pause here, for it requires all my fortitude to express the feelings of portent that overwhelmed me, or to properly recall the frightful events I am about to relate, which in a few moments would overwhelm me, and extinguish in horror and despair all fear of ignominy or death. From the darkness that enveloped my senses, I can only construct this cold procession of facts that were unveiled to me, as if from some great detachment:

—that the body of a man was found on the shore, who was at first supposed to have drowned and been thrown on shore by the waves, but on examination, was found to have his clothes dry, and the black mark of strangulation on his neck;

—that a woman had seen a boat with only one man in it push off from that part of the shore where the corpse was afterwards found;

—that several men conjectured that, with the strong north wind that had arisen during the night, it was very probable that I had beaten about for many hours and had been obliged to return nearly to the same spot from which I had departed;

—and that the magistrate, on hearing this evidence, desired that I should be taken into the room where the body lay for interment, that it might be observed what effect the sight of it would produce upon me.

This idea was probably suggested by the extreme agitation I had exhibited when the mode of the murder had been described. I was accordingly conducted by the magistrate and several other persons to the inn. I entered the room where the corpse lay and was led up to the coffin. How can I describe my sensations on beholding it? I feel yet parched with horror, nor can I reflect on that terrible moment without shuddering and agony. The examination, the presence of the magistrate and witnesses, passed like a dream from my memory when I saw the lifeless form of Henry Clerval stretched before me.

I was spared the disgrace of appearing publicly as a criminal, as the case was not brought before the court that decides on life and death. The grand jury rejected the bill on its being proved that I was on the Orkney Islands at the hour the body of my friend was found, and after my removal I was liberated from detention.

In the weeks after these heart-rending events, I had lain on the point of death with fever. My ravings, as I afterwards heard, were frightful. I called myself the murderer of William, of Justine, and of Clerval. Sometimes I entreated my attendants to assist me in the destruction of the fiend by whom I was tormented, and at others I felt the fingers of the monster already grasping my neck and screamed aloud with agony and terror

During this period, I had briefly recovered sufficiently to send my father the horrific news of Clerval's murder, but had spared him and Elizabeth the distressing account of the unfair accusations that were thrown against me, and the appalling effects all this had manifested upon my physical and mental conditions. It was necessary, as soon as my strength allowed, that I should return without delay to

Geneva, there to watch over the lives of those I so fondly loved and to lie in wait for the murderer.

I was a shattered wreck—the shadow of a human being. I was a mere skeleton, but the fever that night and day had preyed upon my wasted frame was gone. While journeying homeward I became more calm. Misery had her dwelling in my heart, but my pulse beat with a feverish joy when I reflected that I should soon see my sweet and beloved Elizabeth. Some softened feelings stole into my heart and dared to whisper paradisiacal dreams of love and happiness.

Upon my arrival home the sweet girl welcomed me with warm affection, yet tears were in her eyes as she beheld my emaciated frame and feverish cheeks. I saw a change in her also. She was thinner and had lost much of that heavenly vivacity that had before charmed me, but her gentleness and soft looks of compassion made her a more fit companion for one blasted and miserable as I was. In this state of mind, I could not delay my articulation of that which had been so long expressed between us only in looks and warmest admiration and affection: that my dearest hopes were entirely bound in the expectation of our union. But my heart faltered when in place of smiles and joyful acceptance of my passionate proposal, her face displayed lines of concern and stern resolution.

"My poor cousin, how much you must have suffered!" said she. "This winter has passed most miserably, tortured as I have been by anxious suspense. I had hoped to see peace return to your countenance, and to find your heart not totally void of comfort and tranquility. Yet I fear that the same feelings now exist that made you so miserable a year ago, even perhaps augmented by time. Now that you have openly stated your sincere intentions, I dare not any longer postpone that which I have often wished to express to you, but have never had the courage to begin.

"Our union has been the favorite plan of your parents ever since our infancy. We were affectionate playfellows during childhood, and dear and valued friends to one another as we grew older. I confess to you, my friend, that I love you, and that in my airy dreams of futurity you have been my constant soul-mate. But unless it were the dictate of your own free choice and not a stifling sense of family honor that impels your proposal, there is little hope for our mutual happiness in marriage."

"Chase away your idle fears, my beloved girl," said I. "To you alone do I consecrate my life and my endeavors for contentment. Little happiness may remain for us on earth, yet all that I may one day enjoy is centered in you. I have one secret, Elizabeth, a dreadful one. When revealed to you it will chill your frame with horror, and then, far from being surprised at my misery, you will only wonder that I survive what I have endured. I will confide this tale of misery and terror to you the day after our marriage shall take place, for, my sweet cousin, there must be perfect confidence between us. But until then, I conjure you, do not mention or allude to it. This I most earnestly entreat, and I know you will comply."

Preparations were made for our wedding, which was to take place in our family's house by the lake near Bellerive. As the period fixed for the event drew near, I took every precaution to defend my person in case the fiend should openly attack me. I carried pistols and a dagger constantly about me, and was ever on the watch to prevent artifice.

Elizabeth seemed happy. My tranquil demeanor contributed greatly to calm her mind. But on the day that was to fulfill my wishes and my destiny she was melancholy, and a presentiment of evil pervaded her. My father was in the meantime overjoyed, and in the bustle of preparation, and only recognized in the melancholy of his niece the diffidence of a bride.

A large party assembled at my father's, congratulatory visits were received, and all wore a cheerful disposition. I concealed my feelings by an appearance of hilarity that brought smiles and joy to the countenance of my father, but hardly deceived the ever watchful and nicer eye of Elizabeth.

With gentle solemnity, the ceremony was performed. Those were the last moments of my life during which I enjoyed the feeling of happiness.

It was eight o'clock. I had been calm during the day, but so soon as night obscured the shapes of objects, a thousand fears arose in my mind. I was anxious and watchful, while my right hand grasped a pistol which was hidden in my bosom. Every sound terrified me, nor can you wonder that, omnipotent as the fiend had yet been in his deeds of blood, I should almost regard him as invincible, and that when he had pronounced the words, "I shall be with you on your wedding-night," I should regard the threatened fate as unavoidable.

Great God! If for one instant I had thought what might be the hellish intention of my fiendish adversary, I would rather have banished myself forever from my native country, and wandered a friendless outcast over the earth, than have consented to this miserable marriage. As if possessed of magic powers, the monster had blinded me to his real intentions, and when I thought that I had prepared only my own death, I hastened that of a far dearer victim.

Elizabeth observed my agitation for some time in timid and fearful silence, but there was something in my glance which communicated terror to her, and trembling she asked, "What is it that agitates you, my dear Victor? What is it you fear?"

"Oh! peace, peace, my love," replied I, "this night and all will be safe, but this night is dreadful, very dreadful."

I passed an hour in this state of mind, when suddenly I reflected how fearful the combat which I momentarily expected would be to my wife, and I earnestly entreated her to retire, resolving not to join her until I had obtained some knowledge as to the situation of my enemy.

She left me, and I continued some time walking up and down the passages of the house, and inspecting every corner that might afford a retreat to my adversary. But I discovered no trace of him, and was beginning to conjecture that some fortunate chance had intervened to prevent the execution of his menaces, when suddenly I heard a shrill and dreadful scream. It came from the room into which Elizabeth had retired. As I heard it, the whole truth rushed into my mind, my arms dropped, the motion of every muscle and fiber was suspended. I could feel the blood trickling in my veins and tingling in the extremities of my limbs. This state lasted but for an instant, the scream was repeated, and I rushed into the room.

Oh God, why did I not then expire! Why am I here to relate the destruction of the best hope and the purest creature of earth? She was there, lifeless and inanimate, thrown across the bed, her head hanging down, and her pale and distorted features half covered by her hair. Everywhere I turn I see the same figure—her bloodless arms and relaxed form flung by the murderer on its bridal bier. Could I behold this and live? Alas! life is obstinate and clings closest where it is most hated. For a moment only did I lose recollection. I fell senseless on the ground.

When I recovered, I found myself surrounded by the guests. Their countenances expressed a breathless terror, but the horror of others appeared only as a mockery, a shadow of the feelings that oppressed me. I escaped from them to the room where lay the body of Elizabeth, my love, my wife, so lately living, so dear, so worthy. She had been moved from the posture in which I had first beheld her, and now as she lay, her head upon her arm, and a handkerchief thrown across her face and neck, I might have supposed her asleep. I rushed towards her and embraced her with ardor, but the deadly languor and coldness of the limbs told me that what I now held in my arms had ceased to be the Elizabeth whom I had loved and cherished. The murderous mark of the fiend's grasp was on her neck.

While I still hung over her in the agony of despair, I happened to look up. The windows of the room had before been darkened, and I felt a kind of panic on seeing the pale yellow light of the moon illuminate the chamber. The shutters had been thrown back, and with a sensation of horror not to be described, I saw at the open window a figure the most hideous and abhorred. A grin was on the face of the monster. He seemed to jeer as with his fiendish finger he pointed towards the corpse of my wife. I rushed towards the window and, drawing a pistol from my bosom, fired. But he eluded me, leaped from his station, and running with the swiftness of lightning, plunged into the lake.

The report of the pistol brought a crowd into the room. My head whirled round, my steps were like those of a drunken man. I was placed in a chair, hardly conscious of what had happened. My hysterical rantings led them to believe I had shot at a form conjured up by my fancy. I was bewildered in a cloud of wonder and horror. There were women weeping. My eyes wandered round the room as if to seek something that I had lost, and settled on the corpse of my beloved. Even at that moment I knew not that my only remaining friends were safe from the malignity of the fiend. Would my father find himself writhing under his grasp? Would Ernest next fall dead at his feet? A fiend had snatched from me every hope of rest or future happiness.

4.

Mine has been a tale of horrors. I now approach their *acme*. My own strength is exhausted, and I must tell, in a few words, what remains of my hideous narration.

My father and Ernest yet lived, but the former sunk under the crowning loss of Elizabeth. I see him now, excellent and venerable old man! His eyes wandered in vacancy, for they had lost their charm and their delight—his Elizabeth, his more than daughter, whom he doted on with all that affection which a father feels. He could not live under the horrors that were accumulated around him. The springs of existence suddenly gave way. He was unable to rise from his bed, and in a few days he died in my arms.

For a time I lost sensation, and chains and darkness were the only objects that pressed upon me. I awakened to reason, at the same time that I awakened to revenge. When I thought of the miserable demon whom I had sent abroad into the world for my destruction, I desired and ardently prayed that I might have him within my grasp to wreak a great and signal revenge on his cursed head.

I quit Geneva forever. My country, which, when I was happy and beloved, was dear to me, now, in my adversity, became hateful. I provided myself with a sum of money, together with a few jewels which had belonged to my mother, and departed.

And so my wanderings began, which are to cease but with life. I have traversed a vast portion of the earth, and have endured all the hardships which travelers, in deserts and barbarous countries, are wont to meet. How I have lived I hardly know. Many times have I stretched my failing limbs upon the sandy plain and prayed for death. But revenge kept me alive. I dared not die and leave my adversary in being. The fiend had the uncanny skill to stalk me endlessly. I prayed he would again confront me, that we might commence our final duel.

I was answered when, through the stillness of night there broke a loud and fiendish laugh. It rung on my ears long and heavily. The mountains re-echoed it, and I felt as if all hell surrounded me with mockery and laughter. The laughter died away, when a well-known and abhorred voice, apparently close to my ear, addressed me in an audible whisper: "I am satisfied, miserable wretch! You have determined to live, and I am satisfied."

I darted towards the spot from which the sound proceeded, but the devil eluded my grasp. Suddenly the broad disk of the moon arose and shone full upon his ghastly and distorted shape as he fled with more than mortal speed.

I pursued him, and for many months this has been my task. Guided by a slight clue I followed the windings of the Rhone, but vainly. The blue Mediterranean appeared, and by a strange chance I saw the fiend enter by night and hide himself in a vessel bound for the Black Sea. I took my passage in the same ship but he escaped, I know not how.

Amidst the wilds of Tartary and Russia, although he still evaded me, I have ever followed in his track. Sometimes the peasants, scared by this horrid apparition, informed me of his path. Sometimes he himself, who feared that if I lost all trace of him I should despair and die, left some mark to guide me. Indeed, he left marks in writing on the barks of the trees, or cut in stone, that guided me and instigated my fury. "My reign is not yet over," or "You live, and my power is complete," and finally, "Follow me—I seek the everlasting ices of the north, where you will feel the misery of cold and frost to which I am impassive. You will find near this place, if you follow not too tardily, a dead hare. Eat and be refreshed. Come on, my enemy, we have yet to wrestle for our lives, but many hard and miserable hours must you endure until that period shall arrive."

The snows thickened and the cold increased in a degree almost too severe to support. The rivers were covered with ice and no fish could be procured, and thus I was cut off from my chief article of maintenance. Yet I continued with unabated fervor until the ocean appeared at a distance, forming the utmost boundary of the horizon. Oh, how unlike it was to the blue seas of the south! Covered with ice, it was only to be distinguished from land by its superior wildness and ruggedness. The Greeks wept for joy when they beheld the Mediterranean from the hills of Asia, and hailed with rapture the boundary of their toils. I did not weep, but I knelt down and with a full heart, thanked my guiding spirit for conducting me in safety to the place where I hoped, notwithstanding my adversary's gibe, to meet and grapple with him.

Some weeks before this period I had procured a sledge and dogs, and thus traversed the snows with inconceivable speed. I know not whether the fiend possessed the same advantages, but I found that I now gained ground on him, so much so that when I first saw the ocean he was but one day's journey in advance, and I hoped to intercept him before he should reach the beach. With new courage, therefore, I pressed on, and in two days arrived at a wretched hamlet on the sea-shore. I inquired of the inhabitants concerning the fiend. A gigantic monster, they said, had arrived the night before, putting to flight the inhabitants of a solitary cottage. He had carried off their store of winter food, and placing it in a sledge, to the joy of the horror-struck villagers, had pursued his journey across the sea in a direction that led to no land, and they conjectured that he must speedily be destroyed by the breaking of the ice or frozen by the eternal frosts.

On hearing this information I suffered a temporary access of despair. He had escaped me, and I must commence a destructive and almost endless journey across the mountainous ices of the ocean—amidst cold that few of the inhabitants could long endure, and which I, the native of a genial and sunny climate, could not hope to survive.

Now, when I appeared almost within grasp of my foe, my hopes had been extinguished, and I lost all trace of him more utterly than I had ever done before. I pressed on, but in vain. A ground sea was heard. The thunder of its progress, as the waters rolled and swelled beneath me, became every moment more ominous and terrific. The wind arose, the sea roared, and, as with the mighty shock of an earthquake, it split and cracked with a tremendous and overwhelming sound. The work was soon finished. In a few minutes a tumultuous sea rolled between me and my enemy, and I was left drifting on a scattered piece of ice, that was continually lessening, and thus preparing for me a hideous death.

In this manner many appalling hours passed. Several of my dogs died, and I myself was about to sink under the accumulation of distress, when I saw a vessel riding at anchor, and holding forth to me hopes of succor and life. I had no conception that vessels ever came so far north and was astounded at the sight. I quickly destroyed part of my sledge to construct oars, and by these means was enabled, with infinite fatigue, to move my ice-raft in the direction of the ship. I was taken aboard the vessel, which was bound on a voyage of discovery towards the northern pole.

My limbs were nearly frozen, and I was worn down by fatigue and suffering. To my rescuers my body must have appeared dreadfully emaciated. I was carried into the cabin, where, quitting the fresh air, I soon fainted. When I awoke I was wrapped in blankets and lay near the chimney of the kitchen stove. I was forced to swallow a small quantity of brandy, and later offered a little soup, which helped restore me. The captain proved a man of unlimited kindness. When I had in some measure recovered, he removed me to his own cabin, and attended to me as much as his duty would permit. He took pains to keep off the men, who wished to ask me a thousand questions. When one asked why I had come so far upon the ice in so strange a vehicle, I answered, "To seek one who fled from me."

"And did the man whom you pursued travel in the same fashion?"

"Yes."

"Then I fancy we have seen him," reported the sailor, "for the day before we picked you up, we saw some dogs drawing a sledge with a large man in it across the ice."

Later when I was alone with the Captain I said, "I have doubtless excited your curiosity, as well as that of these good people, but you are too considerate to make inquiries."

"Certainly it would indeed be very impertinent and inhuman in me to trouble you with any inquisitiveness of mine."

"And yet you rescued me from a strange and perilous situation. You have benevolently restored me to life."

The boundless kindness of the officer aroused a new spirit of life that animated my decaying frame. In the days that followed, feeling that I owed him some account for his patience, I recounted, sparingly, the sad history that led me to the current circumstance, leaving out all such elements as would threaten my new friend's assurance for my sanity, or our mutual camaraderie which increased to me in value day by day.

When my strength allowed, I would go on deck, where my eyes could not help but seek the sledge which had before appeared.

Oh, when will my guiding spirit allow me the rest I so much desire, or must I die and the demon yet live? His soul is as hellish as his form, full of treachery and fiendlike malice. I call on the names of William, Justine, Clerval, Elizabeth, my father, and of the wretched Victor, and I thrust my mind's sword into his heart!

Though I am rescued from certain death upon the frigid sea, yet there remains something terribly appalling in our situation. We are surrounded by mountains of ice which admit of no escape and threaten every moment to crush our vessel.

Meanwhile my host regards me with the tenderest compassion. He endeavors to fill me with hope, and talks as if life were a possession to be valued. He reminds me how often the same accidents have happened to other navigators who have attempted this sea, and in spite of myself, he fills me with cheerful prognoses. Even the sailors feel the power of his eloquence. When he speaks they no longer despair. He rouses their energies, and while they hear his voice, they believe these vast mountains of ice are molehills which will vanish before the resolutions of man.

On a day when despair had spread among the crew to an alarming and dangerous degree, from my bed I heard his voice address them in a rousing speech. He shamed them, while praising their heretofore show of fortitude:

"Be men, or be more than men. Be steady to your purposes and firm as a rock. This ice is not made of such stuff as your hearts may be. It is mutable and cannot withstand you if you say that it shall not."

The Captain spoke with a voice so modulated to the different feelings expressed in his speech, with an eye so full of lofty design and heroism, none would wonder that these men were moved.

But the cold is excessive, and the scene of desolation weighs down the spirits of many of my unfortunate comrades. I have daily declined in health. A feverish fire will suddenly rouse me to exertion, then, exhausted, I sink into lifelessness. Alas! the strength I relied on is gone. I feel that I shall soon die, and he, my enemy and persecutor, may still be in being.

At length the ice began to brake, and roarings like thunder were heard at a distance as the islands split and cracked in every direction. The ice broke apart behind us and was driven with force towards the north. A breeze sprung from the west and in two days the passage towards the south became perfectly free. When the sailors saw this, a shout of tumultuous joy broke from them, loud and long-continued.

By now my illness has increased in such a degree that I am entirely confined to bed. I am sunk in languor and almost deprived of life. Awakened by the tumult, I ask the cause. From the cabin door, "They shout," answers he who rarely left my side, "because they will soon return to England!" Then, returning to his men, he leaves my sight forever.

The intoxicating cheers suddenly arouse in me an irrational determination that I should yet recover my health and resume my desperate quest assigned to me by Heaven. Exhausted, I breathe with difficulty. I am weak, but surely the spirits who freed the ship will endow me with sufficient strength to continue. I endeavor to spring from the bed, but the exertion is too great for me. I fall back and faint. In my delirium, the forms of the beloved dead flit before me and I hasten to their arms.

Presently I dream that over me looms a form, gigantic in stature, yet uncouth and distorted in its proportions. As he hangs over my bed his face is concealed by long locks of ragged hair, but one vast hand is extended, in color and apparent texture like that of a mummy. Yet I do not look away from his face, of such loathsome yet appalling hideousness. His every feature and gesture seem instigated by the wildest rage of some uncontrollable passion.

"Oh, unfortunate creator, do you see an unpenitent monster before you? my final victim, do you dream?" says the demon, "do you think that I am without agony and remorse? think you that the groans of Clerval were music to my ears? did you not know that you fashioned my heart to be susceptible of love and sympathy? and when wrenched by misery to vice and hatred it would not endure the violent change without pain such as you cannot even imagine?

"I pitied you, Frankenstein. My pity amounted to horror. I abhorred myself. But when I discovered that you, the author at once of my existence and of its unspeakable torments, dared to hope for happiness, that while wretchedness and despair accumulated upon me, you sought enjoyment in feelings and passions from the indulgence of which I was forever barred, then impotent envy and bitter indignation filled me with an insatiable thirst for vengeance. I recollected my threat and resolved that it should be accomplished.

Yet when she died!—nay, then I cast off all feeling, subdued all anguish, to riot in the excess of my despair. And now my insatiable passion is ended, with you, my last victim! In your death my crimes are consummated. The miserable series of my being is wound to its close! Oh, Frankenstein! generous and self-devoted being! what does it avail that I now ask you to pardon me? I, who irretrievably destroyed you by destroying all you loved."

"Wretch!" I cry, though with enfeebled voice, for I am not touched by the his expressions of repentance, imbued as they are with his undiminished powers of eloquence and fraudulent persuasion. "Dare not you come here to whine over the desolation that you have made. Hypocritical fiend! If I whom you mourn lived on, still would I be the object, again the prey, of your accursed vengeance. It is not pity that you feel. You lament only because the victim of your malignity is withdrawn from your power."

"Oh, it is not so—not so," interrupts the being. "I seek not a fellow-feeling in my misery. No sympathy may I ever find. When I first sought it, it was the love of virtue, the feelings of happiness and affection with which my whole being overflowed, that I wished to be participated. Once I falsely hoped to meet with beings who, pardoning my outward form, would love me for the excellent qualities which I was capable of unfolding. I was nourished with high thoughts of honor and devotion. But now crime has degraded me beneath the meanest animal. I have murdered the lovely and the helpless. I have strangled the innocent as they slept, and grasped to death his throat who never injured me or any other living thing. I have devoted you, my creator, the select specimen of all that is worthy of love and admiration among men, to misery.

"Fear not that I shall be the instrument of future mischief. My work is nearly complete. Neither yours nor any man's death is needed to consummate the series of my being, and accomplish that which must be done. But it requires my own. Do not think that I shall be slow to perform this sacrifice. I shall quit your vessel on the ice raft which brought me here and shall seek the most northern extremity of the globe. I shall collect my funeral pile and consume to ashes this miserable frame, that its remains may afford no light to any curious wretch who would create such another as I have been. I shall die.

"Soon he too is dead who called me into being, and when I shall be no more the very remembrance of us both will speedily vanish. I shall no longer see the sun or stars, or feel the winds play on my cheeks. Light, feeling, and sense will pass away, and in this condition must I find my happiness. Some years ago, when the images which this world affords first opened upon me, when I felt the cheering warmth of summer, and heard the rustling of the leaves and the warbling of the birds, and these were all to me, I should have wept to die. Now it is my only consolation.

"Farewell, Frankenstein! Farewell! I leave you, and in you the last of human kind whom these eyes will ever behold."

Saying this, from the cabin window the spectre springs on to the ice raft which lies close to the vessel, and is soon borne away by the waves and lost in darkness and distance.

THE END

DRACULA

Adapted from the novel by
BRAM STOKER

1.

Budapest seemed a wonderful place from the glimpse
which he got of it from the train and the little morning
walk he had through the streets. Jonathan feared to go very
far from the station, as he had arrived late from Vienna
and expected to depart again as near the correct time as
possible. The train left in pretty good time, and came to
Klausenburg after nightfall. Here he stopped for the night
at the Hotel Royale. He had for dinner, or rather supper, a
chicken done up some way with red pepper, which was
very good but made him thirsty. He made a mental note to
get the recipe for Mina. He asked the waiter, who said it
was called "paprika hendl," and, as it was a national dish, it
should be able to be had anywhere along the Carpathians.

Every known superstition in the world is gathered into
the horseshoe of the Carpathians, as if it were the center of
some sort of imaginative whirlpool. If so, his stay might be
very interesting. He would ask the Count all about them.

When in London, he had made search among the
books and maps in the library regarding Transylvania. He
was not able to light on any map or work giving the exact
locality of the Castle Dracula, as there were no maps of the
district to compare with his own Ordnance Survey Maps,

but he found that Bistritz, the post town named by Count Dracula, was a fairly well-known place.

It was on the dark side of twilight when he arrived there. Count Dracula had directed him to go to the Golden Krone Hotel, which he found, to great delight, to be thoroughly old-fashioned, for of course he wanted to see all he could of the ways of the country. He was evidently expected, for when he got near the door he faced a cheery-looking elderly woman in the usual peasant dress-white undergarment with a long double apron, front, and back, of colored stuff fitting almost too tight for modesty. When he came close she bowed and said, "The Herr Englishman?" "Yes," he said, "Jonathan Harker." She smiled, and gave some message to an elderly man in white shirt-sleeves, who had followed her to the door. He went, but immediately returned with a letter:

"My friend.—Welcome to the Carpathians. I am anxiously expecting you. Sleep well tonight. At three tomorrow the diligence will start for Bukovina; a place on it is kept for you. At the Borgo Pass my carriage will await you and will bring you to me. I trust your journey from London has been a happy one, and that you will enjoy your stay in my beautiful land.—Your friend, Dracula."

He and his wife, the old lady who had received Jonathan, looked at each other in a frightened sort of way. When asked if he knew Count Dracula, and could tell anything of his castle, both he and his wife crossed themselves, and saying that they knew nothing at all, simply refused to speak further. It was so near the time of starting that there was no time to ask anyone else. It was all very mysterious and not by any means comforting to the young solicitor.

Just before he was leaving, the old lady came up to Jonathan's room and said in a hysterical way, "Must you go? Oh! Young Herr, it is the eve of St. George's Day. Do you not know that tonight, when the clock strikes midnight, all the evil things in the world will have full sway? Do you know where you are going, and what you are going to?" She was in such evident distress that he tried to comfort her, but without effect. It was all very ridiculous but Jonathan said, as gravely as he could, that his duty was imperative, and that he must go. She then dried her eyes, and taking a crucifix from her neck offered it to him. Jonathan did not know what to do, for, as an English Churchman, he had been taught to regard such things as in some measure idolatrous, and yet it seemed so ungracious to refuse an old lady meaning so well and in such a state of mind. She saw the doubt in his face. She put the rosary round his neck and said, "For your mother's sake," and went out of the room.

Whether it was the old lady's fear, or the many ghostly traditions of this place, or the crucifix itself, he did not know, but he was not feeling nearly as easy in his mind as usual. The coach arrived, of course, late, the crucifix still round his neck.

He soon lost sight and recollection of ghostly fears in the beauty of the scene as they drove along, although had Jonathan known the language, or rather languages, which his fellow-passengers were speaking, he might not have been able to throw them off so easily.

The road was rugged, but still they seemed to fly over it with a feverish haste. Jonathan could not understand then what the haste meant, but the driver was evidently bent on losing no time in reaching Borgo Prund.

As they wound on their endless way, the sun sank lower and lower behind them and the shadows of the evening began to creep round them. It began to get very cold, and the growing twilight seemed to merge the gloom of the trees into one dark mistiness. Sometimes the hills were so steep that, despite the driver's haste, the horses could only go slowly. Jonathan wished to get down and walk up them, as he would at home, but the driver would not hear of it. "No, no," he said. "You must not walk here. The dogs are too fierce." And then he added, with what he evidently meant for grim pleasantry—for he looked round to catch the approving smile of the rest—"And you may have enough of such matters before you go to sleep." The only stop he would make was a moment's pause to light his lamps.

When it grew dark there seemed to be some excitement among the passengers, and they kept speaking to the driver, one after the other, as though urging him to further speed. He lashed the horses unmercifully with his long whip, and with wild cries of encouragement urged them on to further exertions. Then through the darkness could be seen a sort of patch of grey light ahead, as though there were a cleft in the hills. The excitement of the passengers grew greater. The crazy coach rocked on its great leather springs, and swayed like a boat tossed on a stormy sea. Everyone had to hold on. The road grew more level, and they appeared to fly along. Then the mountains seemed to come nearer on each side and to frown down upon them. They were entering on the Borgo Pass.

The driver leaned forward, and on each side the passengers, craning over the edge of the coach, peered eagerly into the darkness. It was evident that something very exciting was either happening or expected, but though he asked each passenger, no one would give Jonathan the slightest explanation. This state of excitement kept on for some little time. And at last the Pass opened out on the eastern side. There were dark, rolling clouds overhead, and in the air the heavy, oppressive sense of thunder. Jonathan was looking out for the conveyance which was to take him to the Count. Each moment he expected to see the glare of lamps through the blackness, but all was dark. The only light was the flickering rays of his own coach's lamps, in which the steam from its hard-driven horses rose in a white cloud. The sandy road lay white before them, but there was on it no sign of a vehicle.

Turning to Jonathan, the driver spoke in German worse than his own.

"There is no carriage here. You are not expected after all. You will now come on to Bukovina, and return tomorrow or the next day, better the next day." While he was speaking the horses began to neigh and snort and plunge wildly, so that the driver had to hold them up. Then, amongst a chorus of screams from the peasants and a universal crossing of themselves, a carriage with four horses drove up behind, overtook and drew up beside the coach. You could see from the flash of lamps as the rays fell on them, that the horses were coal-black and splendid animals. They were driven by a tall man with a great black hat, which seemed to hide his face. The gleam of a pair of very bright eyes seemed red in the lamplight as he turned. He said to the driver, "You are early tonight, my friend."

The man stammered in reply, "The English Herr was in a hurry."

To which the stranger replied, "That is why, I suppose, you wished him to go on to Bukovina. You cannot deceive me, my friend. I know too much, and my horses are swift." As he spoke he smiled, and the lamplight fell on a hard-looking mouth with very red lips and sharp-looking teeth as white as ivory. One of the passengers whispered to another the line from Burger's "Lenore."

"Denn die Todten reiten Schnell." ("For the dead travel fast.")

The strange driver evidently heard the words, for he looked up with a gleaming smile. The passenger turned his face away, at the same time putting out his two fingers and crossing himself.

"Give me the Herr's luggage," said the driver, and with exceeding alacrity Jonathan's bags were handed out and put in the carriage. Then Jonathan descended from the side of the coach, as the carriage was close alongside, the driver helping him with a hand which caught his arm in a grip of steel. Without a word he shook his reins, the horses turned, and they swept into the darkness of the pass. As they sank into the darkness Jonathan felt a strange chill, and a lonely feeling come over him. But a cloak was thrown over his shoulders, and a rug across his knees, and the driver said in excellent German—

"The night is chill, mein Herr, and my master the Count bade me take all care of you. There is a flask of slivovitz (the plum brandy of the country) underneath the seat, if you should require it."

Jonathan did not take any, but it was a comfort to know it was there all the same. He felt a little strangely, and not a little frightened. Had there been any alternative he should have taken it, instead of prosecuting that unknown night journey.

A dog began to howl somewhere in a farmhouse far down the road, a long, agonized wailing, as if from fear. The sound was taken up by another dog, and then another and another, till, borne on the wind which now sighed softly through the Pass, a wild howling began which seemed to come from all over the country. Then, far off in the distance, from the mountains on each side began a louder and a sharper howling, that of wolves, which affected both the horses and Jonathan in the same way. For he was minded to jump from the carriage and run, while they reared again and plunged madly, so that the driver had to use all his great strength to keep them from bolting.

It grew colder and colder still, and fine, powdery snow began to fall, so that soon they and all around them were covered with a white blanket. The baying of the wolves sounded nearer and nearer, as though they were closing round on them from every side. Jonathan grew dreadfully afraid, and the horses shared his fear. The driver, however, was not in the least disturbed. They sped onwards through the gloom, with the howling all around them, as though the wolves were following in a moving circle.

Suddenly, the driver at once checked the horses, for the moon had appeared behind the jagged crest of a jutting, pine-clad rock, and by its light revealed around them a ring of wolves, with white teeth and lolling red tongues, with long, sinewy limbs and shaggy hair. They were a hundred times more terrible in the grim silence which held them than even when they howled. Jonathan felt a sort of paralysis of fear. The horses jumped about and reared, and looked helplessly round with eyes that rolled in a way painful to see. But the living ring of terror encompassed them on every side, and they were forced to remain within it. Suddenly the driver's voice was heard raised in a tone of imperious command. As he swept his long arms, as though brushing aside some impalpable obstacle, the wolves fell back and back further still. Just then a heavy cloud passed across the face of the moon, so that all was again in darkness.

When the cloud lifted, the wolves had disappeared. This was all so strange and uncanny to Jonathan that he was afraid to speak or move. The time seemed interminable as they swept on their way, now in almost complete darkness, for the rolling clouds obscured the moon. The carriage kept on ascending, with occasional periods of quick descent, but in the main always ascending. At last the driver was in the act of pulling up the horses in the courtyard of a vast ruined castle, from whose tall black windows came no ray of light, and whose broken battlements showed a jagged line against the sky.

When the caleche stopped, the driver jumped down and held out his hand to assist Jonathan to alight. Then he took the passenger's traps and placed them on the ground beside a great door, old and studded with large iron nails, and set in a projecting doorway of massive stone. The driver jumped again into his seat and shook the reins. The horses started forward and the carriage disappeared down one of the dark openings.

Jonathan stood in silence where he was, for he did not know what to do. Of bell or knocker there was no sign. Through those frowning walls and dark window openings it was not likely that his voice could penetrate. The time he waited seemed endless, and he felt doubts and fears crowding upon him. What sort of place had he come to, and among what kind of people? What sort of grim adventure was it on which he had embarked? Was this a customary incident in the life of a solicitor's clerk sent out to explain the purchase of a London estate to a foreigner? Solicitor's clerk! Mina would not like that. Solicitor, for just before leaving London he had got word that his examination was successful, and her husband was now a full-blown solicitor!

A heavy step approached behind the great door, and through the chinks was the gleam of a coming light. Then there was the sound of rattling chains and the clanking of massive bolts drawn back. A key was turned with the loud grating noise of long disuse, and the great door swung back.

Within stood a tall old man clad in black from head to foot, without a single speck of color about him anywhere. He held in his hand an antique silver lamp, throwing long quivering shadows as it flickered in the draft of the open door. The old man motioned Jonathan in with his right hand with a courtly gesture, saying in excellent English, but with a strange intonation—

"Welcome to my house! Enter freely and of your own free will!" He made no motion of stepping to meet him, but stood like a statue, as though his gesture of welcome had fixed him into stone. The instant, however, that Jonathan had stepped over the threshold, the old man moved impulsively forward and grasped the other's hand with one as cold as ice, more like the hand of a dead than a living man. The strength of the handshake was so much akin to that of the driver, whose face he had not seen, that for a moment Jonathan doubted if it were not the same person. So to make sure, he said interrogatively, "Count Dracula?"

The man bowed in a courtly way as he replied, "I am Dracula, and I bid you welcome, Mr. Harker, to my house. Come in, the night air is chill, and you must need to eat and rest." As he was speaking, he put the lamp on a bracket on the wall, and stepping out, carried in Jonathan's luggage before he could forestall him.

"Nay, sir, you are my guest. It is late, and my people are not available. Let me see to your comfort myself." He insisted on carrying the traps along the passage, and then up a great winding stair, and along another great passage, on whose stone floor their steps rang heavily. At the end of this he threw open a heavy door, and Jonathan rejoiced to see a well-lit room in which a table was spread for supper, and on whose mighty hearth a great fire of logs, freshly replenished, flamed and flared.

The Count halted, putting down the bags, closed the door, and crossing the room, opened another door, and motioned Jonathan to enter. It was a welcome sight. For there was a great bedroom well lighted and warmed with another log fire.

"You will need, after your journey, to refresh yourself by making your toilet. I trust you will find all you wish. When you are ready you will find your supper prepared."

The light and warmth and the Count's courteous welcome seemed to have dissipated all Jonathan's doubts and fears. Having then reached his normal state, he discovered that he was half famished with hunger. So making a hasty toilet, he went into the other room. His host, who stood on one side of the great fireplace, leaning against the stonework, made a graceful wave of his hand to the table, and said,

"I pray you, be seated and sup how you please. You will I trust, excuse me that I do not join you, but I have dined already, and I do not sup."

As Jonathan ate, the stillness was suddenly broken by the howling of many wolves as if from down below in the valley. The Count's eyes gleamed, and he said,

"Listen to them, the children of the night. What music they make! But you must be tired. Your bedroom is all ready, and tomorrow you shall sleep as late as you will."

Jonathan only slept a few hours, and feeling that he could not sleep any more, got up. He had hung his shaving glass by the window and was just beginning to shave. Suddenly he felt a hand on his shoulder, and heard the Count's voice saying, "Good morning." Jonathan started, for it amazed him that he had not seen him, since the reflection of the glass covered the whole room behind him. In starting he had cut himself slightly. The cut had bled a little, and the blood was trickling over his chin. He laid down the razor, turning as he did so half round to look for some sticking plaster. When the Count saw his face, his eyes blazed with a sort of demoniac fury, and he suddenly made a grab at Jonathan's throat. Jonathan drew away and the Count's hand touched the string of beads which held the crucifix. It made an instant change in him.

"Take care," he said, "take care how you cut yourself. It is more dangerous that you think in this country."

The fury passed so quickly that Jonathan could hardly believe that it was ever there.

When he went into the dining room, breakfast was prepared, and a card on the table, on which was written: *I have to be absent for a while. Do not wait for me.—D.* Jonathan noted that as yet he had not seen the Count eat or drink.

After breakfast he did a little exploring in the castle. He went out on the stairs and found a room looking towards the South, where the view was magnificent. The castle was on the very edge of a terrific precipice. A stone falling from the window would fall a thousand feet without touching anything.

But when he explored further he found nothing but doors, doors everywhere, and all locked and bolted. In no place save from the windows in the castle walls was there an available exit. The castle was like a veritable prison. And Jonathan was the prisoner.

It was late in the afternoon when Jonathan noticed that the lamps were lit in the study or library, and there he found the Count lying on the sofa, reading, of all things in the world, an English Bradshaw's Guide.

"Come," said the Count, upon seeing Jonathan, "tell me of London and of the house which you have procured for me."

With an apology for his remissness, Jonathan went into his own room to get the papers from his bag. While he was placing them in order he heard a rattling of china and silver in the next room, and through the chink of the hinges of the door saw the Count clearing the table, which added to Jonathan's growing suspicion that there were no servants in the house. Was it the Count himself who was the driver of the coach that brought him here? This was a terrible thought, for if so, did it mean that he could control the wolves, by only holding up his hand for silence? How was it that all the people at Bistritz and on the coach had some terrible fear of him? What meant the giving of the crucifix?

When Jonathan came in, the Count motioned for him to be seated, placed a lamp upon the table, and turned his full attention to the plans and deeds and figures. He was interested in everything, and asked a myriad questions about the place and its surroundings. He clearly had studied beforehand all he could get on the subject of the neighborhood, for he evidently at the end knew very much more than Jonathan did. When the latter remarked this, he answered—

"Well, but, my friend, is it not needful that I should? When I go there I shall be all alone in a strange country, and my friend Jonathan Harker will not be by my side to correct and aid me."

The estate the Count would be deeded was named Carfax, no doubt a corruption of the old Quatre Face, as the house was four sided, very large, and contained in all some twenty acres, quite surrounded by a high, heavy stone wall of ancient structure. It sat in the district of Purfleet, near Whitby, where Jonathan had discovered it during a summer visit to some family friends of his wife in the port town. It was part of a keep, and was close to an old chapel or church. There were but few houses close at hand, one being a very large house only recently added to and formed into a private lunatic asylum. It was not, however, visible from the grounds.

"I rejoice also that there is a chapel of old times," the Count said. "We Transylvanian nobles love not to think that our bones may lie amongst the common dead. Moreover, the walls of my castle are broken. The shadows are many, and the wind breathes cold through the broken battlements and casements." Somehow his words and his look did not seem to accord, or else it was that his cast of face made his smile look malignant and saturnine.

After his signature was acquired to the necessary papers, the Count showed no inclination to conclude their conversation. He continued chatting, and asking questions on every conceivable subject, hour after hour. All at once the crow of the cock came with preternatural shrillness through the clear morning air.

Count Dracula, jumping to his feet, said, "Why there is the morning again! How remiss I am to let you stay up so long. You must make your conversation regarding my dear new country of England less interesting, so that I may not forget how time flies by us," then in a sudden change of tone he said, "Have you written to your associate?"

It was with some bitterness in Jonathan's heart that he answered that he had not, that as yet he had not seen any opportunity of sending letters to anybody.

"Then write now, my young friend," said the Count, laying a heavy hand on the seated man's shoulder, "write and say, if it will please you, that you shall stay with me until a month from now."

"Do you wish me to stay so long?" he asked, for his heart grew cold at the thought.

"I desire it much, nay I will take no refusal."

While Count Dracula was speaking, there was that in his eyes and in his bearing which made Jonathan remember that he was a prisoner. The Count saw his victory and his mastery in the troubled face of his visitor, and he began at once to use them in his own smooth, resistless way.

"I pray you, my good young friend, that you will not discourse of things other than business in your letters. It will doubtless please your friends to know that you are well, and that you look forward to getting home to them. Is it not so?"

Jonathan understood as well as if he had been given an unconcealed threat, and determined to write only formal notes at that time, but to write fully to Mina in secret, for to her he could write shorthand, which would puzzle the Count if he did see it.

"Let me advise you, my dear young friend." added the Count, "Nay, let me warn you with all seriousness, that the castle is old, and has many memories, and there are bad dreams for those who sleep unwisely. Be warned! Should sleep ever overcome you, then haste to your own chamber, for your rest will then be safe." And with a courtly bow he quickly left.

Jonathan doubted whether any dream could be more terrible than the unnatural, horrible net of gloom and mystery which seemed closing around him.

"I shall not fear to sleep in any place where he is not," he thought.

When he went to his room, he placed the crucifix over the head of his bed, and blessed the good woman who had placed it round his neck. For it was a comfort and a strength to him whenever he touched it.

As was the usual case, the Count made no appearance during the following day until the evening, when he announced to Jonathan, "I am informed that your supper is ready. I trust you will forgive me, but I have much work to do in private this evening."

Some time after he had finished his meal, Jonathan came out and went up the stone stair to where he could look out towards the South. There was some sense of freedom in the vast expanse, inaccessible though it was to him, as compared with the narrow darkness of the courtyard. Looking out on this, he felt that he was indeed in prison, and he seemed to want a breath of fresh air, though it were of the night. He was beginning to feel the nocturnal existence tell on him. It was destroying his nerve. He would start at his own shadow, and was full of all sorts of horrible imaginings.

Jonathan looked out over the beautiful expanse, bathed in soft yellow moonlight till it was almost as light as day. In the soft light the distant hills became melted, and the shadows in the valleys and gorges of velvety blackness. The mere beauty seemed to cheer him. As he leaned from the window his eye was caught by something moving a story below and somewhat to his left, where the windows of the

Count's own room would be. He drew back behind the stonework and looked carefully out.

What he saw was the Count's head coming out from the window. He did not see the face, but he knew the man by the neck and the movement of his back and arms. He was at first interested and somewhat amused, for it is wonderful how small a matter will interest and amuse a man when he is a prisoner. But his very feelings changed to repulsion and terror when he saw the whole man slowly emerge from the window and begin to crawl down the castle wall over the dreadful abyss, face down with his cloak spreading out around him like great wings. At first he could not believe his eyes. He thought it was some trick of the moonlight, some weird effect of shadow, but he kept looking, and it could be no delusion. He saw the fingers and toes grasp the corners of the stones, worn clear of the mortar by the stress of years, and by thus using every projection and inequality move downwards with considerable speed, just as a lizard moves along a wall in a sidelong way. Some hundred feet down he vanished into some hole or window.

What manner of man was this, or what manner of creature was it in the semblance of man? Jonathan felt the dread of the accursed place overpowering him.

Then a sort of madness came over him. He rushed up and down the stairs, trying every door and peering out of every window he could find, and behaved much as a rat does in a trap. But after a little the conviction of his helplessness overpowered all other feelings and he was about to give up hope, when one door at the top of the stairway, though it seemed locked, gave a little under pressure. With many efforts he forced it back so that he could enter. This was evidently the portion of the castle occupied by the ladies in bygone days, for the furniture had more an air of comfort than any he had seen.

The windows were curtainless, and the yellow moonlight, flooding in through the diamond panes, softened the wealth of dust which lay over all and disguised in some measure the ravages of time and moth. Still, it was better than the rooms which he had come to hate from the presence of the Count.

He felt sleepy. The Count's warning came to mind, but he took pleasure in disobeying it. The sense of sleep was upon him, and with it the obstinacy which sleep brings as outrider. The soft moonlight soothed, and the wide expanse without gave a sense of freedom which, though false, lulled him.

He drew a great couch out of its place near the corner, so that as he lay, he could look at the lovely view to east and south, and unthinking of and uncaring for the dust, composed himself for sleep here, where, of old, ladies had sat and sung and lived sweet lives while their gentle breasts were sad for their menfolk away in the midst of remorseless wars.

He was not alone. In the moonlight opposite him were three young women. He thought for a while that he must be dreaming. They threw no shadow on the floor. They came close to him, and looked at him for some time, and then whispered together. Two were dark and had high aquiline noses, like the Count, and great dark, piercing eyes that seemed to be almost red when contrasted with the pale yellow moon. The other was fair, as fair as can be, with great masses of golden hair and eyes like pale sapphires. All three had brilliant white teeth that shone like pearls against the ruby of their voluptuous lips. There was something about them that made him uneasy, some longing and at the same time some deadly fear. He felt in his heart a wicked, burning desire that they would kiss him with those red lips. He tried to think of Mina, to no effect. That he loved his wife more dearly than any living being on earth was a cold fact, with no attendant emotion. The three whispered together, and then they all three laughed, such a silvery, musical laugh, but as hard as though the sound never could have come through the softness of human lips. It was like the intolerable, tingling sweetness of water glasses when played on by a cunning hand.

Jonathan lay quiet, looking out from under his eye-lashes in an agony of delightful anticipation. The fair girl advanced and bent over him till he could feel the move-ment of her breath upon him. Sweet it was in one sense, honey-sweet, but with a bitter underlying the sweet, a bitter offensiveness, as one smells in blood.

The girl went on her knees, and bent over him, simply gloating. She had a deliberate voluptuousness which was both thrilling and repulsive. Lower and lower went her head as her lips went below the range of his mouth and chin and seemed to fasten on his throat. Then she paused, and he could hear the churning sound of her tongue as it licked her teeth and lips, and he could feel the hot breath on his neck. Then the skin of his throat began to tingle as one's flesh does when the hand that is to tickle it ap-proaches nearer, nearer. He could feel the soft, shivering touch of the lips on the super sensitive skin of his throat, and the hard dents of two sharp teeth, just touching and pausing there. He closed his eyes in languorous ecstasy and waited, waited with beating heart.

But at that instant, another sensation swept through him as quick as lightning. He was conscious of the pres-ence of the Count, and of his being as if lapped in a storm of fury. As Jonathan's eyes opened involuntarily he saw the Count's strong hand grasp the slender neck of the fair woman and with giant's power draw it back, her blue eyes transformed with fury, her white teeth champing with rage, and her fair cheeks blazing red with passion. But the Count! No one could imagine such wrath and fury, even to the demons of the pit. His eyes were positively blazing. The red light in them was lurid, as if the flames of hell blazed behind them. With a fierce sweep of his arm, he hurled the woman from him, and then motioned to the others, as though he were beating them back. It was the same imperious gesture that he had used to the wolves. In a voice which, though low and almost in a whisper seemed to cut through the air and then ring in the room he said—

"How dare you touch him, any of you? How dare you cast eyes on him when I had forbidden it? Back, I tell you all! This man belongs to me! Beware how you meddle with him, or you'll have to deal with me."

The fair girl, with a laugh of ribald coquetry, turned to answer him. "You yourself never loved. You never love!" On this the other women joined, and a mirthless, hard, soulless laughter rang through the room. It seemed like the pleasure of fiends.

Then the Count turned, after looking at the young man's face attentively, and said in a soft whisper, "Yes, I too can love. You yourselves can tell it from the past. Is it not so? When I am done with him you may have him. Now go! Go!"

"Are we to have nothing tonight?" said one of them as she pointed to the bag which he had thrown upon the floor, and which moved as though there were some living thing within it. For answer he nodded his head. One of the women jumped forward and opened it. There was a gasp and a low wail, as of a half smothered child. The women closed round, while Jonathan was aghast with horror.

What they did next was blocked from his view, and so were all things from conscious sanity, by the growing face of Dracula, as it sank ever closer to his. Silently, he said goodbye to Mina.

From without came an agonized cry. In the courtyard below, a woman with disheveled hair leaned against the corner of the gateway and held her hands over her heart as one distressed with running. When she saw the Count's face appear at the window, she shouted in a voice laden with menace—

"Monster, give me my child!"

She threw herself forward on her knees, and raising up her hands, cried the same words in heart-wringing tones. Then she tore her hair and abandoned herself to all the violences of extravagant emotion. Finally, she threw herself forward, beating her naked hands against the door.

The Count called in his harsh, metallic whisper. His call seemed to be answered from far and wide by the howling of wolves. Before many minutes had passed a pack of them poured, like a pent-up dam when liberated, through the wide entrance into the courtyard.

There was no cry from the woman, and the howling of the wolves was but short. Before long they streamed away singly, licking their lips.

2.

Whitby Abbey was a most noble ruin, of immense size, and full of beautiful and romantic bits. Between it and the town there was another church, the parish one, round which was a big graveyard, all full of tombstones.

This was to Mina's mind the nicest spot in Whitby, for it lay right over the town, and had a full view of the harbor. In one place part of the stonework of the graves stretched out over the sandy pathway far below. There were walks, with seats beside them, through the churchyard, and people would go and sit there all day long looking at the beautiful view and enjoying the breeze.

Lucy Westenra had been chattering away for some time. She was looking sweetly pretty in her white lawn frock. But Mina Harker was uneasy. She had not heard from her husband, and was very concerned.

Then, too, her dear friend who sat beside her had lately taken to her old habit of walking in her sleep. Lucy's mother had spoken to Mina about it, and they decided that Mina was to lock the door of their room every night. Mrs. Westenra had got an idea that sleep-walkers always go out on roofs of houses and along the edges of cliffs and then get suddenly wakened and fall over with a despairing cry that echoes all over the place.

Lucy was to be married to a young doctor in the autumn, and she was already planning out her dresses and how her house was to be arranged. Mina sympathized with her, for she did the same with her home in Exeter, only Jonathan and she had to start in life in a very simple way, and have had an ongoing struggle to make both ends meet.

"He is really clever," said Lucy, referring to her fiancé. "Just fancy! He is only nine-and-twenty, and he has an immense lunatic asylum all under his own care.

"He has a curious habit of looking one straight in the face, as if trying to read one's thoughts. What a wonderful power he must have over his patients! He tries this on very much with me, but I flatter myself he has got a tough nut to crack. Oh, Mina, couldn't you guess? I love him. Am I blushing? But, oh, Mina, I love him. I love him! There, that does me good."

Of Jonathan Harker no one had heard a word for a whole month. For Mina the suspense was getting dreadful. She could only pray to God for patience. She pulled his last letter from her pocket. It was only a line that said his stay would be a little longer than he had planned. It did not read like him, and yet it was his writing. There was no mistake of that.

Watching Mina study the letter, Lucy understood, and silently took hold of her hand.

"I wonder where Jonathan is," said Mina, "and if he is thinking of me."

It was mid-afternoon when the two women decided it was time to leave, as the day had turned grey, with the sun hidden in thick clouds. The sea was tumbling in over the shallows and the sandy flats with a roar, muffled in the sea-mists drifting inland. Dark figures on the beach here and there were half shrouded in the mist. The fishing boats were racing for home, and rose and dipped in the ground swell as they swept into the harbor.

As Mina and Lucy gathered themselves, the coast guard came along with his spyglass under his arm. He stopped to talk with the young women as he always did, but all the time kept looking at a strange ship.

"I can't make her out," he said. "She's a Russian by the look of her. But she's knocking about in the queerest way. She doesn't know her mind a bit. She seems to see the storm coming, but can't decide whether to run up north in the open or to put in here. Look there again! She is steered mighty strangely, for she doesn't mind the hand on the wheel, changes about with every puff of wind. We'll hear more of her before this time tomorrow."

The sun's downward way marked the prelude to the great storm with so very beautiful, so grand masses of splendidly colored clouds, that it drew quite an assemblage on the walk along the cliff in the old churchyard. Shortly before ten o'clock the stillness of the air grew quite oppressive. There came a strange sound from over the sea, and high overhead the air began to carry a faint, hollow booming.

Then without warning the tempest broke. The whole aspect of nature at once became convulsed. White-crested waves beat madly on the level sands and rushed up the shelving cliffs. Others broke over the piers, and with their spume swept the lanterns of the lighthouses which rose from the end of either pier of Whitby Harbor. The wind roared like thunder, and blew with such force that it was with difficulty that even strong men kept their feet, or clung with grim clasp to the iron stanchions. It was found necessary to clear the entire pier from the mass of onlookers, or else the fatalities of the night would have increased manifold.

Before long the searchlight discovered some distance away the schooner which had been noticed earlier by the coast guard. The wind had by this time backed to the east, and there was tenseness among the watchers on the cliff as they realized the terrible danger in which she now was.

The wind suddenly shifted to the northeast, and the remnant of the sea fog melted in the blast. And then, amazingly, between the piers, leaping from wave to wave as it rushed at headlong speed, swept the strange schooner before the blast, with all sail set, and gained the safety of the harbor. The searchlight followed her, and a shudder ran through all who saw her, for lashed to the helm was a corpse, with drooping head, which swung horribly to and fro at each motion of the ship. No other form could be seen on the deck at all. It turned out that he was the captain. It was believed he tied himself to the wheel when his strength failed to support him against the storm. The schooner turned out to be Russian from Varna, and was almost entirely in ballast of silver sand, with only a small amount of cargo.

But, strangest of all, the very instant the shore was touched, an immense dog sprang up on deck from below, as if shot up by the concussion, and running forward, jumped from the bow on the sand, and seemed to have disappeared entirely from the town. It may be that it was frightened and made its way on to the moors, where it remained hiding in terror.

Early next morning a large dog, a half-bred mastiff belonging to a coal merchant close to Tate Hill Pier, was found dead in the roadway opposite its master's yard. It had been fighting, and manifestly had had a savage opponent, for its throat was torn away and its belly was slit open as if with a savage claw.

Lucy was very restless all night, and Mina too could not sleep. The storm was fearful, and as it boomed loudly among the chimney pots it made her shudder. When a sharp puff came it seemed to be like a distant gun. Somehow she felt glad that Jonathan was not on the sea, but on land. But, oh, was he on land or sea? Where was he, and how? She was getting fearfully anxious about him, and soothed herself to sleep with repeated prayers.

It was well past midnight when suddenly Mina became broad awake, and sat up with a horrible sense of fear upon her, and of some feeling of emptiness around her. The room was dark, so she could not see Lucy's bed. She stole across and felt for her. The bed was empty. She lit a match and found that Lucy was not in the room. The door was shut, but not locked as Mina had left it. She feared to wake Lucy's mother, who had been more than usually ill lately, so threw on some clothes and got ready to look for her.

She ran downstairs and looked in the sitting room. Not there! Then she looked in all the other rooms of the house, with an ever-growing fear chilling her heart. Finally, she came to the hall door and found it open. She feared that Lucy must have gone out as she was. There was no time to think of what might happen. A vague over-mastering fear obscured all details.

She took a big, heavy shawl and ran out. The clock was striking one as she was in the Crescent, and there was not a soul in sight. She ran along the North Terrace, but could see no sign of the white figure which she expected. At the edge of the West Cliff above the pier she looked across the harbor to the East Cliff, in the hope or fear, she didn't know which, of seeing Lucy in their favorite seat.

There was a bright full moon with heavy black, driving clouds, which threw the whole scene into a fleeting diorama of light and shade as they sailed across. She could see the ruins of the abbey coming into view, and as the edge of a narrow band of light as sharp as a sword-cut moved along, the church and churchyard became gradually visible. Whatever her expectation was, it was not disappointed, for there, on their favorite seat, the silver light of the moon struck a half-reclining figure, snowy white. It seemed as though something dark stood behind the seat, and bent over it. What it was, whether man or beast, she could not tell.

Mina did not wait to catch another glance, but flew down the steep steps to the pier and along by the fishmarket to the bridge, which was the only way to reach the East Cliff. The town seemed as dead, for not a soul did she see. She rejoiced that it was so, for she wanted no witness of poor Lucy's condition. The time and distance seemed endless, and her knees trembled and her breath came labored as she toiled up the endless steps to the abbey.

When she got almost to the top she could see Lucy half reclining with her head lying over the back of the seat. She was quite alone, and there was not a sign of any living thing about.

When Mina approached her she could see that she was still asleep. Her lips were parted, and she was breathing, not softly as usual with her, but in long, heavy gasps, as though striving to get her lungs full at every breath. As Mina came close, Lucy put up her hand in her sleep and pulled the collar of her nightdress close around her, as though she felt the cold. Mina flung the warm shawl over her, and drew the edges tight around her neck, and then began very gently to wake her.

The young doctor had lain tossing about, and had heard the clock strike only twice, when the night watchman came, sent up from the ward, to say that Renfield had escaped.

Dr. Seward threw on his clothes and ran down at once. The patient was too dangerous a person to be roaming about. Committed by the magistrate just earlier that evening, he had been found cowering in the stores of the mystery ship, and raving, an apparent stowaway, and the only living thing on board, apart from a scattering of rats. After a brief interview the doctor had made some preliminary notes, indicating among other things, that the patient's behavior was consistent with undeveloped homicidal mania.

The attendant was waiting and said he had seen him not ten minutes before, seemingly asleep in his bed, when he had looked through the observation trap in the door. His attention was called by the sound of the window being wrenched out. He ran back and saw his feet disappear through the window. He was only in his night gear, and could not be far off.

The attendant was a bulky man and couldn't get through the window. Dr. Seward was thin, so, with the attendant's aid got out, feet foremost, and as they were only a few feet above ground landed unhurt.

The attendant reported the patient had gone to the left and had taken a straight line, so Dr. Seward ran as quickly as he could. As he got through the belt of trees he saw a white figure reaching up the high wall which separates the grounds from those of the deserted house.

He was talking, apparently to someone, but the doctor was afraid to go near enough to hear what he was saying, lest he might frighten him, and he should run off.

Chasing an errant swarm of bees is nothing to following a naked lunatic when the fit of escaping is upon him! After a few minutes, however, the doctor could see that the patient did not take note of anything around him and so ventured to draw nearer to him. He heard him say...

"I am here to do your bidding, Master. I am your slave, and you will reward me, for I shall be faithful. I have worshipped you and tended you through our long journey. Now that we have arrived, I await your commands, and you will not pass me by, will you, dear Master, in your distribution of good things?"

Seward was amazed as he watched him then scale the high wall with ease and disappear behind it. The doctor drew a whistle from his pocket and sounded a high pitched signal which brought several trained dogs, who leapt the wall with agility equal to the patient and cornered him with frantic barking before he could reach the house. Three or four attendants, having brought a ladder, had now crossed the wall. When they closed in on him he fought more like a wild beast than a man. The doctor had never seen a lunatic in such a paroxysm of rage before, and hoped he would not again.

Soon he was safe in a strait waistcoat and chained to the wall in a padded room. His cries were at times awful, but the silences that followed were more deadly still, for he meant murder in every turn and movement. When the patient thought he was alone, the doctor heard him whisper, "I shall be patient, Master. It is coming, coming, coming!"

R. M. Renfield, age about 30. Sanguine temperament, great physical strength, morbidly excitable, periods of gloom, ending in some fixed idea which I cannot make out. I presume that the sanguine temperament itself and the disturbing influence end in a mentally-accomplished finish, a possibly dangerous man.

So began the case history of Renfield as recorded by Dr. Seward. Renfield's case grew more interesting to the doctor the more he got to observe the man. The subject had certain qualities very largely developed, selfishness, secrecy, and purpose. His redeeming quality was a love of animals, though he had such curious turns in it that it might be that he was only abnormally cruel. His pets were of odd sorts.

His hobby was catching flies. He had accumulated such a quantity that the doctor had to object. He did not break out into a fury, as feared, but took the matter in simple seriousness. He thought for a moment, and then said, "May I have three days? I shall clear them away."

He then turned his mind to spiders, and got several very big fellows into a box, to which he began feeding his flies.

When a horrid blowfly, bloated with some carrion food, buzzed into the room. He caught it, held it exultantly for a few moments between his finger and thumb, and before the doctor knew what he was going to do, put it in his mouth and ate it. He argued quietly that it was very good and very wholesome, that it was life, strong life, and gave life to him. The doctor decided to observe how he got rid of his spiders.

Renfield kept a little folder in which he was always jotting down something. Whole pages of it were filled with masses of tiny figures or symbols, grouped into batches, and neatly grouped again, some horizontally and some alongside, vertically. The doctor wondered if he might be keeping some sort of log of his insect population. The overall appearance was like an auditor's notebook, but it was all completely unintelligible.

Mina Harker was off by train to London to visit her ailing father. During her stay, she would visit the law offices of Hawkins & Harker, where she would seek some clue regarding her husband's situation from Mr. Hawkins, in whose service Jonathan had grown into manhood, and with whom he was now the junior partner. At least, she hoped, he could share some information about the client her husband was visiting.

She had been somewhat reluctant to leave her dear friend in Whitby to the attendance of her frail mother, and was inclined to post a note of concern to Dr. Seward. But

Lucy had recovered so remarkably in the preceding few days, that she decided not to impose her opinion upon the doctor, whom she had not yet met, and whose visits to Lucy, she knew, would reveal all.

Alas, her friend's rally was short-lived. No sooner had Mina departed, than the sleepwalks began again, and with increasing detriment to Lucy's health. When he called on her, Dr. John Seward was so appalled at her condition that he proposed to her mother that he should take her to, that is to say admit her, as a patient in the asylum immediately. Sleepwalking was, after all, in its severest form, a potentially dangerous mental condition. Lucy's mother felt most fortunate to have her daughter's well-being entrusted to the affianced young doctor, for whom she had the utmost respect and affection.

The transition was made, yet Lucy grew weaker. Dr. Seward could not understand her fading away as she was doing. She ate well and slept well, and enjoyed the fresh air, but all the time the roses in her cheeks were fading, and she got weaker and more languid day by day. At night he watched her gasping as if for air.

He was in doubt, and so did the best thing he knew. He wrote to his old friend and master, Professor Van Helsing of Amsterdam, who knew as much about obscure diseases as anyone in the world. He asked him to come.

Renfield had managed to get a sparrow, and partially tamed it. His means of taming was simple, for the spiders had diminished. Those that did remain, however, were well fed, for he still brought in the flies by tempting them with his food. Soon he had a whole colony of sparrows, and his flies and spiders were almost obliterated.

One morning when Dr. Seward visited Renfield very early, before the attendant went his rounds, he found him up and humming a tune. He was spreading out his sugar, which he had saved, in the window, and was manifestly beginning his fly catching again, and beginning it cheerfully and with a good grace.

The doctor looked around for his birds, and not seeing them, asked him where they were. He replied, without turning round, that they had all flown away. There were a few feathers about the room and on his pillow a drop of blood.

Van Helsing was a seemingly arbitrary man, but would, for a personal reason, do anything for his former pupil. He was a philosopher and a metaphysician, and one of the most advanced scientists of his day. He was known for his iron nerve, his temper of the ice-brook, and his indomitable resolution, and together with the kindliest and truest heart that beat, an absolutely open mind.

Upon his arrival, the Professor was shown into the young doctor's study, and quickly reached for Seward's hand, while with his other he deposited upon the table a bag in which were many instruments and drugs, "the ghastly paraphernalia of our beneficial trade," as he once called them in one of his lectures. He immediately asked about Lucy's symptoms. When Seward said they were the same as in his letter, but infinitely more marked, Van Helsing looked very grave, but said nothing.

When they walked into her room, both men were horrified. She was ghastly, chalkily pale. The red seemed to have gone even from her lips, and the bones of her face stood out prominently. Her breathing was painful to see or hear. Van Helsing's face grew set as marble, and his eyebrows converged till they almost touched over his nose. Lucy lay motionless, and did not seem to have strength to speak, so for a while they were all silent. Then Van Helsing beckoned to Seward, and they went gently out of the room. The instant he had closed the door he stepped quickly along the passage to the next door, which was open. Then he pulled the young doctor quickly in with him and closed the door. "My god!" he said. "This is dreadful. There is not time to be lost. She will die for sheer want of blood to keep the heart's action as it should be. There must be a transfusion of blood at once. Is it you or me?"

"I'll get ready at once," said the younger man in reply.

"Then I will bring up my bag. I am prepared."

With swiftness, but with absolute method, Van Helsing began the operation. As the transfusion went on, something like life seemed to come back to poor Lucy's cheeks, and through Seward's growing pallor the joy of his face seemed absolutely to shine.

No man knows, till he experiences it, what it is to feel his own lifeblood drawn away into the veins of the woman he loves.

After a bit Van Helsing began to grow anxious, for the loss of blood was telling on Seward, strong man as he was. It gave an idea of what a terrible strain Lucy's system must have undergone that what weakened Seward only partially restored her.

Van Helsing held up a warning finger. "Do not stir," he said. "I fear that with growing strength she may wake, and that would make danger, oh, so much danger. But I shall precaution take. I shall give hypodermic injection of morphia." He proceeded then, swiftly and deftly, to carry out his intent.

The effect on Lucy was not bad, for the faint seemed to merge subtly into the narcotic sleep. It was with a feeling of personal pride that Seward could see a faint tinge of color steal back into the pallid cheeks and lips.

The Professor watched him critically. "That will do," he said. "Already?" the young man remonstrated. To which Van Helsing smiled a sad sort of smile as he replied,

"You have work, much work to do for her and for others, and the present will suffice."

When they stopped the operation, he attended to Lucy, while Seward applied digital pressure to his own incision. He laid down and waited his leisure to attend to him, for he felt faint and a little sick. By and by Van Helsing bound up his wound and sent him downstairs to get a glass of wine for himself.

When Seward came back he found the Professor examining two small punctures in the patients neck which had revealed themselves as he had adjusted the pillow to the patient's head. There was no sign of disease, but the edges were white and worn looking, as if by some trituration.

Seward asked the Professor if he thought that this wound, or whatever it was, might be the means of that manifest loss of blood, but he abandoned the idea himself before the Professor could answer. "No," he said, "such a thing could not be. The whole bed would have been drenched with the blood which the girl must have lost to leave such a pallor as she had before the transfusion."

The Professor looked at him carefully, and then said, "You are not much the worse. Go have much breakfast, then go lie on your sofa and rest awhile."

Seward followed out his orders, for he knew how right and wise they were. He had done his part, and now his next duty was to keep up his strength. He felt very weak, and in the weakness lost something of the amazement at what had occurred. He fell asleep on his sofa, however, wondering over and over again how Lucy had made such a retrograde movement, and how she could have been drained of so much blood with no sign anywhere to show for it but for the two small wounds on her neck.

The opiate worked itself off towards noon, and Lucy waked naturally. She looked a different being from what she had been before the operation. Her spirits even were good, and she was full of a happy vivacity, but there were evidences of the absolute prostration which she had undergone.

At dusk Seward made preparations for his long vigil. When the nurse had prepared her for the night he came in, having in the meantime had supper, and took a seat by the bedside. He would sit up all night with her.

Lucy did not in any way make objection, but looked at him gratefully whenever he caught her eye.

"I owe you so much, John, for all you have done, but you really must now take care not to overwork yourself. You are looking pale yourself. You want a wife to nurse and look after you a bit, that you do!" As she spoke, Lucy turned crimson, though it was only momentarily, for her poor wasted veins could not stand for long an unwonted drain to the head. The reaction came in excessive pallor as she turned imploring eyes on her betrothed. He smiled and nodded, and laid his finger on his lips. With a sigh, she sank back amid her pillows.

After a long spell she seemed sinking off to sleep, but with an effort seemed to pull herself together and shook it off. Seward tackled the subject at once.

"You do not want to sleep?"

"No. I am afraid."

"Afraid to go to sleep! Why so? It is not the boon we all crave for?"

"Ah, not if you were like me, if sleep was to you a presage of horror!"

"A presage of horror! What on earth do you mean?"

"I don't know. Oh, I don't know. And that is what is so terrible. All this weakness comes to me in sleep, until I dread the very thought."

"But, my dear, you may sleep tonight. I am here watching you, and I can promise that nothing will happen."

"Ah, I can trust you!" she said.

He seized the opportunity and said, "I promise that if I see any evidence of bad dreams I will wake you at once."

"You will? Oh, will you really? Then I will sleep." And with this she gave a deep sigh of relief, and just before she sank back into sleep, "How good you are to me, John!"

Presently she moved uneasily. At the same moment there came a sort of dull flapping or buffeting at the window. Seward went over to it softly and peeped out by the corner of the blind. There was a full moonlight and he could see that the noise was made by a great bat which wheeled around, doubtless attracted by the light, although so dim, and every now and again struck the window with its wings.

He came back to his seat, and all night long he watched by her. She never stirred, but slept on and on in a deep, tranquil, life-giving, health-giving sleep. Her lips were slightly parted, and her breast rose and fell with the regularity of a pendulum. There was a smile on her face, and it was evident that no bad dreams had come to disturb her peace of mind, or his.

*

Seward was conscious of the Professor's hand on his head and started awake all in a second. That is one of the things they learn in an asylum.

"And how is our patient? Come, let us see." Van Helsing stepped with his soft, cat-like tread, over to the bed.

As Seward gently raised the blind, and the morning sunlight flooded the room, he heard the Professor's low hiss of inspiration, and knowing its rarity, a deadly fear shot through his heart. As he passed over, the Professor moved back, and his exclamation of horror, "Gott in Himmel!" needed no enforcement from his agonized face. He raised his hand and pointed to the bed, and his iron face was drawn and ashen white. Seward felt his knees begin to tremble.

There on the bed, seemingly in a swoon, lay poor Lucy, more horribly white and wan-looking than ever. The lips were white, and the gums seemed to have shrunken back from the teeth, as we sometimes see in a corpse after a prolonged illness.

"Quick!" he said. "Bring the brandy."

The young man flew to the dining room and returned with the decanter. The other wetted the poor white lips with it, and together they rubbed palm and wrist and heart. Van Helsing felt her heart, and after a few moments of agonizing suspense said—

"All our work is undone. She is dying. There is no more we can do. It will not be long now." Then in more matter-of-fact tones, he added, "It will be much difference, mark me, whether she dies conscious or in her sleep."

The young doctor covered his face with his hands and slid down on his knees by the bed, where he remained, perhaps a minute, with his head buried. Van Helsing took him by the hand and raised him up. "Come," he said, "my dear old fellow, summon all your fortitude. It will be best and easiest for her."

With his usual forethought, Van Helsing began putting matters straight and making everything look as pleasing as possible. He even brushed Lucy's hair, so that it lay on the pillow in its usual sunny ripples. For a little bit her breast heaved softly, and her breath came and went like a tired child's.

And then insensibly there came a strange change, as her breathing grew stertorous, the mouth opened, and the pale gums, drawn back, made the teeth look long and sharp. In a sort of sleep-waking, vague, unconscious way she opened her eyes, which were dull and hard at once, and whispered in a soft, voluptuous voice, such as her betrothed had never heard from her lips, "John! Oh, my love, I am so glad you have come! Kiss me!"

He bent eagerly over to kiss her, but at that instant Van Helsing, who had been startled by her voice, swooped upon him, and catching him by the neck with both hands, dragged him back with a fury of strength which one would never have thought he possessed, and actually hurled him almost across the room.

"Not on your life!" he said, "not for your living soul and hers!" And he stood between them like a lion at bay.

Seward was so taken aback that he did not for a moment know what to do or say.

Van Helsing kept his eyes fixed on Lucy, and saw a spasm as of rage flit like a shadow over her face. The sharp teeth clamped together. Then her eyes closed, and she breathed heavily.

Very shortly after, she opened her eyes in all their soft-ness, and putting out her poor, pale, thin hand, took Van Helsing's great brown one, drawing it close to her, she kissed it. "My true friend," she said in a faint voice, but with untellable pathos, "My true friend, and his! Oh, guard him, and give me peace!"

"I swear it!" he said solemnly, kneeling beside her and holding up his hand, as one who registers an oath. Then he turned to Seward, and said to him, "Come, my child, take her hand in yours, and kiss her on the forehead, and only once."

Then Lucy's breathing became stertorous again, and all at once it ceased.

"It is all over," said Van Helsing. "She is dead!"

The young man sat down, and covered his face with his hands, sobbing in a way that should have broken his men-tor down to see, yet Van Helsing was looking at Lucy, and his face was sterner than ever. Some change had come over her body. Death had given back part of her beauty, for her brow and cheeks had recovered some of their flow-ing lines. Even the lips had lost their deadly pallor. It was as if the blood, no longer needed for the working of the heart, had gone to make the harshness of death as little rude as might be.

We thought her dying whilst she slept, and sleeping when she died.

Seward stood beside Van Helsing, and said, "There is peace for my poor girl at last. It is the end!"

The Professor turned to him and said with grave so-lemnity, "Not so, alas! Not so. It is only the beginning!"

The funeral was arranged, and with Mrs. Westenra's blessing, Dr. Seward attended to all the ghastly formalities. She had provided the address of the father of Lucy's dear friend, Mrs. Harker, and he was engaged in his study preparing to send a telegram to London, when suddenly the door was burst open, and in rushed Renfield, his face distorted with passion. The doctor was thunderstruck, for such a thing as a patient getting of his own accord into the Superintendent's study is almost unknown.

Without an instant's notice he made straight at Seward. He had a dinner knife in his hand. Seward tried to keep the table between them. Renfield was too quick and too strong for him, however, for before he could get his balance the madman had struck at him and cut his left wrist rather severely.

Before he could strike again, however, Seward got in his right hand and the patient was sprawling on his back on the floor. Seward's wrist bled freely, and quite a little pool trickled on to the carpet. Seeing that his friend was not intent on further effort, Seward occupied himself binding up his wrist, keeping a wary eye on the prostrate figure all the time. When the attendants rushed in, and they turned their attention to the patient, his employment positively sickened them. He was lying on his belly on the floor licking up, like a dog, the blood which had fallen from the wounded wrist. He was easily secured, and to the doctor's surprise, went with the attendants quite placidly, simply repeating over and over again, "The blood is the life! The blood is the life!"

Seward took his way to Paddington, where he arrived about fifteen minutes before the train came in.

The crowd melted away, after the bustling fashion common to arrival platforms, and he was beginning to feel uneasy, lest he might miss his guest, when a sweet-faced, dainty looking girl stepped up to him, and after a quick glance said, "Dr. Seward, is it not?"

"And you are Mrs. Harker!" he answered at once, whereupon she held out her hand.

"I knew you from the description of poor dear Lucy, but..." She stopped suddenly, and a quick blush overspread her face.

The blush that rose to his own cheeks somehow set them both at ease, for it was a tacit answer to her own. She inquired about the well-being of Mrs. Westenra. The doctor replied that she was too weak to even attend her daughter's funeral, and, he feared, she was beginning to suffer mental lapses.

He got her luggage, which included a typewriter, and they took the Underground to Fenchurch Street, after he had sent a wire to his housekeeper to have a sitting room and a bedroom prepared at once for Mrs. Harker.

In due time they arrived. She knew, of course, that the place was a lunatic asylum, but he could see that she was unable to repress a shudder when they entered.

Poor woman! She looked desperately sad and broken. She seemed to have shrunk somewhat under the strain of her much-tried emotions. She had been very genuinely and devotedly attached to her father, and to come straight from his funeral, to another, was a bitter blow to her. With Seward she was warm, but he could see that there was some constraint with her.

After she tidied herself, she asked that he bring her to Lucy. He did so, and at the door she turned to him, saying hoarsely—

"You loved her too. There was no friend who had a closer place in my heart than she. I don't know how to thank you for all you have done for her. I can't think yet…"

Here she suddenly broke down, crying, "Oh, Dr. Seward! What shall I do? The whole of life seems gone from me all at once, and there is nothing in the wide world for me to live for."

He stood still and silent till her sobs died away, and then said softly, "Come and look at her."

The room had been turned into a small chapelle ardente. There was a wilderness of beautiful white flowers, and death was made as little repulsive as might be. Together they moved over to the bed, and the doctor lifted the lawn from Lucy's face. God! How beautiful she was. Every hour seemed to be enhancing her loveliness. It frightened and amazed him somewhat. As for Mina, she fell to trembling, and finally was shaken with doubt as with an ague. At last, after a long pause, she said in a faint whisper, "Doctor, is she really dead?"

He assured her sadly that it was so, that it often happened that after death faces become softened and even resolved into their youthful beauty. After kneeling beside the couch for a while and looking at her lovingly and long, Mina turned aside. He told her that that must be goodbye, as the coffin had to be prepared, so she went back and took Lucy's dead hand in hers and kissed it, and bent over and kissed her forehead. She came away, fondly looking back over her shoulder.

He left Mina in the drawing room, and went to the kitchen to tell the undertaker's men to proceed with the preparations and to screw up the coffin. When he came out of the room again he led her to his study to offer some tea and sympathy before showing her to her room. When he heard her tell of her husband's mysterious disappearance, added to her other griefs, he could not wonder at Mina's breakdown. Before he could decide whether to approach the situation as doctor or friend, she startled him by saying—

"You helped to attend dear Lucy at the end. Let me hear how she died, for all that I know of her, I shall be very grateful. She was very, very dear to me."

To her surprise, he grew to a positively deathly pallor as he said, "No! No! No! For all the world. I wouldn't let you know that terrible story!"

Then it was terrible. Mina's intuition was right!

"The fact is," he continued awkwardly, "we do not yet know the reasons that led to her death... We are yet in the process of studying her case, and..."

For a moment her eyes ranged the room, unconsciously looking for something or some opportunity to aid her, they lit on a great batch of note paper on the table. His eyes caught the look in hers, and without his thinking, followed their direction and saw an opportunity to change the subject.

"You are wondering at the strange hieroglyphics on those papers. No, they are not a secret physician's code, only the meaningless scribblings of one of our most deranged patients."

With a look of unusual interest, she picked up and perused the top sheet. "These are not meaningless scribblings," she said. "This is shorthand."

"Shorthand!"

"Yes. It is not the most adept in style, but..." and she began to interpret aloud what was in her hand.

"*We went thoroughly into the business of the purchase of the estate at Purfleet. When I had got his signature to the necessary papers...*"

Suddenly she froze. Then she stood and grasped the next page from the table, and continued reading silently. Seward rose, astonished by the wild look in her eyes, and said, "Miss Harker, please!"

"This was written by Jonathan! He is here! What have you done with him!" she screamed. The papers fell from her hands and scattered, she reached out for Seward, then stumbled forward and swooned into his arms.

Seward rang for assistance, then he lifted her and carried her up to her room. He placed her on the bed, where she rested for the remainder of the night in a fever.

At 8:00 a.m., Seward found the Professor in the kitchen, intently studying the Westminster Gazette over a cup of tea. He poured himself a cup and sat down. After a moment, impatient for the elder's attention, he reflected aloud about the strange behavior of Mrs. Harker, which he had reported to the Professor the previous night, as if he were resuming a conversation left off a minute ago.

"We have both seen this type of self-delusion before, though it is unusual that it originates in the marks upon a page made by a lunatic. It is not surprising when you consider the stress put upon that poor woman by the loss of her father and her best friend almost at the same time, and the unknown whereabouts of her husband."

"So you are quick to dismiss it as hallucination, my young friend?" said the Professor, without lifting his eyes from the newspaper.

"Either that, or she is misinterpreting what the shorthand says—if it *is* shorthand—reading into innocuous phrases signals and clues that support what she so desperately wishes to believe—that her husband is alive and well."

"Remarkable!"

Van Helsing removed his glasses and put down the paper. "You must have her put down a complete transcript of the collected notes of Mr. Renfield as soon as madame is up to it. If nothing else, it may help unravel the mystery of your prize patient.

"But for now another task is at hand, concerning the corpse of Miss Lucy. Before night, I want you to bring me a set of post-mortem knives."

"Must we make an autopsy?"

"Yes and no. I want to operate, but not what you think. Let me tell you now, but not a word to another. I want to cut off her head and take out her heart. Ah! You a surgeon, and so shocked! You, whom I have seen with no tremble of hand or heart, do operations of life and death that make the rest shudder. Oh, but I must not forget, my dear friend John, that you loved her, and I have not forgotten it, for is I that shall operate, and you must not help. When she is coffined ready for tomorrow, you and I shall come when all sleep. We shall unscrew the coffin lid, and shall do our operation, and then replace all, so that none know save we alone."

"But why do it at all? The girl is dead. Why mutilate her poor body without need? And if there is no necessity for a post-mortem and nothing to gain by it, no good to her, to us, to science, to human knowledge, why do it? Without such it is monstrous. I cannot permit it!"

For answer Van Helsing put his hand on the young doctor's shoulder, and said, with infinite tenderness, "Friend John, I pity your poor bleeding heart, and I love you the more because it does so bleed. If I could, I would take on myself the burden that you do bear.

"But to your authority must I bow. If faith in me you will not have, perhaps I am wrong. I hope I am wrong, and we shall be blessed that that which I seek to prevent will never come to pass, but I fear there are strange and terrible days before us."

A week after Lucy's interment, Dr. Seward took Mina with him to visit poor Mrs. Westenra, after which he had hoped to arrange for her going back to Exeter, where he believed daily tasks in her own home would benefit her mental state. Upon seeing Lucy's mother in such frail spirits, however, Mina decided to remain and keep her company for a few days. It would provide a strange comfort to herself as well, to spend time in the home where the spirit of her long friendship with Lucy yet resided, and far from the neighborhood of lunatics.

After reassuring Mina that her quarters at his building would remain available for her use, the doctor returned home, and was standing at his own gate under a cold mist, when once more he heard yelling from Renfield's room. The poor wretch was doubtless torturing himself, after the manner of the insane, with needless thoughts of pain. Then there was the sound of a struggle, and he knew that the attendants were dealing with him.

The mist was spreading, and was lying thick against the east wall, as though it were stealing up to the windows. It was a shock to Seward to turn from the wonderful smoky beauty of sunset over Whitby Harbor, and to realize all the grim sternness of his own cold stone building, with its wealth of breathing misery, and his own desolate heart to endure it all.

At about half-past five o'clock Seward was undressing in his own room, when, with a premonitory tap at the door, Van Helsing entered, and thrust the "Westminster Gazette" into his hand.

"What do you think of that?" he asked as he more or less flopped into a chair and wiped his forehead.

Seward sat on his bed and looked over the paper, not knowing what he meant, but the Professor took it from him and read aloud a paragraph with the headline, "The Hampstead Horror."

"We have just received intelligence that another child was discovered late in the morning under a furze bush at the less frequented side of Hampstead Heath. It had the same tiny wounds in the throat as has been noticed in other cases. It was weak and emaciated, and told a similar story of being lured away by the 'bloofer lady.'

"And what do you make of it?" the Professor repeated.

"It is like poor Lucy's."

"You think then that those so small holes in the children's throats were made by the same that made the holes in Miss Lucy?"

"I suppose so."

Van Helsing said solemnly, "Then you are wrong. Oh, would it were so! But alas! No. It is worse, far, far worse."

"In God's name, Professor, what do you mean?"

Van Helsing covered his face with his hands as he spoke.

"They were made by Miss Lucy!"

For a while sheer anger mastered Seward. It was as if the Professor had during her life struck Lucy on the face. Seward rose up as he said to him, "Dr. Van Helsing, are you mad?"

"Would I were!" he said. "Madness were easy to bear compared with truth like this. Oh, my friend, I do not expect you should believe so sad a concrete truth, and of such a one as Miss Lucy. Tonight I go to prove it. Dare you come with me?"

This staggered Seward. The Professor saw his hesitation, and spoke:—

"Come, I tell you what I propose. First, that we go off now and see that child in the hospital. Dr. Vincent, of the North Hospital, where the papers say the child is, is a friend of mine, and I think of yours since you were in class at Amsterdam. He will let two scientists see his case, if he will not let two friends. We shall tell him nothing, but only that we wish to learn. And then…"

"And then?"

Van Helsing took a key from his pocket and held it up. "And then we spend the night, you and I, in the churchyard where Lucy lies. This is the key that lock the tomb."

His pupil's heart sank within him, for he felt that there was some fearful ordeal before them. He could do nothing, however, so he plucked up what heart he could and said that they had better hasten, as the afternoon was passing.

They found the child awake. It had had a sleep and taken some food, and altogether was going on well. Dr. Vincent took the bandage from its throat, and showed them the punctures. There was no mistaking the similarity to those which had been on Lucy's throat. They were smaller, and the edges looked fresher, that was all.

Vincent attributed them to a bite of some animal, perhaps a rat, but was inclined to think it was one of the bats which are so numerous on the northern heights of London.

The visit to the hospital took more time than they had reckoned on, and the sun had dipped before they came out. When Van Helsing saw how dark it was, he said, "It is

more late than I thought. Come, let us seek somewhere
that we may eat, and then we shall go on our way."

They dined at 'Jack Straw's Castle' along with a little
crowd of bicyclists and others who were genially noisy.
About ten o'clock they started from the inn. It was then
very dark, and the scattered lamps made the darkness
greater when they were once outside their individual radius.
The Professor had noted the road they were to go, and he
went on unhesitatingly, but Seward was in quite a mix-up
as to locality. As they went further, they met fewer and
fewer people. At last they reached the wall of the churchyard, which they climbed over. With some little difficulty
they found the Westenra tomb. The Professor took the
key, opened the creaky door, and standing back, politely,
but quite unconsciously, motioned his student to precede
him. There was a delicious irony in the offer, in the court-
liness of giving preference on such a ghastly occasion. The
Professor followed quickly, and cautiously drew the door
to, after carefully ascertaining that the lock was a falling,
and not a spring one. In the latter case they should have
been in a bad plight. Then he fumbled in his bag, and taking out a matchbox and a piece of candle, proceeded to
make a light.

The tomb in the daytime, and when wreathed with
fresh flowers, had looked grim and gruesome enough, but
now, some days afterwards, when the flowers hung lank
and dead, their whites turning to rust and their greens to
browns, when the spider and the beetle had resumed their
accustomed dominance, when the rusty, dank iron, and
tarnished brass gave back the feeble glimmer of a candle,
the effect was more miserable and sordid than could have
been imagined.

Van Helsing went about his work systematically. Holding his candle so that he could read the coffin plates, and so holding it that the sperm dropped in white patches which congealed as they touched the metal, he made assurance of Lucy's coffin. Another search in his bag, and he took out a turnscrew.

"What are you going to do?" Seward asked.

"To open the coffin. You shall yet be convinced."

Straightway he began taking out the screws, and finally lifted off the lid, showing the casing of lead beneath. To Seward it seemed to be too much—as much an affront to the dead as it would have been to have stripped off her clothing in her sleep while living. He actually took hold of the Professor's hand to stop him.

He only said, "You shall see," and taking the edge of the loose flange, he bent it back towards the foot of the coffin, and holding up the candle into the aperture, motioned to his companion to look.

He drew near and looked. The coffin was empty. It was a considerable shock to him, but Van Helsing was unmoved. He was now more sure than ever of his ground, and so emboldened to proceed in his task. "Are you satisfied now, friend John?" he asked.

"I am satisfied only that Lucy's body is not in that coffin."

"But how do you, how can you, account for it not being there?"

"Perhaps a body-snatcher," he suggested. "Some of the undertaker's people may have stolen it." He felt that he was speaking folly, and yet it was the only real cause which he could suggest.

The Professor sighed. "Ah well!" he said, "we must have more proof. Come with me."

He put on the coffin lid again, gathered up all his things and placed them in the bag, blew out the light, and placed the candle also in the bag. He opened the door and both went out. Behind them he closed the door and locked it. Then he took from his bag a packet, and from it pulled what looked like a thin, wafer like biscuit, which was carefully rolled up in a white napkin. He asked Seward to give him his handkerchief, and wrapped the wafer inside it. Then, taking hold of Seward's arm, he tied the loose ends of the handkerchief around the wrist.

With both his hands in a firm hold on the doctor's arm, he said in all solemnity, "You must keep and protect this with your life."

By now Seward was too appalled at the whole business even to ask the Professor what it was.

Then the Professor told him to watch at one side of the churchyard while he would watch at the other.

Seward took up his place behind a yew tree, and saw Van Helsing's dark figure move until the intervening headstones and trees hid it from sight. He was too cold and too sleepy to be keenly observant, and not sleepy enough to betray his trust, so altogether he was in for a dreary, miserable time. He was angry with the Professor for taking him on such an errand and with himself for coming. Just after his lonely vigil began, John heard a distant clock strike one, and in time came two, but when he heard the toll of three, he was for some reason chilled and unnerved. He, who had up to an hour ago repudiated the proofs, felt his heart sink within him. Never did tombs look so ghastly white. Never did cypress, or yew, or juniper so seem the embodiment of funereal gloom. Never did tree or grass wave or rustle so ominously. Never did bough creak so mysteriously, and never did the far-away howling of dogs send such a woeful presage through the night.

There was a long spell of silence, big, aching, void, and then from the Professor a keen "S-s-s-s!" He pointed, and far down the avenue of yews they saw a white figure advance, a dim white figure, which held something dark at its breast. The figure stopped, and at the moment a ray of moonlight fell upon the masses of driving clouds, and showed in startling prominence a dark-haired woman, dressed in the cerements of the grave. They could not see the face, for it was bent down over what appeared to be a fair-haired child. There was a pause and a sharp little cry, such as a child gives in sleep, or a dog as it lies before the fire and dreams. Seward was starting forward, but the Professor's warning hand kept him back. And then the white figure moved forwards again. It was now near enough for them to see clearly, and the moonlight still held. Seward's heart grew cold as ice, and he uttered a gasp, as he recognized the features of Lucy Westenra. Lucy Westenra, but yet how changed. The sweetness was turned to adamantine, heartless cruelty, and the purity to voluptuous wantonness.

Van Helsing raised his lantern and drew the slide. By the concentrated light that fell on Lucy's face they could see that the lips were crimson with fresh blood, and that the stream had trickled over her chin and stained the purity of her lawn death-robe. They both shuddered with horror. Even Van Helsing's iron nerve had failed.

When the thing that bore the shape of Lucy saw them she drew back with an angry snarl, such as a cat gives when taken unawares, then her eyes ranged over them. Lucy's eyes in form and color, but Lucy's eyes unclean and full of hell fire, instead of the pure, gentle orbs they knew. At that moment the remnant of Seward's love passed into hate and loathing. Had she then to be killed, he could have done it with savage delight. As she looked at him, her eyes blazed with unholy light, and the face became wreathed with a voluptuous smile. It made him shudder to see it. With a careless motion, she flung to the ground, callous as a devil, the child that up to now she had clutched strenuously to her breast, growling over it as a dog growls over a bone. The child gave a sharp cry and lay there moaning. There was a cold-bloodedness in the act which wrung a groan from Seward. When she advanced to him with out-stretched arms and a wanton smile he fell back and hid his face in his hands.

She still advanced, however, and with a languorous, voluptuous grace, said, "Come to me, John. My arms are hungry for you. Come, and we can rest together. Come, be my husband, come!"

There was something diabolically sweet in her tones, something of the tinkling of glass when struck, which rang through the brain. Seward seemed suddenly under a spell, moving his hands from his face, he opened wide his arms. She was leaping for them, when suddenly she recoiled as if arrested by some irresistible force. Shown in the clear burst of moonlight was her distorted face, full of rage and baffled malice. The beautiful color became livid, the eyes seemed to throw out sparks of hell-fire, the brows were wrinkled as though the folds of flesh were the coils of Medusa's snakes, and the lovely, blood-stained mouth grew to an open square, as in the passion masks of the Greeks and Japanese. If ever a face meant death, if looks could kill, they saw it at that moment.

She turned as if to make for the entrance to her tomb. Van Helsing sprang forward and held before her his little golden crucifix, which again thwarted her advance.

And so for full half a minute, which seemed an eternity, the sacred crucifix sealed her means of passage. Van Helsing broke the silence by asking Seward, "Answer me, oh my friend! Am I to proceed in my work?"

"Do as you will. Do as you will. There can be no horror like this ever any more." He groaned in spirit, and looked on with horrified amazement as he saw, when Van Helsing stood back, the woman, with a corporeal body as real at that moment as their own, pass through the crevice between the door and its setting, where scarce a knife blade could have gone.

"In little more than an hour, the dawn will break. She dare not leave her coffin again tonight," said Van Helsing.

He reached for Seward's arm and untied the handkerchief, removing the wafer, then gently placed it in it's packet and back into his bag.

Then he went and he lifted the child and said, "As for this little one, he is not much harmed, and by tomorrow night he shall be well."

They took the child to the edge of Hampstead Heath. When they heard a policeman's heavy tramp, they lay the child on the pathway, then waited and watched until he saw it as he flashed his lantern to and fro. They heard his exclamation of astonishment, and then they went away silently.

On the way back, Seward asked about the curious wafer, and was stopped in his tracks by the Professor's reply—

"The Host. I brought it from Amsterdam. I have dispensation."

This he stated as casually as if he were commenting on the weather. Seward fell silent in the presence of such earnest purpose, impossible to distrust, that the Professor had so armed them with what was to him the most sacred of things.

As they approached the tomb, coming close to his friend, the Professor said, "John, you have had a sore trial, but after, when you look back, you will see how it was necessary. You are now in the bitter waters, my child. By this time tomorrow you will, please God, have passed them, and have drunk of the sweet waters. So do not mourn over-much. Till then I shall not ask you to forgive me."

When they were certain they were alone, they silently proceeded to the tomb. The Professor unlocked the door and they entered, closing it behind them. Then he took from his bag the lantern, which he lit, and also two wax candles, which, when lighted, he stuck by melting their own ends on other coffins, so that they might give light sufficient to work by. When he again lifted the lid off Lucy's coffin they both looked, Seward trembling like an aspen, and saw that the corpse lay there in all its death beauty. But there was no love in her betrothee's heart, nothing but loathing for the foul Thing which had taken Lucy's shape without her soul. His face grew hard as he looked. Presently he said to Van Helsing, "Is this really Lucy's body, or only a demon in her shape?"

"It is her body, and yet not it. But wait a while, and you shall see her as she was, and is."

She seemed like a nightmare of Lucy as she lay there, the pointed teeth, the blood stained, voluptuous mouth, the whole carnal and unspirited appearance, seeming like a devilish mockery of Lucy's sweet purity. Van Helsing, with his usual methodicalness, began taking the various contents from his bag and placing them ready for use. First he took out a soldering iron and some plumbing solder, and then a small oil lamp, then his operating knives, which he placed to hand, and last a round wooden stake, some two and a half or three inches thick and about three feet long. One end of it was hardened by charring in the fire, and was sharpened to a fine point. With this stake came a heavy hammer, such as in households is used in the coal cellar for breaking the lumps.

When all was ready, Van Helsing said, "Before we do anything let me tell you this. It is out of the lore and experience of the ancients and of all those who have studied the powers of the UnDead. When they become nosferatu, as they call it in Eastern Europe, there comes with the change the curse of immortality. They cannot die, but must go on age after age adding new victims. For all that die from the preying of the Undead become themselves Undead, and prey on their kind. And so the circle goes on ever widening, like as the ripples from a stone thrown in the water. The career of this so unhappy dear lady is but just begun. But if this now UnDead be made to rest as true dead, then the soul of the poor lady whom we love shall again be free. Instead of working wickedness by night and growing more debased in the assimilating of it by day, she shall take her place with the other Angels. So that, my friend, it will be a blessed hand for her that shall strike the blow that sets her free. To this I am willing, but would it not be a comfort to you, my friend, in future days, when sleep is not, to think, 'It was my hand that sent her to the stars. It was the hand of him that loved her best, the hand that of all she would herself have chosen, had it been to her to choose?'"

Seward stepped forward.

Van Helsing laid a hand on his shoulder, and said, "Brave lad! A moment's courage, and it is done. This stake must be driven through her. It will be a fearful ordeal, be not deceived in that, but you must not falter when once you have begun."

Said Seward hoarsely, "Tell me what I am to do."

"Take this stake in your left hand, ready to place to the point over the heart, and the hammer in your right. Then when we begin our prayer for the dead, strike in God's name."

Seward took the stake and the hammer. Van Helsing opened his missal and began to read. Seward rested the point over the heart, then he struck with all his might.

The thing in the coffin writhed, and a hideous, blood-curdling screech came from the opened red lips. The body shook and quivered and twisted in wild contortions. The sharp white teeth champed together till the lips were cut, and the mouth was smeared with a crimson foam. But Seward never faltered. He looked like a figure of Thor as his untrembling arm rose and fell, driving deeper and deeper the mercy-bearing stake, while the blood from the pierced heart welled and spurted up around it.

And then the writhing and quivering of the body became less, and the teeth seemed to champ, and the face to quiver. Finally it lay still. The terrible task was over.

The hammer fell from Seward's hand. He reeled and would have fallen had Van Helsing not caught him. The great drops of sweat sprang from his forehead, and his breath came in broken gasps. It had indeed been an awful strain on him, and had he not been forced to his task by more than human considerations he could never have gone through with it. For a few minutes both were so taken up with him that they did not look towards the coffin. When they did, however, a murmur of startled surprise ran from one to the other. A glad strange light broke over Seward's face and dispelled altogether the gloom of horror that lay upon it.

There, in the coffin lay no longer the foul Thing that they had so dreaded and grown to hate, but Lucy as they had seen her in life, with her face of unequalled sweetness and purity. True that there were there, as they had seen them in life, the traces of care and pain and waste. But these were all dear to them, for they marked her truth to what they knew. They felt that the holy calm that lay like sunshine over the wasted face and form was only an earthly token and symbol of the calm that was to reign forever.

Van Helsing came and laid his hand on Seward's shoulder, and said to him, "And now, my friend, dear lad, am I not forgiven?"

The reaction of the terrible strain came as Seward took the old man's hand in his, and raising it to his lips, pressed it, and said, "Forgiven! God bless you that you have given my dear one her soul again, and me peace." He put his hands on the Professor's shoulder, and laying his head on his breast, cried for a while silently, while both stood unmoving.

When he raised his head Van Helsing said to him, "And now, my child, you may kiss her. Kiss her dead lips if you will, as she would have you to, if for her to choose. For she is not a grinning devil now, not any more a foul Thing for all eternity. She is God's true dead, whose soul is with Him!"

Seward bent and kissed her, and then the Professor sent him out of the tomb that he might be spared the final procedure, which would be made hard now that she had none of the malign in her appearance.

He sawed the top off the stake, leaving the point of it in the body. Then he cut off the head and filled the mouth with garlic. He soldered up the leaden coffin, screwed on the coffin lid, and gathering up his belongings, came away. When the Professor locked the door he gave the key to Seward.

Outside the air was sweet, the sun was rising, and the birds sang, and it seemed as if all nature were tuned to a different pitch. There was gladness and mirth and peace everywhere, for the two men were at rest themselves on one account, and they were glad, though it was with a tempered joy.

3.

Van Helsing was off to the British Museum, looking up some authorities on ancient medicine, searching for witch and demon cures which might be useful to him. Sometimes Seward thought they must be all mad and that they should wake in strait waistcoats—then from the wings would enter Renfield, to dispense the rational wisdom that would restore them all to sanity.

Seward was making his rounds, when he was surprised by Mina's voice behind him.

"Dr. Seward, may I ask a favor? I want to see your patient, Mr. Renfield."

She had returned unannounced. He was slightly thrown by her direct manner. He quickly deemed this the best way, and possibly the only way, to resolve the issue in her mind, so he consented.

When he went into the room, he told the man that a lady would like to see him, to which the patient simply answered, "Why?"

"She is going through the house, and wants to see everyone in it."

"Oh, very well," he said, "let her come in, by all means, but just wait a minute till I tidy up the place."

His method of tidying was to simply swallow all the flies and spiders in the boxes before Seward could stop him. It was quite evident that he feared, or was jealous of some interference. When he had got through his disgusting task he said cheerfully, "Let the lady come in," and sat down on the edge of his bed with his head down, but with his eyelids raised so that he could see her as she entered. For a moment the doctor thought that he might have some homicidal intent and took care to stand where he could seize him at once if he attempted to make a spring at her.

She came into the room with an easy gracefulness which would at once command the respect of any lunatic, for easiness is one of the qualities mad people most respect. She walked over to him, smiling pleasantly, and held out her hand.

"Good evening, Mr. Renfield," said she. "You see, I know you, for Dr. Seward has told me of you." He made no immediate reply, but eyed her all over intently with a set frown on his face. This look gave way to one of wonder, which merged in doubt, then to Seward's intense astonishment he said, "You're not the girl the doctor wanted to marry, are you? You can't be, you know, for she's dead."

Mina smiled sweetly as she replied, "Oh no! I have a husband of my own, to whom I was married before I ever saw Dr. Seward, or he me. I am Mrs. Harker."

"Then what are you doing here?"

"My husband and I are staying on a visit with Dr. Seward."

"Then don't stay."

"But why not?"

Seward thought that this style of conversation might not be pleasant to Mrs. Harker, any more than it was to him, so he joined in, "How did you know I wanted to marry anyone?"

Renfield's reply was simply contemptuous, given in a pause in which he turned his eyes from Mina to Seward, instantly turning them back again, "What an asinine question!"

"I don't see that at all, Mr. Renfield," said Mina.

He replied to her with as much courtesy and respect as he had shown contempt to Seward, "You will, of course, understand, Mrs. Harker, that when a man is so loved and honored as our host is, everything regarding him is of interest in our little community. Dr. Seward is loved not only by his household and his friends, but even by his patients, who, being some of them hardly in mental equilibrium, are apt to distort causes and effects. Since I myself have been an inmate of a lunatic asylum, I cannot but notice that the sophistic tendencies of some of its inmates lean towards the errors of non causa and ignoratio elenche."

Seward positively opened his eyes at this new development. Here was his own pet lunatic, the most pronounced of his type that he had ever met with, talking elemental philosophy, and with the manner of a polished gentleman. It was hard to imagine that he had seen him eat up his spiders and flies not five minutes before. He wondered if it was Mrs. Harker's presence which had touched some chord in his memory.

They continued to make small talk for some time. Looking at his watch, the doctor saw that he should go to the station to meet Van Helsing, so he told Mrs. Harker that it was time to leave.

She came at once, after saying pleasantly to Mr. Renfield, "Goodbye, and I hope I may see you again, under auspices pleasanter to yourself."

To which, to Seward's astonishment, he replied, "Goodbye, my dear. I pray God I may never see your sweet face again. May He bless and keep you!"

Back within the study, Mina let fall the mask of composure, and gently collapsed into the upholstered chair.

"Is that the man you believed to be Mr. Harker?" asked Seward, as he seated himself across from her.

"It is him. And it is not him," said she, quavering. "The face and figure... and voice are his, but the person I spoke with in that room is a stranger to me."

Before Seward could react to this, she pulled from her purse a typed manuscript, which she placed on his desk.

"This is the transcript of Mr.... Renfield's diary." And placing her hand to her temple, "Dr. Seward, you will excuse me, I must lie down."

Seward rose, but she had already left the study.

"Alas! How that dear woman must have suffered as she read her husband's terrible account!" said the Professor. "Oh, Madam Mina, how can I say what I owe to her? This paper is as sunshine. It opens the gate to me."

He stopped, his voice was breaking, and Seward did not know if rage or terror predominated in his own heart. There was no need to put their fear, nay their conviction, into words, they shared them in common.

For more than an hour Seward and Van Helsing had been studying and analyzing the bundle of papers typed by Mina. In fearful detail, the horror which Jonathan Harker had lived through was brought before them, as it had been before Mina, like the slow unveiling of a hideous painting.

"What is here told," the Professor laid his hand heavily and gravely on the packet of papers as he spoke, "may foretell the beginning of the end to you and me and many another, or it may sound the knell of the UnDead who walk the earth, for is not information the greatest weapon?"

Now they knew that it was this Count Dracula who killed Lucy, attacking her first in her own home, then here at the asylum; that the house which Dracula had bought, and was his hiding place, was the one next door to the very one in which they now sat; and that in this very building, the moods and behavior of one of its own patients were powerfully connected to the doings of the Count.

Could it be that the vulnerability of the monster might be carried to Renfield in some subtle way? If they could only get some hint as to what passed in his mind... The patient had been seemingly quiet for some time. Was he? That wild yell seemed to come from his room...

The attendant came bursting into the doctor's study and announced that Renfield had somehow met with some accident. He had heard him yell, and when he went to him found him lying on his face on the floor, all covered with blood.

Seward looked to Van Helsing, who gave him a nod, and he hurried to the patient's room. There Seward found him lying on the floor on his left side, in a pool of blood. When he went to move him, it became at once apparent that he had received some terrible injuries. There seemed none of the unity of purpose between the parts of the body which marks even lethargic sanity. As the face was exposed he could see that it was horribly bruised, as though it had been beaten against the floor.

The attendant who was kneeling beside the body said to Seward as they turned him over, "I think, sir, his back is broken. See, both his right arm and leg and the whole side of his face are paralyzed." The attendant seemed quite bewildered, "I can't understand the two things. He could mark his face like that by beating his own head on the floor. I saw a young woman do it once at the Eversfield Asylum before anyone could lay hands on her. And I suppose he might have broken his neck by falling out of bed, if he got in an awkward kink. But for the life of me I can't imagine how the two things occurred at once."

Seward said to him, "Go to Dr. Van Helsing, and ask him to kindly come here at once."

The man ran off and found the Professor already on his way, bearing with him his surgical case. Seward sent the attendant off to his round, and they went into a strict examination of the patient. The wounds of the face were superficial. The real injury was a depressed fracture of the skull, extending right up through the motor area.

The Professor thought a moment and said, "The rapidity of the suffusion shows the terrible nature of his injury. The whole motor area seems affected. The suffusion of the brain will increase quickly. There's no use. His time is short."

Each instant the poor man seemed as though he would open his eyes and speak, but then would follow a prolonged stertorous breath.

For a few moments the breathing continued to be stertorous. There was a nervous suspense over them, as though overhead some dread bell would peal out powerfully when they should least expect it. Then there came a breath so prolonged that it seemed as though it would tear open his chest. Suddenly his eyes opened and became fixed in a wild, helpless stare. This was continued for a few moments, then it was softened into a glad surprise, and from his lips came a sigh of relief. He moved convulsively, and as he did so, said, "I'll be quiet, Doctor. Tell them to take off the strait waistcoat. I have had a terrible dream, and it has left me so weak that I cannot move. What's wrong with my face? It feels all swollen, and it smarts dreadfully."

He tried to turn his head, but even with the effort his eyes seemed to grow glassy again, so Seward gently put it back. Then Van Helsing said in a quiet grave tone, "Tell us your dream, Mr. Renfield."

As he heard the voice his face brightened through its mutilation, and he said, "That is Dr. Van Helsing. How good it is of you to be here. Give me some water, my lips are dry, and I shall try to tell you. I dreamed…"

He stopped and seemed fainting. Seward hurried to his study and returned with a glass, a decanter of brandy and a carafe of water. They moistened the parched lips, and the patient quickly revived. He looked at Seward piercingly with an agonized confusion and said, "I must not deceive myself. It was no dream, but all a grim reality." Then his eyes roved round the room.

For an instant his eyes closed, not with pain or sleep but voluntarily, as though he were bringing all his faculties to bear. When he opened them he said, hurriedly, and with more energy than he had yet displayed, "Quick, Doctor, quick, I am dying! I feel that I have but a few minutes, and then I must go back to death, or worse! Wet my lips with brandy again. I have something that I must say before I die. Or before my poor crushed brain dies anyhow. Thank you!"

As he spoke, Van Helsing's eyes never blinked, but his hand came out and met Seward's and gripped it hard. He did not, however, betray himself. He nodded slightly and said, "Go on," in a low voice.

Renfield proceeded. "The Master came up to the window in the mist, as I had seen him often before, but he was solid then, not a ghost, and his eyes were fierce like a man's when angry. I wouldn't ask him to come in at first, though I knew he wanted to, just as he had wanted all along. Then he began promising me things, not in words but by doing them."

He was interrupted by a word from the Professor, "How?"

"By making them happen. Just as he used to send in the flies when the sun was shining. Great big fat ones with steel and sapphire on their wings. And big moths in the night, with skull and cross-bones on their backs."

Van Helsing nodded to him as he whispered to Seward unconsciously, "The Acherontia Atropos of the Sphinges, what you call the 'Death's-head Moth'."

The patient went on without stopping. "Then the dogs howled, away beyond the dark trees in His house. He beckoned me to the window. I got up and looked out, and He raised his hands and seemed to call out without using any words. A dark mass spread over the grass, coming on like the shape of a flame of fire. And then He moved the mist to the right and left, and I could see that there were thousands of rats, millions of them, with their eyes blazing red, like His only smaller. He held up his hand and they all stopped, and I thought he seemed to be saying, 'All these lives will I give you, ay, and many more and greater, through countless ages, if you will fall down and worship me!' And then a red cloud, like the color of blood, seemed to close over my eyes, and before I knew what I was doing, I found myself opening the sash and saying to Him, 'Come in, Lord and Master!' The rats were all gone, but He slid into the room through the sash, though it was only open an inch wide, just as the Moon herself has often come in through the tiniest crack and has stood before me in all her size and splendor, but he did not bring me anything, not even a blowfly. I was pretty angry with him. He sneered at me, and his white face looked out of the mist with his red eyes gleaming, and he went on as though he owned the whole place, and I was no one. He didn't even smell the same as he went by me.

"When Mrs. Harker came in to see me this afternoon she looked too pale."

The Professor started and quivered. His face, however, grew grimmer and sterner still. Renfield went on without noticing

"I don't care for the pale people. I like them with lots of blood in them, and hers all seemed to have run out. I didn't think of it at the time, but when she went away I began to think, and it made me mad to know that He had been taking the life out of her.

"So when He came tonight I was ready for Him. I saw the mist stealing in and I grabbed it tight. I had heard that madmen have unnatural strength. And as I knew I was a madman, at times anyhow, I resolved to use my power. Ay, and He felt it too, for He had to come out of the mist to struggle with me. I held tight, and I thought I was going to win, for I didn't mean Him to take any more of her life, till I saw His eyes. They burned into me, and my strength became like water. He slipped through it, and when I tried to cling to Him, He raised me up and flung me down. There was a red cloud before me, and a noise like thunder, and the mist seemed to steal away under the door."

At last there came a time when it was evident that the patient was sinking fast. He might die at any moment. His voice was becoming fainter and his breath more stertorous. Van Helsing stood up instinctively.

Just then Renfield's face underwent a remarkable change. Looking past both men, his eyes seemed to light up, as he breathed his final words.

"Wilhelmina!" —his voice more tender than they had ever heard from him. "It's all right. I've come home."

In the doorway, they turned and saw Mina standing, pale and emotionless, except for a single teardrop that descended slowly down her cheek.

Throughout the institution there was an undercurrent of terror, and simpering sounds from the patients, and nervousness and confusion amongst the staff. Was it the howling of the dogs mingled with distant thunder? or the agitated voices in the corridor that spoke in muffled tones of crisis?

Seward and Van Helsing stood in the archway off the drawing room, where they had gently placed Mina. There she sat, erect and dreamy eyed. Van Helsing pulled Seward aside and with great agitation, whispered—

"Mein Gott! Mein Gott! Could I have been so stupid! We attributed the poor lady's languid state to mental anguish, when it is so much worse, so much worse! We took Lucy away from him, now the Being sets his sights on Mina, and has been assaulting her as she slept!"

They made a quick consult about the dead body. If the coroner should demand it, there would be a formal inquest. It would never do to put forward the truth, as no one would believe it. As it was, Seward thought that on the attendant's evidence he could give a certificate of death by misadventure in falling from bed.

"Let her safely rest there," said the Professor, "while I go to gather my sacred tools for her protection, belatedly, alas, alas! We know the worst now. He is here, and we know his purpose. It may not be too late. Let us lose no time, there is not an instant to spare."

Seward instructed the attendants to search the premises and report anything unusual immediately, but under no circumstances to approach or confront any stranger.

The Professor was on his way to Mina's room to secure the premises with his sacred weaponry, when Seward suddenly emerged from the archway and cried, "Dr. Van Helsing, Mina is gone!"

They both raced up the steps. Outside Mina's door they paused and Van Helsing said "Friend John, when I turn the handle, if the door does not open, do you put your shoulder down and shove. Now!"

He turned the handle as he spoke, but the door did not yield. They threw themselves against it. With a crash it burst open and they almost fell headlong into the room. The Professor did actually fall, and Seward saw across him as the old man gathered himself up from hands and knees. What he saw appalled him. He felt his hair rise like bristles on the back of his neck, and his heart seemed to stand still.

The moonlight was so bright that through the thick yellow blind the room was light enough to see. Kneeling on the near edge of the bed facing outwards was the white-clad figure of Mina. By her side stood a tall, thin man, clad in black. His face was turned from them, but the instant they saw they instinctively recognized the Count. With his left hand he held both Mina's hands, keeping them away with her arms at full tension. His right hand gripped her by the back of the neck, forcing her face down on his bosom. Her white nightdress was smeared with blood, and a thin stream trickled down the man's bare chest which was shown by his torn-open dress. The attitude of the two had a terrible resemblance to a child forcing a kitten's nose into a saucer of milk to compel it to drink. With a wrench that threw his victim back upon the bed as though hurled from a height, the Count turned his face, and a hellish look seemed to leap into it. His eyes flamed red with devilish passion. The great nostrils of the white aquiline nose opened wide and quivered at the edge, and a horrible sort of snarl passed over his face, showing the eyeteeth long and pointed. But the evil smile as quickly passed into a cold stare of lion-like disdain. He adjusted his shirt and stood erect, a caricature of false dignity, in abominable contrast to the pathetic figure on the bed.

The two men stood paralyzed, as if spellbound.

He spoke to them mockingly—

"Professor Van Helsing! Such an undignified entrance for such a noble adversary!

"And you, Dr. Seward, who stole from me your best beloved one, let me thank you for providing me this replacement," with grotesque mockery he swept his arm over Mina, "my bountiful wine-press, where more than once my thirst has been appeased," —and throwing open his shirt, he proclaimed, "She is now flesh of my flesh, blood of my blood, kin of my kin, the prize bride of all my horde!

"You think to confound me, you with your pale faces, like sheep in a butcher's. My revenge is just begun! I spread it over centuries. Your girls that you all love are mine already. And through them others shall yet be mine, my creatures, to do my bidding and to be my jackals when I want to feed!

"And you play wits against *me*, against *me* who commanded nations! Then learn what it is to cross my path, when with one of you in each hand, I dash out both your brains!"

It would be impossible to describe the expression of hatred and malignity which came over the Count's face as he rushed toward them.

As his control succumbed to beastly rage, it was enough to release Van Helsing from his spell. The Professor quickly pulled out the sacred wafer and thrust it forward in his hand to within inches of the Count's face.

The Count suddenly stopped, just as poor Lucy had done outside the tomb, and cowered back. Seward raised his crucifix. Further and further back the Count cowered, as the two men advanced. The moonlight suddenly failed, as a great black cloud sailed across the sky. And when the gaslight sprang up under Seward's match, they saw nothing but a faint vapor. This, as they looked, trailed under the door, which with the recoil from its bursting open, had swung back to its old position.

For a few seconds Mina lay in her helpless attitude and disarray. Her face was ghastly, with a pallor which was accentuated by the blood which smeared her lips and cheeks and chin. From her throat trickled a thin stream of blood. Her eyes were mad with terror. Then she put before her face her poor crushed hands, which bore on their whiteness the red mark of the Count's terrible grip, and from behind them came a low desolate wail, the expression of an endless grief. Professor Van Helsing stepped forward and drew the coverlet gently over her body, and said with wonderful calmness, "Do not fear, my dear. We are here. You are safe." And to Seward he added, "He will not be back tonight, for the sky is reddening in the east, and the dawn is close. We must work tomorrow!"

For a space of perhaps a couple of minutes there was silence, and Seward fancied that he could hear the sound of their hearts beating.

The Professor gently lifted Mina's hand. "Now, Madam Mina, I will prepare your chamber by the placing of things of which we know, so that He may not enter. But now let me guard yourself. On your forehead I touch this piece of Sacred Wafer in the name of the Father, the Son, and..."

There was a fearful scream so wild, so ear-piercing, so despairing that it almost froze all hearts to hear. As he had placed the Wafer on Mina's forehead, it had seared it... had burned into the flesh as though it had been a piece of white-hot metal. The poor darling's mind had told her the significance of the fact as quickly as her nerves received the pain of it.

The echo of the scream had not ceased to ring on the air when she rose from the bed and sank on her knees on the floor in an agony of abasement. Pulling her beautiful hair over her face, as the leper of old his mantle, she wailed out.

"Unclean! Unclean! Even the Almighty shuns my polluted flesh! I must bear this mark of shame upon my forehead until the Judgment Day."

Seward turned away his eyes that ran tears silently. Then Van Helsing said gravely, so gravely that even Mina could not help feeling that he was in some way inspired, and was stating things outside himself.

"It may be that you may have to bear that mark till God himself see fit, as He most surely shall, on the Judgment Day, to redress all wrongs of the earth and of His children that He has placed thereon. And oh, Madam Mina, my dear, my dear, may we who love you be there to see, when that red scar, the sign of God's knowledge of what has been, shall pass away and leave your forehead as pure as the heart we know. For so surely as we live, that scar shall pass away when God sees right to lift the burden that is hard upon us. Till then we bear our Cross, as His Son did in obedience to His Will. It may be that we are chosen instruments of His good pleasure, and that we ascend to His bidding as that other through scourge and shame. Through tears and blood. Through doubts and fear, and all that makes the difference between God and man."

4.

Breakfast was a strange meal to the three of them. They tried to be cheerful and encourage each other. Decisive action was required to kill the monster and save Mina's soul, and time was of the essence. They must strike while Dracula was still unaware that they knew the location of his lair. With any luck, he would be caught napping in his grisly litter, and at his most vulnerable. Beyond killed, beyond destroyed, his very essence must be totally obliterated. The tools for this accomplishment lay collected on the table before them. The Professor placed them in his bag, one by one, save their greatest weapon of all, their unified unwavering determination.

The Professor pulled a large bowie knife half out of its sheath, momentarily perused it, locked eyes with Mina, and slid it back in, and with a look of uncertainty on his face, placed it in the bag alongside his great Gurkha blade. Seward glanced at Mina. She was of God's army, despite the sign of the devil's illness in the terrible red scar on her forehead.

They had been surprised when she had stated so matter-of-factly that she would be accompanying them on their bleak mission. The rising sun had turned her heart from despairing to vengeful. Seward had objected, but the Professor saw in this amazing woman a spiritual resilience that was only short of miraculous, along with a strength of will and steel resolve that would not be challenged. "Perhaps it is safest, after all," said he, "if we three all stay together always now, until the matter is ended. It may be that one more armed hand will increase our chance of victory against the enemy."

Dr. Seward gave procedural instructions to the attendants for the continued operation of the asylum in case the two doctors' return should be unusually delayed, and the three of them set forth on their noble quest.

At breakfast, Mina had asked only two questions, neither of them self-serving.

Firstly, she wanted to know what would become of the remains of the man who called himself Renfield. Seward explained that there would be an inquest, after which the hospital would arrange a proper interment for the unclaimed body... in consult with herself.

Secondly, Mina wondered if a diagnosis had been put forth to explain the patients behavior, to which Professor Van Helsing had responded in this manner:

"In mental conditions, diagnosis always is in part guesswork. From the unusual circumstance that surround that poor man's case, we theorize this way:

"Your husband's so nightmare-like experience in Castle Dracula did bring out his so great strength of will, certainly made strong by thoughts that he must come home to you.

He knows he is descending to vampirism, so he makes his conscious soul to withdraw to dormancy, safely behind a new personality that does emerge, whom he names Renfield, who shall absorb all the madness brought by the real life nightmare, including the sick blood lust. Through unconscious influence, Renfield's bloodthirsty instinct he keeps at bay, satisfying the insane part of his brain with blood from the tiny living creatures, instead of from the humans. On the voyage at sea, the Count, who needs a servant to guard his sleep during the day, finds his victim will be more valuable in the human state, and feasts instead on the hapless crew.

"Your husband escaped the curse of vampirism, and, we are certain, died a blessed death as a human being, and a hero unsung, who delivered to us, through you, my blessed woman, the knowledge we need to destroy his and Lucy's murderer."

They took a circuitous route to Carfax through the back wood, and having passed the wall, headed towards the rear of the house, taking care to keep in the shadows of the trees on the lawn. When they got to the porch the Professor opened his bag and took out a lot of things, which he laid on the step, sorting them into three groups as he spoke.

"My friends, we are going into a terrible danger, and we need arms of many kinds. Our enemy is not merely spiritual. Remember that he has the strength of twenty men, and that, though our necks or our windpipes are of the common kind, and therefore breakable or crushable, his are not amenable to mere strength.

"Keep this near your heart." As he spoke he lifted a little silver crucifix and held it out to Seward. "Put these flowers round your neck." Here he handed to Mina a wreath of withered garlic blossoms, and then brought out several weapons normally reserved for enemies more mundane. For aid in all, he distributed small electric lamps, which they fastened to their clothes, then he said, "And for all, and above all at the last, this, which we must not desecrate needless." This was the Sacred Wafer, which he kept in his pouch.

The depleted bag was placed on the porch aside the door, while Seward pulled a ring of skeleton keys from his pocket, attached to which also was the small silver whistle he had used to call the dogs into pursuit of Renfield when the patient had escaped. He tried one or two keys, his mechanical dexterity as a surgeon standing him in good stead. Presently he got one to suit, after a little play back and forward the bolt yielded, and with a rusty clang, shot back. He pressed on the door, the rusty hinges creaked, and it slowly opened. The Professor was the first to move forward, and stepped into the open door.

"In manus tuas, Domine!" he said, crossing himself as he passed over the threshold. Before they closed the door behind them, the Professor carefully tried the lock, lest they might not be able to open it from within should they be in a hurry making their exit. To Seward it was startlingly like the image of the opening of Lucy's tomb. Then they all lit their lamps and proceeded on their search.

The light from the tiny lamps fell in all sorts of odd forms, as the rays crossed each other, or the opacity of their bodies threw great shadows. The feeling that there was someone else among them was common to all three, as they kept looking over their shoulders at every sound and every new shadow.

The whole place was thick with dust. The floor was seemingly inches deep, except where there were recent footsteps, in which one could see marks of hobnails where the dust was cracked. The walls were fluffy and heavy with dust, and in the corners were masses of spider's webs whereon the dust had gathered till they looked like old tattered rags as the weight had torn them partly down.

The house floor plan was among the original correspondence Mina had brought from London. The old map was confusing, but gave Seward an idea of the direction to the chapel, so he led the way. After a few wrong turnings they found themselves opposite a low, arched oaken door, ribbed with iron bands.

"This is the spot," said the Professor. With a little trouble they were able to push open the heavy door that decades-long settling of the foundation had tightened. They were prepared for some unpleasantness, for as they were opening the door a faint, malodorous air seemed to exhale through the gaps, but none of them ever expected such an odor as they encountered. The place was small and close, and the long disuse had made the air stagnant and foul. There was an earthy smell, as of some dry miasma, which came through the fouler air. But as to the odor itself, it was not alone that it was composed of all the ills of mortality and with the pungent, acrid smell of blood, but it seemed as though corruption had become itself corrupt. Every breath exhaled by that monster seemed to have clung to the place and intensified its loathsomeness.

"Faugh! How sickening!" said Seward.

Under ordinary circumstances such a stench would have brought any enterprise to an end, but this was no ordinary case, and the high and terrible purpose in which they were involved gave them a strength which rose above merely physical considerations. As of one mind, they proceeded into the chamber.

Mina suddenly turned and looked out of the vaulted doorway into the dark passage behind them, causing Seward to look too, and for an instant his heart stood still. Somewhere, looking out from the shadow, he seemed to see the highlights of the Count's evil face, the ridge of the nose, the red eyes, the red lips, the awful pallor. It was only for a moment, and when Mina said, "I thought I saw a face, but it was only the shadows," he turned his lamp in the direction, and stepped into the passage. There was no sign of anyone, and as there were no corners, no doors, no aperture of any kind, but only the solid walls of the passage, there could be no hiding place even for him. He took it that fear had helped imagination in both of them, and said nothing.

To the left was a huge, elaborately carved and bolted door. This was the entry to the chapel from without. The dust on the ground had been much disturbed. The boxed coffin had been brought in this way. Unconsciously they all moved towards the door. A moment later Van Helsing stepped suddenly back from a corner which he was examining. The other two followed his movements with their eyes, and they saw a whole mass of phosphorescence, which twinkled like stars. They all instinctively drew back. The whole place was becoming alive with rats.

For a moment or two they stood appalled, then Seward, who had an antidote on call, rushed up to the great iron-bound oaken door, he turned the lock, drew the huge bolts, and swung the door open. Then, taking the whistle from his pocket, he blew a low, shrill call. It was answered from behind the doctor's house by the yelping of dogs, and after about a minute three terriers came dashing round the corner of the house. But even in the minute that had elapsed the number of the rats had vastly increased. They seemed to swarm over the place all at once, till the lamplight, shining on their moving dark bodies and glittering, baleful eyes, made the place look like a bank of earth set with fireflies. The dogs dashed on, but at the threshold suddenly stopped and snarled, and then, simultaneously lifting their noses, began to howl in most lugubrious fashion. The rats were multiplying in the hundreds.

Seward lifted one of the dogs, and carrying him in, placed him on the floor. The instant his feet touched the ground he seemed to recover his courage, and rushed at his natural enemies. They fled before him so fast that before he had shaken the life out of a score, the other dogs, who had by now been lifted in the same manner, had but small prey ere the whole mass had vanished.

With their going it seemed as if some evil presence had departed, for the dogs frisked about and barked merrily as they made sudden darts at their prostrate foes, and turned them over and over and tossed them in the air with vicious shakes. The trio of vampire hunters seemed to find their spirits rise. With the purifying of the deadly atmosphere by the opening of the chapel door, the shadow of dread seemed to slip from them like a robe, and the occasion lost something of its grim significance—until the daylight from the open door drew their attention to the outline of a coffin near the far wall.

Mina was the first to approach. As if drawn by invisible bonds, she glided towards it along the dust-free path that had been scraped out by the dragged box. Seward and Van Helsing moved quickly past her.

The Professor's heart leapt as he stood above the chest, for he felt that the end was coming. He did not know if the

Thing was imprisoned there or not, or if so, would it awake and elude them, as it might in any of many powerful forms. Would all advantage of surprise attack be lost, and the demon escape with no possibility of capture, to spread his curse upon untold victims?

After a moment's pause, he, with desperate energy, attacked one end of the chest, attempting to prize off the lid with his great Kukri knife, while Seward frantically followed suit on the other end with a crowbar. Under the efforts of both men the lid began to yield. A frightened howl came from one of the dogs. Another gave a low growl. The nails drew with a screeching sound, and the top of the box was thrown back.

They saw the Count lying within the box upon the earth. Some rot had fallen from the manhandled lid and scattered over him. He was deathly pale, just like a waxen image, but the eyes were not closed. They glared red with a horrible vindictive look, and seeing Mina standing at the foot of his coffin in an apparent trance-like state, the look turned to triumph.

The UnDead Thing sprung from the coffin with fangs gleaming and lunged for her! The dogs barked insanely.

But, on the instant, came the sweep and flash of Van Helsing's great knife. Mina shrieked as she saw it shear through the Count's throat. At the same moment, Seward, in shock, had dropped the stake and hammer and reflexively rushed to place himself between Mina and the attacking monster. He was too late, and the sharpened stake lay on the ground behind him, thenceforth and forever a purposeless shard of timber, for in his plunge at her, the Vampire had impaled his chest directly upon the upheld bowie knife, which Mina gripped before her in two hands that were like the jaws of a vice. It struck deep, and point-blank, through the small, self-inflicted wound over the Count's heart, where with his long sharp nails he had opened a vein to force-feed her his blood.

Before their very eyes, and almost in the drawing of a breath, the whole body of the Count crumbled into dust and fell away from their sight. The death that should have come centuries ago at last asserted itself.

One of the dogs approached warily and sniffed the ground. The three stood for a moment, blank and stunned, that so suddenly it was all over. The nightmare had ended. Mina, saint that she was, would always be glad that in that moment of final dissolution, she perceived in the face of the Count a look of peace, such as none could have imagined might have rested there.

Just then, the strain of the confrontation, and all that had led up to it, caught up with the old Professor and took him to his knees. Seward tried to catch him but missed, and the gallant gentleman fell to the ground, where Mina quickly bent to aid him.

"Oh, God!" he cried suddenly, struggling to a sitting posture and pointing to her. "It was worth for this to die! Look! Look!"

The sun was now right over the hills and, filtered by the high stained glass window, the beams fell upon Mina's face, so that it was bathed in golden light. Seward followed the pointing of the Professor's finger, and from him broke a deep and earnest "Amen."

All had not been in vain. The purest ivory was not more stainless than her forehead. The curse had passed away.

THE END

THE INVISIBLE MAN

Adapted from the novel by
H. G. Wells

1.

About a mile and a half out of Iping the warming winds of May were drawing up over the down towards Adderdean, and Mr. Thomas Marvel was sitting with his feet in a ditch by the roadside.

You must picture Mr. Thomas Marvel as a person of copious, flexible visage, a nose of cylindrical protrusion, a liquorish, ample, fluctuating mouth, and a beard of bristling eccentricity. His figure inclined to plumpness, his short limbs accentuate this inclination. He wears a furry silk hat, and the frequent substitution of twine and shoe-laces for buttons, apparent at critical points of his costume, mark a man essentially bachelor. His feet, save for socks of irregular open-work, are bare, his big toes are broad, and pricked like the ears of a watchful dog.

In a leisurely manner—he did everything in a leisurely manner—he was contemplating trying on a pair of boots. They were the soundest boots he had come across for a long time, but too large for him, whereas the ones he had were, in dry weather, a very comfortable fit, but too thin-soled for damp. Mr. Thomas Marvel hated roomy shoes, but then he hated damp. He had never properly thought out which he hated most, and it was a pleasant day, and there was nothing better to do. So he put the four shoes in a graceful group on the turf and looked at them. And seeing them there among the grass and springing agrimony, it suddenly occurred to him that both pairs were exceedingly ugly to see. He was not at all startled by a voice behind him.

"They're boots, anyhow," said the Voice.

"They are—charity boots," said Mr. Thomas Marvel, with his head on one side regarding them distastefully, "and which is the ugliest pair in the whole blessed universe, I'm darned if I know!"

"H'm," said the Voice.

"I've worn worse—in fact, I've worn none. But none so owdacious ugly—if you'll allow the expression. I've been hunting boots, in particular, for days. Because I was sick of *them*. They're sound enough, of course. But a gentleman on tramp sees such a thundering lot of his boots. And if you'll believe me, I've raised nothing in the whole blessed country, try as I would, but *them*. Look at 'em! And a good country for boots, too, in a general way. But it's just my promiscuous luck. I've got my boots in this country ten years or more. And then they treat you like this."

"It's a beast of a country," said the Voice. "And pigs for people."

"Ain't it?" said Mr. Thomas Marvel. "Lord! But them boots! It beats it."

He turned his head over his shoulder to the right, to look at the boots of his interlocutor with a view to comparisons, and lo! where the boots of his interlocutor should have been were neither legs nor boots. He was irradiated by the dawn of a great amazement. "Where *are* yer?" said Mr. Thomas Marvel over his shoulder and coming on all fours. He saw a stretch of empty downs with the wind swaying the remote green-pointed furze bushes.

"Am I drunk?" said Mr. Marvel. "Have I had visions? Was I talking to myself? What the—"

"Don't be alarmed," said a Voice.

"None of your ventriloquising *me*," said Mr. Thomas Marvel, rising sharply to his feet. "Where *are* yer? Alarmed, indeed!"

"Don't be alarmed," repeated the Voice.

"*You'll* be alarmed in a minute, you silly fool," said Mr. Thomas Marvel. "Where *are* yer? Lemme get my mark on yer...

"Are yer *buried*?" said Mr. Thomas Marvel, after an interval.

There was no answer. Mr. Thomas Marvel stood bootless and amazed, his jacket nearly thrown off.

"Peewit," said a peewit, very remote.

"Peewit, indeed!" said Mr. Thomas Marvel. "This ain't no time for foolery." The down was desolate, east and west, north and south. The road with its shallow ditches and white bordering stakes, ran smooth and empty north and south, and, save for that peewit, the blue sky was empty too. "So help me," said Mr. Thomas Marvel, shuffling his coat on to his shoulders again. "I could have swore I heard a voice. It's the drink! I might ha' known."

"It's not the drink," said the Voice. "You keep your nerves steady."

"It's there again," said Mr. Marvel, closing his eyes and clasping his hand on his brow with a tragic gesture. He was suddenly taken by the collar and shaken violently, and left more dazed than ever. "Don't be a fool," said the Voice.

"I'm—off—my—blooming—chump," said Mr. Marvel. "It's no good. It's fretting about them blarsted boots. I'm off my blessed blooming chump. Or it's spirits."

"Neither one thing nor the other," said the Voice. "Listen!"

"Chump," said Mr. Marvel.

"One minute," said the Voice, penetratingly, tremulous with self-control.

"Well?" said Mr. Thomas Marvel, with a strange feeling of having been dug in the chest by a finger.

"You think I'm just imagination? Just imagination?"

"What else *can* you be?" said Mr. Thomas Marvel, rubbing the back of his neck.

"Very well," said the Voice, in a tone of relief. "Then I'm going to throw flints at you till you think differently."

"But where *are* yer?"

The Voice made no answer. Whizz came a flint, apparently out of the air, and missed Mr. Marvel's shoulder by a hair's-breadth. Mr. Marvel, turning, saw a flint jerk up into the air, trace a complicated path, hang for a moment, and then fling at his feet with almost invisible rapidity. He was too amazed to dodge. Whizz it came, and ricocheted from a bare toe into the ditch. Mr. Thomas Marvel jumped a foot and howled aloud. Then he started to run, tripped over an unseen obstacle, and came head over heels into a sitting position.

"*Now*," said the Voice, as a third stone curved upward and hung in the air above the tramp. "Am I imagination?"

Mr. Marvel by way of reply struggled to his feet, and was immediately rolled over again. He lay quiet for a moment. "If you struggle anymore," said the Voice, "I shall throw the flint at your head."

"It's a fair do," said Mr. Thomas Marvel, sitting up, taking his wounded toe in hand and fixing his eye on the third missile. "I don't understand it. Stones flinging themselves. Stones talking. Put yourself down. Rot away. I'm done."

The third flint fell.

"It's very simple," said the Voice. "I'm an invisible man."

"Tell us something I don't know," said Mr. Marvel, gasping with pain. "Where you've hid—how you do it—I *don't* know. I'm beat."

"That's all," said the Voice. "I'm invisible. That's what I want you to understand."

"But whereabouts?" interrupted Mr. Marvel.

"Here! Six feet in front of you."

"Oh, *come*! I ain't blind. You'll be telling me next you're just thin air. I'm not one of your ignorant tramps—"

"I am just a human being—solid, needing food and drink, needing covering too—But I'm invisible. You see? Invisible. Simple idea. Invisible."

"What, real like?"

"Yes, real."

"Let's have a hand of you," said Marvel, "if you *are* real. It won't be so darn out-of-the-way like, then—*Lord*!" he said, "how you made me jump!—gripping me like that!"

He felt the hand that had closed round his wrist with his disengaged fingers, and his fingers went timorously up the arm, patted a muscular chest, and explored a bearded face. Marvel's face was astonishment.

"I'm dashed!" he said. "If this don't beat cock-fighting! Most remarkable!—And there I can see a rabbit clean through you, 'arf a mile away! Not a bit of you visible—except—"

He scrutinized the apparently empty space keenly. "You 'aven't been eatin' bread and cheese?" he asked, holding the invisible arm.

"You're quite right, and it's not quite assimilated into the system."

"I tell you, the whole business fairly beats me," said Mr. Marvel.

"It's a simple matter: I need help. I have come to that—I came upon you suddenly. I was wandering, mad with rage, naked, impotent. I could have murdered. And I saw you—"

"*Lord!*" said Mr. Marvel.

"'Here,' I said, 'is an outcast like myself. This is the man for me.' A man needs a friend after all, doesn't he?—especially an invisible one."

"*Lord!*" said Mr. Marvel. "But I'm all in a tizzy. May I ask—How is it? And what you may be requiring in the way of help?—Invisible!"

"You're simply going to help me retrieve some of my belongings at the inn."

"Look here," said Mr. Marvel. "I'm too flabbergasted. Don't knock me about any more. You've pretty near broken my toe. It's all so unreasonable. Empty downs, empty sky. Nothing visible for miles. And then comes a voice. A voice out of heaven! And stones! And a fist—Lord!"

"Pull yourself together," said the Voice, "for you have to do the job I've chosen for you."

Mr. Marvel blew out his cheeks, and his eyes were round.

"I've chosen you," said the Voice. "You are the only man except some of those fools down there, who knows there is such a thing as an invisible man. You have to be my helper. Help me—and I will do great things for you.

An invisible man is a man of power." He stopped for a moment to sneeze violently.

"But if you betray me" he said, "if you fail to do as I direct you—" He paused and tapped Mr. Marvel's shoulder smartly. Mr. Marvel gave a yelp of terror at the touch. "I don't want to betray you," said Mr. Marvel, edging away from the direction of the fingers. "Don't you go a-thinking that, whatever you do. All I want to do is to help you—just tell me what I got to do. (Lord!) Whatever you want done, that I'm most willing to do."

After the first gusty panic had spent itself Iping became argumentative. Skepticism suddenly reared its head—rather nervous skepticism, not at all assured of its back, but skepticism nevertheless. It is so much easier not to believe in an invisible man, and those who had actually watched him dissolve into air one section at a time as he disrobed, or felt the strength of his invisible arm, could be counted on the fingers of two hands.

Iping was gay with bunting, and everybody was in gala dress. Whit Monday had been looked forward to for a month or more. By the afternoon even those who believed in the Unseen were beginning to resume their little amusements in a tentative fashion, on the supposition that he had quite gone away.

Haysman's meadow had sprouted a tent, in which Mrs. Bunting and other ladies were preparing tea, while, without, the Sunday-school children ran races and played games under the noisy guidance of the curate and the Misses Cuss and Sackbut. Down the village street stood a row of nearly a dozen booths, a shooting gallery, and on the green an inclined strong, down which, clinging the while to a pulley-swung handle, one could be hurled violently against a sack at the other end. This came in for considerable favor among the adolescent, as also did the swings and the cocoanut shies. There was also promenading—the gentlemen wore blue jerseys, the ladies white aprons and quite fashionable hats with heavy plumes—and the steam organ attached to a small roundabout filled the air with a pungent flavor of oil, and with equally pungent music. Old Fletcher, whose conceptions of holiday-making were severe, was visible through the jasmine about his window or through the open door (whichever way you chose to look), poised delicately on a plank supported on two chairs, and whitewashing the ceiling of his front room.

About four o'clock a stranger entered the village from the direction of the downs. He was a short, stout person in an extraordinarily shabby top hat, and he appeared to be very much out of breath. His cheeks were alternately limp and tightly puffed. His mottled face was apprehensive, and he moved with a sort of reluctant alacrity. He turned the corner of the church, and directed his way to the "Coach and Horses." Among others old Fletcher remembers seeing him, and indeed the old gentleman was so struck by his peculiar agitation that he inadvertently allowed a quantity of whitewash to run down the brush into the sleeve of his coat while regarding him.

At that precise moment Mr. Cuss and Mr. Bunting were in the parlor of the "Coach and Horses." They were seriously investigating the strange occurrences of the morning, and were, with Mr. Hall's permission, making a thorough examination of the Invisible Man's belongings.

The stranger's scattered garments had been removed by Mrs. Hall. "'Tas sperits, I know 'tas sperits," she had mumbled to herself as she tidied up the room. "I've read in papers of en. Tables and chairs leaping and dancing... I half guessed—I might ha' known. With them goggling eyes and bandaged head, and never going to church of a Sunday. And all they bottles—more'n it's right for any one to have. He's put the sperits into the furniture.... My good old furniture! 'Twas in that very chair my poor dear mother used to sit when I was a little girl. To think it should rise up against me now!"

And on the table under the window where the stranger had been wont to work, Cuss had hit almost at once on three big books in manuscript labeled "Diary."

"Diary!" said Cuss, putting the three books on the table. "Now, at any rate, we shall learn something." While the Vicar stood with his hands on the table the general practitioner, Cuss, sitting down, put two volumes to support the third, and opened it.

Not two days past had the stranger welcomed Cuss into this very parlor with a genial handshake. The bandages had excited the physician's professional interest. The report of the thousand and one bottles had aroused his jealous regard. But there was no mistaking the sincerity of his panic when he later related to Bunting, after his nerves had been steadied by a glass of cheap sherry—the only drink the good Vicar had available—that the hand that had grasped his firmly turned out to be no hand at all, reaching out from an empty sleeve.

"Diary," repeated Cuss. "H'm—no name on the flyleaf. Bother!—cipher. And figures."

The Vicar came round to look over his shoulder.

Cuss turned the pages over with a face suddenly disappointed. "I'm—dear me! It's all cipher, Bunting."

"There are no diagrams?" asked Mr. Bunting. "No illustrations throwing light—"

"See for yourself," said Mr. Cuss. "Some of it's mathematical and some of it's Russian or some such language (to judge by the letters), and some of it's Greek. Now the Greek I thought *you*—"

"Of course," said Mr. Bunting, taking out and wiping his spectacles and feeling suddenly very uncomfortable—for he had no Greek left in his mind worth talking about. "Yes—the Greek, of course, may furnish a clue."

"I'll find you a place."

"I'd rather glance through the volumes first," said Mr. Bunting, still wiping. "A general impression first, Cuss, and *then*, you know, we can go looking for clues."

He coughed, put on his glasses, arranged them fastidiously, coughed again, and wished something would happen to avert the seemingly inevitable exposure. Then he took the volume Cuss handed him in a leisurely manner. And then something did happen.

The door opened suddenly.

Both gentlemen started violently, looked round, and were relieved to see a sporadically rosy face beneath a furry silk hat. "Tap?" asked the face, and stood staring.

"No," said both gentlemen at once.

"Over the other side, my man," said Mr. Bunting. And "Please shut that door," said Mr. Cuss, irritably.

"All right," said the intruder, as it seemed in a low voice curiously different from the huskiness of its first inquiry. "Right you are," said the intruder in the former voice. "Stand clear!" and he vanished and closed the door.

"A sailor, I should judge," said Mr. Bunting. "Amusing fellows, they are. Stand clear! indeed. A nautical term, referring to his getting back out of the room, I suppose."

"I daresay so," said Cuss. "My nerves are all loose today. It quite made me jump—the door opening like that."

Mr. Bunting smiled as if he had not jumped. "And now," he said with a sigh, "these books."

Someone sniffed as he did so.

"One thing is indisputable," said Bunting, drawing up a chair next to that of Cuss. "There certainly have been very strange things happen in Iping during the last few days—very strange. I cannot of course believe in this absurd invisibility story—"

"It's incredible," said Cuss—"incredible. But the fact remains that I saw—I certainly saw right down his sleeve—"

"But did you—are you sure? Suppose a mirror, for instance—hallucinations are so easily produced. I don't know if you have ever seen a really good conjuror—"

"I won't argue again," said Cuss. "We've thrashed that out, Bunting. And just now there's these books—Ah! here's some of what I take to be Greek! Greek letters certainly."

He pointed to the middle of the page. Mr. Bunting flushed slightly and brought his face nearer, apparently finding some difficulty with his glasses. Suddenly he became aware of a strange feeling at the nape of his neck. He tried to raise his head, and encountered an immovable resistance. The feeling was a curious pressure, the grip of a heavy, firm hand, and it bore his chin irresistibly to the table. "Don't move, little men," whispered a voice, "or I'll brain you both!" He looked into the face of Cuss, close to his own, and each saw a horrified reflection of his own sickly astonishment.

"I'm sorry to handle you so roughly," said the Voice, "but it's unavoidable."

"Since when did you learn to pry into an investigator's private memoranda," said the Voice, and two chins struck the table simultaneously, and two sets of teeth rattled.

"Since when did you learn to invade the private rooms of a man in misfortune?" and the concussion was repeated.

"Where have they put my clothes?"

"Listen," said the Voice. "The windows are fastened and I've taken the key out of the door. I am a fairly strong man, and I have the poker handy—besides being invisible. There's not the slightest doubt that I could kill you both and get away quite easily if I wanted to—do you understand? Very well. If I let you go will you promise not to try any nonsense and do what I tell you?"

The Vicar and doctor looked at one another, and the doctor pulled a face. "Yes," said Mr. Bunting, and the doctor repeated it. Then the pressure on the necks relaxed, and the doctor and the vicar sat up, both very red in the face and wriggling their heads.

"Please keep sitting where you are," said the Invisible Man. "Here's the poker, you see."

"When I came into this room," continued the Invisible Man, after presenting the poker to the tip of the nose of each of his visitors, "I did not expect to find it occupied, and I expected to find, in addition to my books of memoranda, an outfit of clothing. Where is it? No—don't rise. I can see it's gone. Now, just at present, though the days are quite warm enough for an invisible man to run about stark, the evenings are quite chilly. I want clothing—and other accommodation, and I must also have those three books."

While these things were going on in the parlor, not a dozen yards away were Mr. Hall, husband to the hostess at the "Coach and Horses," and Teddy Henfrey, the clock-jobber, discussing in a state of cloudy puzzlement the one Iping topic.

Suddenly there came a violent thud against the door of the parlor, a sharp cry, and then—silence.

"Hul-lo!" said Teddy Henfrey.

"Hul-lo!" from the Tap.

Mr. Hall took things in slowly but surely, as was his way. "That ain't right," he said, and came round from behind the bar towards the parlor door.

He and Teddy approached the door together, with intent faces. Their eyes considered. "Summat wrong," said Hall, and Henfrey nodded agreement. Whiffs of an unpleasant chemical odor met them, and there was a muffled sound of conversation, very rapid and subdued.

"You all right thur?" asked Hall, rapping.

The muttered conversation ceased abruptly, for a moment silence, then the conversation was resumed, in hissing whispers, then a sharp cry of "No! no, you don't!" There came a sudden motion and the oversetting of a chair, a brief struggle. Silence again.

"What the dooce?" exclaimed Henfrey, *sotto voce*.

"You—all—right thur?" asked Mr. Hall, sharply, again.

The Vicar's voice answered with a curious jerking intonation: "Quite ri-right. Please don't—interrupt."

"Odd!" said Mr. Henfrey.

"Odd!" said Mr. Hall.

"Says, 'Don't interrupt,'" said Henfrey.

"I heerd'n," said Hall.

"And a sniff," said Henfrey.

They remained listening. The conversation was rapid and subdued. "I *can't*," said Mr. Bunting, his voice rising. "I tell you, sir, I *will* not."

"What was that?" asked Henfrey.

"Says he wi' nart," said Hall. "Warn't speaking to us, wuz he?"

"Disgraceful!" said Mr. Bunting, within.

"'Disgraceful,'" said Mr. Henfrey. "I heard it—distinct."

"Who's that speaking now?" asked Henfrey.

"Mr. Cuss, I s'pose," said Hall. "Can you hear—anything?"

Silence. The sounds within indistinct and perplexing.

"Sounds like throwing the table-cloth about," said Hall.

Mrs. Hall appeared behind the bar. Hall made gestures of silence and invitation. This aroused Mrs. Hall's wifely opposition. "What yer listenin' there for, Hall?" she asked. "Ain't you nothin' better to do—busy day like this?"

Hall tried to convey everything by grimaces and dumb show, but Mrs. Hall was obdurate. She raised her voice. So Hall and Henfrey, rather crestfallen, tiptoed back to the bar, gesticulating to explain to her.

At first she refused to see anything in what they had heard at all. Then she insisted on Hall keeping silence, while Henfrey told her his story. Could it be the furniture "sperits" had come back, she wondered with some alarm. "I heerd'n say 'disgraceful'; *that* I did," said Hall.

"*I* heerd that, Mrs. Hall," said Henfrey.

"Like as not—" began Mrs. Hall.

"Hsh!" said Mr. Teddy Henfrey. "Didn't I hear the window?"

"What window?" asked Mrs. Hall.

"Parlor window," said Henfrey.

Simultaneously came a tumult from the parlor, and a sound of windows being closed.

Hall, Henfrey, and the human contents of the tap rushed out at once pell-mell into the street. They saw someone whisk round the corner towards the road, and

Mr. Huxter, the general dealer from over the road, executing a complicated leap in the air that ended on his face and shoulder. Down the street people were standing astonished or running towards them.

Mr. Huxter was stunned. Henfrey stopped to discover this, but Hall and the two laborers from the Tap rushed at once to the corner, shouting incoherent things, and saw Mr. Marvel vanishing by the corner of the church wall. They appear to have jumped to the impossible conclusion that this was the Invisible Man suddenly become visible, and set off at once along the lane in pursuit. But Hall had hardly run a dozen yards before he gave a loud shout of astonishment and went flying headlong sideways, clutching one of the laborers and bringing him to the ground. He had been charged just as one charges a man at football. The second laborer came round in a circle, stared, and conceiving that Hall had tumbled over of his own accord, turned to resume the pursuit, only to be tripped by the ankle just as Huxter had been. Then, as the first laborer struggled to his feet, he was kicked sideways by a blow that might have felled an ox.

As he went down, the rush from the direction of the village green came round the corner. The first to appear was the proprietor of the cocoanut shy, a burly man in a blue jersey. He was astonished to see the lane empty save for three men sprawling absurdly on the ground. And then something happened to his rear-most foot, and he went headlong and rolled sideways just in time to graze the feet of his brother and partner, following headlong. The two were then kicked, knelt on, fallen over, and cursed by quite a number of over-hasty people.

Now when Hall and Henfrey and the laborers ran out of the house, Mrs. Hall, who had been disciplined by years of experience, remained in the bar next the till. And suddenly the parlor door was opened, and Mr. Cuss appeared, and without glancing at her rushed at once down the steps toward the corner. "Hold him!" he cried. "Don't let him drop that parcel."

He knew nothing of the existence of Marvel. For the Invisible Man had handed over the books and bundle in the yard. The face of Mr. Cuss was angry and resolute, but his costume was defective, a sort of limp white kilt that could only have passed muster in Greece. "Hold him!" he bawled. "He's got my trousers! And every stitch of the Vicar's clothes!"

"'Tend to him in a minute!" he cried to Henfrey as he passed the prostrate Huxter, and, coming round the corner to join the tumult, was promptly knocked off his feet into an indecorous sprawl. Somebody in full flight trod heavily on his finger. He yelled, struggled to regain his feet, was knocked against and thrown on all fours again, and became aware that he was involved not in a capture, but a rout. Everyone was running back to the village. He rose again and was hit severely behind the ear. He staggered and set off back to the "Coach and Horses" forthwith, leaping over the deserted Huxter, who was now sitting up, on his way.

Behind him as he was halfway up the inn steps he heard a sudden yell of rage, rising sharply out of the confusion of cries, and a sounding smack in someone's face. He recognized the voice as that of the Invisible Man, and the note was that of a man suddenly infuriated by a painful blow.

In another moment Mr. Cuss was back in the parlor. "He's coming back, Bunting!" he said, rushing in. "Save yourself!"

Mr. Bunting was standing in the window engaged in an attempt to clothe himself in the hearth-rug and a *West Surrey Gazette*. "Who's coming?" he said, so startled that his costume narrowly escaped disintegration.

"Invisible Man," said Cuss, and rushed on to the window. "We'd better clear out from here! He's fighting mad! Mad!"

In another moment he was out in the yard.

"Good heavens!" said Mr. Bunting, hesitating between two horrible alternatives. He heard a frightful struggle in the passage of the inn, and his decision was made. He clambered out of the window, adjusted his costume hastily, and fled up the village as fast as his fat little legs would carry him.

From the moment when the Invisible Man screamed with rage and Mr. Bunting made his memorable flight up the village, it became impossible to give a consecutive account of affairs in Iping. Possibly the Invisible Man's original intention was simply to cover Marvel's retreat with the clothes and books. But his temper, at no time very good, seems to have gone completely at some chance blow, and forthwith he set to smiting and overthrowing for the mere satisfaction of hurting.

You must figure the street full of running figures, of doors slamming and fights for hiding-places. You must figure the tumult suddenly striking on the unstable equilibrium of old Fletcher's planks and two chairs—with cataclysmic results. You must figure an appalled couple caught dismally in a swing. And then the whole tumultuous rush has passed and the Iping street with its gauds and flags is deserted save for the still raging unseen, and littered with cocoanuts, overthrown canvas screens, and the scattered stock in trade of a sweetstuff stall. Everywhere there is a sound of closing shutters and shoving bolts, and the only visible humanity is an occasional flitting eye under a raised eyebrow in the corner of a window pane.

The Invisible Man amused himself for a little while by breaking all the windows in the "Coach and Horses," and then he thrust a street lamp through the parlor window of Mrs. Gribble. He it must have been who cut the telegraph wire to Adderdean just beyond Higgins' cottage on the Adderdean road. And after that, as his peculiar qualities allowed, he passed out of human perceptions altogether, and he was neither heard, seen, nor felt in Iping anymore. He vanished absolutely.

But it was the best part of two hours before any human being ventured out again into the desolation of Iping street.

2.

In the early evening time Dr. Kemp was sitting in his study in the belvedere on the hill overlooking Burdock. It was a pleasant little room with three windows—north, west, and south—and bookshelves covered with books and scientific publications, and a broad writing-table, and under the north window, a microscope, glass slips, minute instruments, some cultures, and scattered bottles of rea-gents. Dr. Kemp's solar lamp was lit, albeit the sky was still bright with the sunset light, and his blinds were up because there was no offence of peering outsiders to require them pulled down. Dr. Kemp was a tall and slender young man, with flaxen hair and a moustache almost white, and the work he was upon would earn him, he hoped, the fellow-ship of the Royal Society, so highly did he think of it.

And his eye, presently wandering from his work, caught the sunset blazing at the back of the hill that is over against his own. For a minute perhaps he sat, pen in mouth, admiring the rich golden color above the crest, and then his attention was attracted by the little figure of a man, inky black, running over the hill-brow towards him. He was a shortish little man, and he wore a high hat, and he was running so fast that his legs verily twinkled.

"Another of those fools," said Dr. Kemp. "Like that ass who ran into me this morning round a corner, with the "Visible Man a-coming, sir!' I can't imagine what possesses people. One might think we were in the thirteenth century."

But those who saw the fugitive nearer, and perceived the abject terror on his perspiring face, being themselves in the open roadway, did not share in the doctor's contempt. The man pounded by, and as he ran he chinked like a well-filled purse that is tossed to and fro. And as they wondered the reason of his haste, something—a wind—a pad, pad, pad—a sound like a panting breathing, rushed by.

People screamed. People sprang off the pavement: It passed in shouts, it passed by instinct down the hill.

"The Invisible Man is coming! The Invisible Man!"

Dr. Kemp continued writing in his study until the shots aroused him. Crack, crack, crack, they came one after the other.

"Hullo!" said Dr. Kemp, putting his pen into his mouth again and listening. "Who's letting off revolvers in Burdock? What are the asses at now?"

He went to the south window, threw it up, and leaning out stared down on the network of windows, beaded gas-lamps and shops, with its black interstices of roof and yard that made up the town at night. "Looks like a crowd down the hill," he said, "by 'The Cricketers,'" and remained watching. Thence his eyes wandered over the town to far away where the ships' lights shone, and the pier glowed—a little illuminated, facetted pavilion like a gem of yellow light. The moon in its first quarter hung over the westward hill, and the stars were clear and almost tropically bright.

After five minutes, during which his mind had traveled into a remote speculation of social conditions of the future, and lost itself at last over the time dimension, Dr. Kemp roused himself with a sigh, pulled down the window again, and returned to his writing desk.

It must have been about an hour after this that the front doorbell rang. He had been writing slackly, and with intervals of abstraction, since the shots. He sat listening. He heard the servant answer the door, and waited for her feet on the staircase, but she did not come. "Wonder what that was," said Dr. Kemp.

He tried to resume his work, failed, got up, went downstairs from his study to the landing, rang, and called over the balustrade to the housemaid as she appeared in the hall below. "Was that a letter?" he asked.

"Only a runaway ring, sir," she answered.

"I'm restless to-night," he said to himself. He went back to his study, and this time attacked his work resolutely. In a little while he was hard at work again, and the only sounds in the room were the ticking of the clock and the subdued shrillness of his quill, hurrying in the very centre of the circle of light his lampshade threw on his table.

It was two o'clock before Dr. Kemp had finished his work for the night. He rose, yawned, and went downstairs to bed. He had already removed his coat and vest, when he noticed that he was thirsty. He took a candle and went down to the dining-room in search of a siphon and whiskey.

Dr. Kemp's scientific pursuits have made him a very observant man, and as he recrossed the hall, he noticed a dark spot on the linoleum near the mat at the foot of the stairs. He went on upstairs, and then it suddenly occurred to him to ask himself what the spot on the linoleum might be. Apparently some subconscious element was at work. At any rate, he turned with his burden, went back to the hall, put down the siphon and whiskey, and bending down, touched the spot. Without any great surprise he found it had the stickiness and color of drying blood.

He took up his burden again, and returned upstairs, looking about him and trying to account for the blood-spot. On the landing he saw something and stopped astonished. The door-handle of his own room was blood-stained.

He looked at his own hand. It was quite clean, and then he remembered that the door of his room had been open when he came down from his study, and that consequently he had not touched the handle at all. He went straight into his room, his face quite calm—perhaps a trifle more resolute than usual. His glance, wandering inquisitively, fell on the bed. On the counterpane was a mess of blood, and the sheet had been torn. He had not noticed this before because he had walked straight to the dressing-table. On the further side the bedclothes were depressed as if someone had been recently sitting there.

Then he had an odd impression that he had heard a low voice say, "Good Heavens!—Kemp!" But Dr. Kemp was no believer in voices.

He stood staring at the tumbled sheets. Was that really a voice? He looked about again, but noticed nothing further than the disordered and blood-stained bed. Then he distinctly heard a movement across the room, near the wash-hand stand. All men, however highly educated, retain some superstitious inklings. The feeling that is called "eerie" came upon him. He closed the door of the room, came forward to the dressing-table, and put down his burdens. Suddenly, with a start, he perceived a coiled and blood-stained bandage of linen rag hanging in mid-air, between him and the wash-hand stand.

He stared at this in amazement. It was an empty bandage, a bandage properly tied but quite empty. He would have advanced to grasp it, but a touch arrested him, and a voice speaking quite close to him.

"Kemp!" said the Voice.

"Eh?" said Kemp, with his mouth open.

"Keep your nerve," said the Voice. "I'm an Invisible Man."

Kemp made no answer for a space, simply stared at the bandage. "Invisible Man," he said.

"I am an Invisible Man," repeated the Voice.

"Have you a bandage on?" he asked.

"Yes," said the Invisible Man.

"Oh!" said Kemp, and then roused himself. "I say!" he said. "But this is nonsense. It's some trick." He stepped forward suddenly, and his hand, extended towards the bandage, met invisible fingers.

He recoiled at the touch and his color changed.

"Keep steady, Kemp, for God's sake! I want help badly. Stop!"

The hand gripped his arm. He struck at it.

"Kemp!" cried the Voice. "Kemp! Keep steady!" and the grip tightened.

A frantic desire to free himself took possession of Kemp. The hand of the bandaged arm gripped his shoulder, and he was suddenly tripped and flung backwards upon the bed. He opened his mouth to shout, and the corner of the sheet was thrust between his teeth. The Invisible Man had him down grimly, but his arms were free and he struck and tried to kick savagely.

"Listen to reason, will you?" said the Invisible Man, sticking to him in spite of a pounding in the ribs. "By Heaven! you'll madden me in a minute!"

Kemp struggled for another moment and then lay still.

"Lie still! If you shout, I'll smash your face," said the Invisible Man, relieving his mouth.

"I'm an Invisible Man. It's no foolishness, and no magic. I really am an Invisible Man. And I want your help. I don't want to hurt you, but if you behave like a frantic rustic, I must. Don't you remember me, Kemp? Griffin, of University College?"

"Let me get up," said Kemp. "I'll stop where I am. And let me sit quiet for a minute."

He sat up and felt his neck.

"I am Griffin, of University College, and I have made myself invisible. I am just an ordinary man—a man you have known—made invisible."

"Griffin?" said Kemp.

"Griffin," answered the Voice. "A younger student than you were, almost an albino, six feet high, and broad, with a pink and white face and red eyes, who won the medal for chemistry."

"I am confused," said Kemp. "My brain is rioting. What has this to do with Griffin?"

"I *am* Griffin."

Kemp thought. "It's horrible," he said. "But what devilry must happen to make a man invisible?"

"It's no devilry. It's a process, sane and intelligible enough—"

"It's horrible!" said Kemp. "How on earth—?"

"It's horrible enough. But I'm wounded and in pain, and tired ... Great God! Kemp, you are a man. Take it steady. Give me some food and drink, and let me sit down here."

Kemp stared at the bandage as it moved across the room, then saw a basket chair dragged across the floor and come to rest near the bed. It creaked, and the seat was depressed the quarter of an inch or so. He rubbed his eyes and felt his neck again. "This beats ghosts," he said, and laughed stupidly.

"That's better. Thank Heaven, you're getting sensible!"

"Or silly," said Kemp, and knuckled his eyes.

"Give me some whiskey. I'm near dead."

"It didn't feel so. Where are you? If I get up shall I run into you? *There*! all right. Whiskey? Here. Where shall I give it to you?"

The chair creaked and Kemp felt the glass drawn away from him. He let go by an effort, his instinct was all against it. It came to rest poised twenty inches above the front edge of the seat of the chair. He stared at it in infinite perplexity. "This is—this must be—hypnotism. You have suggested you are invisible."

"Nonsense," said the Voice.

"It's frantic."

"Listen to me. I'm starving," said the Voice, "and the night is chilly to a man without clothes."

"Food?" said Kemp.

The tumbler of whiskey tilted itself. "Yes," said the Invisible Man rapping it down. "Have you a dressing-gown?"

Kemp made some exclamation in an undertone. He walked to a wardrobe and produced a robe of dingy scarlet. "This do?" he asked. It was taken from him. It hung limp for a moment in mid-air, fluttered weirdly, stood full and decorous buttoning itself, and sat down in his chair. "Drawers, socks, slippers would be a comfort," said the Unseen, curtly. "And food."

"Anything. But this is the insanest thing I ever was in, in my life!"

He turned out his drawers for the articles, and then went downstairs to ransack his larder. He came back with some cold cutlets and bread, pulled up a light table, and placed them before his guest. "Never mind knives," said his visitor, and a cutlet hung in mid-air, with a sound of gnawing.

"Invisible!" said Kemp, and sat down on a bedroom chair.

"I always like to get something about me before I eat," said the Invisible Man, with a full mouth, eating greedily. "Queer fancy!"

"I suppose that wrist is all right," said Kemp.

"Trust me," said the Invisible Man. "But it's odd I should blunder into *your* house to get my bandaging. My first stroke of luck! Anyhow I meant to sleep in this house tonight. You must stand that! It's a filthy nuisance, my blood showing, isn't it? Quite a clot over there. Gets visible as it coagulates, I see. It's only the living tissue I've changed, and only for as long as I'm alive.... I've been in the house three hours."

"But how's it done?" began Kemp, in a tone of exasperation. "Confound it! The whole business—it's unreasonable from beginning to end."

"Quite reasonable," said the Invisible Man. "Perfectly reasonable."

He reached over and secured the whiskey bottle. Kemp stared at the devouring dressing gown. A ray of candlelight penetrating a torn patch in the right shoulder, made a triangle of light under the left ribs. "What were the shots?" he asked. "How did the shooting begin?"

"There was a real fool of a man—a sort of assistant of mine—curse him!—who tried to steal my money. *Has* done so."

"Is *he* invisible too?"

"No."

"Well?"

"Can't I have some more to eat before I tell you all that? I'm hungry—in pain. And you want me to tell stories!"

Kemp got up. "*You* didn't do any shooting?" he asked.

"Not me," said his visitor. "Some fool I'd never seen fired at random. A lot of them got scared. They all got scared at me. Curse them!—I say—I want more to eat than this, Kemp."

"I'll see what there is to eat downstairs," said Kemp. "Not much, I'm afraid."

After he had done eating, and he made a heavy meal, the Invisible Man demanded a cigar. He bit the end savagely before Kemp could find a knife, and cursed when the outer leaf loosened. It was strange to see him smoking. His mouth, and throat, pharynx and nares, became visible as a sort of whirling smoke cast.

"This blessed gift of smoking!" he said, and puffed vigorously. "I'm lucky to have fallen upon you, Kemp. I'm in a devilish scrape—I've been mad, I think. The things I have been through! Let me smoke in peace for a little while, and then I will begin to tell you."

But the story was not told that night. The Invisible Man's wrist was growing painful. He was feverish, exhausted, and his mind came round to brood upon his chase down the hill and the struggle about the inn. He spoke in fragments of Marvel, he smoked faster, his voice grew angry. Kemp tried to gather what he could.

"He was afraid of me, I could see that he was afraid of me," said the Invisible Man many times over. "He meant to give me the slip—he was always casting about! What a fool I was! The cur! I should have killed him!"

"Where did you get the money?" asked Kemp, abruptly.

The Invisible Man was silent for a space. "I can't tell you tonight," he said.

He groaned suddenly and leant forward, supporting his invisible head on invisible hands. "Kemp," he said, "I've had no sleep for near three days, except a couple of dozes of an hour or so. I must sleep soon."

"Well, have my room—have this room."

"I'm sorry," said the Invisible Man, "if I cannot tell you all that I have done tonight. But I am worn out. It's grotesque, no doubt. It's horrible! But believe me, Kemp, in spite of your arguments of this morning, it is quite a possible thing. I have made a discovery. I meant to keep it to myself. I can't. I must have a partner. And you.... We can do such things ... But tomorrow. Now, Kemp, I feel as though I must sleep or perish."

Kemp stood in the middle of the room staring at the headless garment. "I suppose I must leave you," he said.

"It's—incredible. Three things happening like this, over-turning all my preconceptions—would make me insane. But it's real! Is there anything more that I can get you?"

"Only bid me good-night," said Griffin.

"Good-night," said Kemp, and shook an invisible hand. He walked sideways to the door. Suddenly the dressing-gown walked quickly towards him. "Understand me!" said the dressing-gown. "No attempts to hamper me, or capture me! Or—"

Kemp's face changed a little. "I give you my word," he said.

Kemp closed the door softly behind him, and the key was turned upon him forthwith. Then, as he stood with an expression of passive amazement on his face, the rapid feet came to the door of the dressing-room and that too was locked. Kemp slapped his brow with his hand. "Am I dreaming? Has the world gone mad—or have I?"

He laughed, and put his hand to the locked door. "Barred out of my own bedroom, by a flagrant absurdity!" he said.

He walked to the head of the staircase, turned, and stared at the locked doors. "It's fact," he said. He put his fingers to his slightly bruised neck. "Undeniable fact!

"But—"

He shook his head hopelessly, turned, and went down-stairs into his little consulting-room and lit the gas there. It was a little room, because Dr. Kemp did not live by prac-tice, and in it were the day's newspapers. The morning's paper lay carelessly opened and thrown aside. He caught it up, turned it over, and read the account of a "Strange Story from Iping." He rent the paper open. A couple of columns confronted him. "An Entire Village in Sussex goes Mad" was the heading.

"Good Heavens!" said Kemp, reading eagerly an incredulous account of the events in Iping, of the previous afternoon— "Ran through the streets striking right and left. The village constable insensible. Mr. Huxter in great pain—still unable to describe what he saw. Painful humiliation—vicar. Woman ill with terror! Windows smashed."

He dropped the paper and stared blankly in front of him. He caught up the paper again, and re-read the whole business. He sat down abruptly on the surgical bench. "He's not only invisible," he said, "but he's mad! Homicidal!"

3.

When dawn came to mingle its pallor with the lamplight and cigar smoke of the dining-room, Kemp was still pacing up and down, trying to grasp the incredible.

He was altogether too excited to sleep. His servants, descending sleepily, discovered him, and were inclined to think that over-study had worked this ill on him. He gave them extraordinary but quite explicit instructions to lay breakfast for two in the belvedere study—and then to confine themselves to the basement and ground-floor. Then he continued to pace the dining-room until the morning's paper came. That had much to say and little to tell, beyond the confirmation of the evening before, and a very badly written account of another remarkable tale from Port Burdock. This gave Kemp the essence of the happenings at the "Jolly Cricketers," and the name of Marvel. "He has made me keep with him twenty-four hours," Marvel testified. Certain minor facts were added to the Iping story, notably the cutting of the village telegraph-wire. But there was nothing to throw light on the connection between the

Invisible Man and the Tramp, for Mr. Marvel had supplied no information about the three books, or the money with which he was lined. The incredulous tone had vanished and a shoal of reporters and inquirers were already at work elaborating the matter.

Kemp read every scrap of the report and sent his housemaid out to get everyone of the morning papers she could. These also he devoured.

"He is invisible!" he said. "And it reads like rage growing to mania! The things he may do! The things he may do! And he's upstairs free as the air. What on earth ought I to do?"

"For instance, would it be a breach of faith if—? No."

He went to a little untidy desk in the corner, and began a note. He tore this up half written, and wrote another. He read it over and considered it. Then he took an envelope and addressed it to "Colonel Adye, Port Burdock."

The Invisible Man awoke even as Kemp was doing this. He awoke in an evil temper, and Kemp, alert for every sound, heard his pattering feet rush suddenly across the bedroom overhead. Then a chair was flung over and the wash-hand stand tumbler smashed. Kemp hurried upstairs and rapped eagerly.

"What's the matter?" asked Kemp, when the Invisible Man admitted him.

"Nothing," was the answer.

"But, confound it! The smash?"

"Fit of temper," said the Invisible Man. "Forgot this arm, and it's sore."

"You're rather liable to that sort of thing."

"I am."

Kemp walked across the room and picked up the fragments of broken glass. "All the facts are out about you," said Kemp, standing up with the glass in his hand, "all that happened in Iping, and down the hill. The world has become aware of its invisible citizen. But no one knows you are here."

The Invisible Man swore.

"The secret's out. I gather it was a secret. I don't know what your plans are, but of course I'm anxious to help you."

The Invisible Man sat down on the bed.

"There's breakfast upstairs," said Kemp, speaking as easily as possible, and he was delighted to find his strange guest rose willingly. Kemp led the way up the narrow staircase to the belvedere.

"Before we can do anything else," said Kemp, "I must understand a little more about this invisibility of yours." He had sat down, after one nervous glance out of the window, with the air of a man who has talking to do. His doubts of the sanity of the entire business flashed and vanished again as he looked across to where Griffin sat at the breakfast-table—a headless, handless dressing-gown, wiping unseen lips on a miraculously held serviette.

"It's simple enough—and credible enough," said Griffin, putting the serviette aside and leaning the invisible head on an invisible hand.

"No doubt, to you, but—" Kemp laughed.

"Well, yes, to me it seemed wonderful at first, no doubt. But now, great God! ... But we will do great things yet! I came on the stuff first at Chesilstowe."

"Chesilstowe?"

"I went there after I left London. You know I dropped medicine and took up physics? No, well, I did. *Light* fascinated me."

"Ah!"

"Optical density! The whole subject is a network of riddles—a network with solutions glimmering elusively through. And being but two-and-twenty and full of enthusiasm, I said, 'I will devote my life to this. This is worthwhile.' You know what fools we are at two-and-twenty?"

"Fools then or fools now," said Kemp.

"As though knowing could be any satisfaction to a man!

"But I went to work—like a slave. And I had hardly worked and thought about the matter six months, before light came through one of the meshes suddenly—blindingly! I found a general principle of pigments and refraction—a formula, a geometrical expression involving four dimensions. Fools, common men, even common mathematicians, do not know anything of what some general expression may mean to the student of molecular physics. In the books—the books that tramp has hidden—there are marvels, miracles! But this was not a method, it was an idea that might lead to a method by which it would be possible, without changing any other property of matter—except, in some instances colors—to lower the refractive index of a substance, solid or liquid, to that of air—so far as all practical purposes are concerned."

"Phew!" said Kemp. "That's odd! But still I don't see quite ... I can understand that thereby you could spoil a valuable stone, but personal invisibility is a far cry."

"Precisely," said Griffin. "But consider, visibility depends on the action of the visible bodies on light. Either a body absorbs light, or it reflects or refracts it, or does all these things. If it neither reflects nor refracts nor absorbs light, it cannot of itself be visible. You see an opaque red box, for instance, because the color absorbs some of the light and reflects the rest, all the red part of the light, to you. If it did not absorb any particular part of the light, but reflected it all, then it would be a shining white box. Silver! A diamond box would neither absorb much of the light nor reflect much from the general surface, but just here and there where the surfaces were favorable the light would be reflected and refracted, so that you would get a brilliant appearance of flashing reflections and translucencies—a sort of skeleton of light. A glass box would not be so brilliant, not so clearly visible, as a diamond box, because there would be less refraction and reflection. See that? From certain points of view you would see quite clearly through it. Some kinds of glass would be more visible than others, a box of flint glass would be brighter than a box of ordinary window glass. A box of very thin common glass would be hard to see in a bad light, because it would absorb hardly any light and refract and reflect very little. And if you put a sheet of common white glass in water, still more if you put it in some denser liquid than water, it would vanish almost altogether, because light passing from water to glass is only slightly refracted or reflected or indeed affected in any way. It is almost as invisible as a jet of coal gas or hydrogen is in air. And for precisely the same reason!"

"Yes," said Kemp, "that is pretty plain sailing."

"And here is another fact you will know to be true. If a sheet of glass is smashed, Kemp, and beaten into a powder, it becomes much more visible while it is in the air—it becomes at last an opaque white powder. This is because the powdering multiplies the surfaces of the glass at which refraction and reflection occur. In the sheet of glass there are only two surfaces. In the powder the light is reflected or refracted by each grain it passes through, and very little gets right through the powder. But if the white powdered glass is put into water, it forthwith vanishes. The powdered glass and water have much the same refractive index, that is, the light undergoes very little refraction or reflection in passing from one to the other.

"And if you will consider only a second, you will see also that the powder of glass might be made to vanish in air as well, if its refractive index could be made the same as that of air, for then there would be no refraction or reflection as the light passed from glass to air."

"Yes, yes," said Kemp. "But a man's not powdered glass!"

"No," said Griffin. "He's more transparent!"

"Nonsense!"

"That from a doctor! How one forgets! Have you already forgotten your physics, in ten years? Just think of all the things that are transparent and seem not to be so. Paper, for instance, is made up of transparent fibers, and it is white and opaque only for the same reason that a powder of glass is white and opaque. Oil white paper, fill up the interstices between the particles with oil so that there is no longer refraction or reflection except at the surfaces, and it becomes as transparent as glass. And not only paper, but cotton fiber, linen fiber, wool fiber, woody fiber, and *bone*, Kemp, *flesh*, Kemp, *hair*, Kemp, *nails* and *nerves*, Kemp, in fact the whole fabric of a man except the red of his blood and the black pigment of hair, are all made up of transparent, colorless tissue. So little suffices to make us visible one to the other. For the most part the fibers of a living creature are no more opaque than water."

"Great Heavens!" cried Kemp. "Of course, of course! I was thinking only last night of the sea larvae and all jelly-fish!"

"*Now* you have me! And all that I knew and had in mind a year after I left London—six years ago. But I kept it to myself. I had to do my work under frightful disadvantages. I told no living soul, because I meant to flash my work upon the world with crushing effect and become famous at a blow. I took up the question of pigments to fill up certain gaps. And suddenly, not by design but by accident, I made a discovery in physiology."

"Yes?"

"You know the red coloring matter of blood—it can be made white—colorless—and remain with all the functions it has now!"

Kemp gave a cry of incredulous amazement.

The Invisible Man rose and began pacing the little study. "You may well exclaim. I remember that night. It was late at night—in the daytime one was bothered with the gaping, silly students—and I worked then sometimes till dawn. It came suddenly, splendid and complete in my mind. I was alone, the laboratory was still, with the tall lights burning brightly and silently. In all my great moments I have been alone. 'One could make an animal—a tissue—transparent! One could make it invisible! All except the pigments—I could be invisible!' I said, suddenly realizing what it meant to be an albino with such knowledge. It was overwhelming. I left the filtering I was doing, and went and stared out of the great window at the stars. 'I could be invisible!' I repeated.

"To do such a thing would be to transcend magic. And I beheld, unclouded by doubt, a magnificent vision of all that invisibility might mean to a man—the mystery, the power, the freedom. Drawbacks I saw none. You have only to think! And I, a shabby, poverty-struck, hemmed-in demonstrator, teaching fools in a provincial college, might suddenly become—this. I ask you, Kemp if *you* ... Anyone, I tell you, would have flung himself upon that research.

And I worked three years, and every mountain of difficulty I toiled over showed another from its summit. The infinite details! And the exasperation! A professor, a provincial professor, always prying. 'When are you going to publish this work of yours?' was his everlasting question. And the students, the cramped means! Three years I had of it—

"And after three years of secrecy and exasperation, I found that to complete it was impossible—impossible."

"How?" asked Kemp.

"Money," said the Invisible Man, and went again to stare out of the window.

He turned around abruptly. "I robbed the old man—robbed my father.

"The money was not his, and he shot himself."

For a moment Kemp sat in silence, staring at the back of the headless figure at the window. Then he started, struck by a thought, rose, took the Invisible Man's arm, and turned him away from the outlook.

"You are tired," he said, "and while I sit, you walk about. Have my chair."

He placed himself between Griffin and the nearest window.

For a space Griffin sat silent, and then he resumed abruptly.

"I did not feel a bit sorry for my father. He seemed to me to be the victim of his own foolish sentimentality. The current cant required my attendance at his funeral, but it was really not my affair.

"Re-entering my room seemed like the recovery of reality. There were the things I knew and loved. There stood the apparatus, the experiments arranged and waiting. And now there was scarcely a difficulty left, beyond the planning of details.

"I will tell you, Kemp, sooner or later, all the complicated processes. We need not go into that now. For the most part, saving certain gaps I chose to remember, they are written in cipher in those books that tramp has hidden. But the essential phase was to place the transparent object whose refractive index was to be lowered between two radiating centers of a sort of ethereal vibration, of which I will tell you more fully later. No, not those Röntgen vibrations—I don't know that these others of mine have been described. Yet they are obvious enough. I needed two little dynamos, and these I worked with a cheap gas engine. My first experiment was with a bit of white wool fabric. It was the strangest thing in the world to see it in the flicker of the flashes soft and white, and then to watch it fade like a wreath of smoke and vanish.

"I could scarcely believe I had done it. I put my hand into the emptiness, and there was the thing as solid as ever. I felt it awkwardly, and threw it on the floor. I had a little trouble finding it again.

"And then came a curious experience. I heard a meow behind me, and turning, saw a lean white cat, very dirty, on the cistern cover outside the window. A thought came into my head. 'Everything ready for you,' I said, and went to the window, opened it, and called softly.

"It took three or four hours. The bones and sinews and the fat were the last to go, and the tips of the colored hairs. But, the back part of the eye, tough, iridescent stuff it is, wouldn't go at all.

"I remember the shock—the round eyes shining green—and nothing round them. It wouldn't be quiet, it just sat down and meowed at the door. I tried to catch it, with an idea of putting it out of the window, but it wouldn't be caught, it vanished. Then it began meowing in different parts of the room. At last I opened the window and made a bustle. I suppose it went out at last. I never saw any more of it."

"You don't mean to say there's an invisible cat at large!" said Kemp.

"If it hasn't been killed," said the Invisible Man. "Why not?"

"Why not?" said Kemp. "I didn't mean to interrupt."

He was silent for the best part of a minute.

"I remember that morning before the change very vividly.

"At the thought of the possibility of my work being exposed or interrupted at its very climax, I became very anxious and active. I hurried out with my three books of notes, my check-book—the tramp has them now—and directed them from the nearest Post Office to a house of call for letters and parcels in Great Portland Street.

"Walking home, I remember the barracks in Albany Street, and the horse soldiers coming out, and at last I found the summit of Primrose Hill. It was a sunny day in January—one of those sunny, frosty days that came before the snow this year. My weary brain tried to formulate the position, to plot out a plan of action.

"All I could think clearly was that the thing had to be carried through. The fixed idea still ruled me. And soon, for the money I had was almost exhausted. I looked about me at the hillside, with children playing and girls watching them, and tried to think of all the fantastic advantages an invisible man would have in the world. After a time I crawled home, took some food and a strong dose of strychnine, and went to sleep in my clothes on my unmade bed. Strychnine is a grand tonic, Kemp, to take the flabbiness out of a man."

"It's the devil," said Kemp. "It's the paleolithic in a bottle."

"I awoke vastly invigorated and rather irritable. You know?"

"I know the stuff."

"And there was someone rapping at the door. It was my landlord with threats and inquiries, an old Polish Jew in a long grey coat and greasy slippers. I had been tormenting a cat in the night, he was sure—the old woman's tongue had been busy. He insisted on knowing all about it. The laws in this country against vivisection were very severe—he might be liable. I tried to keep between him and the concentrating apparatus I had arranged, and that only made him more curious. What was I doing? Why was I always alone and secretive? Was it legal? Was it dangerous? Suddenly my temper gave way. I told him to get out. He began to protest, to jabber of his right of entry. In a moment I had him by the collar, something ripped, and he went spinning out into his own passage.

"For a moment he gaped. Then he gave a sort of inarticulate cry, dropped candle and writ together, and went blundering down the dark passage to the stairs. I shut the door, locked it, and went to the looking-glass. Then I understood his terror.... My face was white—like white stone.

"But it was all horrible. I had not expected the suffering. A night of racking anguish, sickness and fainting. I set my teeth, though my skin was presently afire, all my body afire, but I lay there like grim death. I understood now how it was the cat had howled until I chloroformed it. Lucky it was I lived alone and untended in my room. There were times when I sobbed and groaned and talked. But I stuck to it.... I became insensible and woke languid in the darkness.

"The pain had passed. I thought I was killing myself and I did not care. I shall never forget that dawn, and the strange horror of seeing that my hands had become as clouded glass, and watching them grow clearer and thinner as the day went by, until at last I could see the sickly disorder of my room through them, though I closed my transparent eyelids. My limbs became glassy, the bones and arteries faded, vanished, and the little white nerves went last. I gritted my teeth and stayed there to the end. At last only the dead tips of the fingernails remained, pallid and white, and the brown stain of some acid upon my fingers.

"I struggled up. At first I was as incapable as a swathed infant—stepping with limbs I could not see. I was weak and very hungry. I went and stared at nothing in my shaving-glass, at nothing save where an attenuated pigment still remained behind the retina of my eyes, fainter than mist. I had to hang on to the table and press my forehead against the glass.

"It was only by a frantic effort of will that I dragged myself back to the apparatus and completed the process.

"I slept during the forenoon, pulling the sheet over my eyes to shut out the light, and about midday I was awakened again by a knocking. My strength had returned. I sat up and listened and heard a whispering. I sprang to my feet and as noiselessly as possible began to detach the connections of my apparatus, and to distribute it about the room, so as to destroy the suggestions of its arrangement. Presently the knocking was renewed and voices called, first my landlord's, and then two others. To gain time I answered them. The invisible rag and pillow came to hand and I opened the window and pitched them out on to the cistern cover. As the window opened, a heavy crash came at the door. Someone had charged it with the idea of smashing the lock. But the stout bolts I had screwed up some days before stopped him. That startled me, made me angry. I began to tremble and do things hurriedly.

"I tossed together some loose paper, straw, packing paper and so forth, in the middle of the room, and turned on the gas. Heavy blows began to rain upon the door. I could not find the matches. I beat my hands on the wall with rage. I turned down the gas again, stepped out of the window on the cistern cover, very softly lowered the sash, and sat down, secure and invisible, but quivering with anger, to watch events. They split a panel, I saw, and in another moment they had broken away the staples of the bolts and stood in the open doorway. It was the landlord and his two stepsons, sturdy young men of three or four and twenty. Behind them fluttered the old hag of a woman from downstairs.

"You may imagine their astonishment to find the room empty. One of the younger men rushed to the window at once, flung it up and stared out. His staring eyes and thick-lipped bearded face came a foot from my face. I was half minded to hit his silly countenance, but I arrested my doubled fist. He stared right through me. So did the others as they joined him. The old man went and peered under the bed, and then they all made a rush for the cupboard. They had to argue about it at length in Yiddish and Cockney English. They concluded I had not answered them, that their imagination had deceived them. A feeling of extraordinary elation took the place of my anger as I sat outside the window and watched these four people—for the old lady came in, glancing suspiciously about her like a cat, trying to understand the riddle of my behavior.

"The old man, so far as I could understand his *patois*, agreed with the old lady that I was a vivisectionist. The sons protested in garbled English that I was an electrician, and appealed to the dynamos and radiators.

"It occurred to me that the radiators, if they fell into the hands of some acute well-educated person, would give me away too much, and watching my opportunity, I came into the room and tilted one of the little dynamos off its fellow on which it was standing, and smashed both apparatus. Then, while they were trying to explain the smash, I dodged out of the room and went softly downstairs.

"I went into one of the sitting-rooms and waited until they came down, still speculating and argumentative, all a little disappointed at finding no 'horrors,' and all a little puzzled how they stood legally towards me. Then I slipped up again with a box of matches, fired my heap of paper and rubbish, put the chairs and bedding thereby, led the gas to the affair, by means of an india-rubber tube, and waving a farewell to the room left it for the last time."

"You fired the house!" exclaimed Kemp.

"Fired the house. It was the only way to cover my trail—and no doubt it was insured. I slipped the bolts of the front door quietly and went out into the street. I was invisible, and I was only just beginning to realize the extraordinary advantage my invisibility gave me. My head was already teeming with plans of all the wild and wonderful things I had now impunity to do.

"In going downstairs the first time I found an unexpected difficulty because I could not see my feet. Indeed I stumbled twice, and there was an unaccustomed clumsiness in gripping the bolt. By not looking down, however, I managed to walk on the level passably well.

"My mood, I say, was one of exaltation. I felt as a seeing man might do, with padded feet and noiseless clothes, in a city of the blind. I experienced a wild impulse to jest, to startle people, to clap men on the back, fling people's hats astray, and generally revel in my extraordinary advantage.

"But hardly had I emerged upon Great Portland Street, however (my lodging was close to the big draper's shop there), when I heard a clashing concussion and was hit violently behind, and turning saw a man carrying a basket of soda-water siphons, and looking in amazement at his burden. Although the blow had really hurt me, I found something so irresistible in his astonishment that I laughed aloud. 'The devil's in the basket,' I said, and suddenly twisted it out of his hand. He let go incontinently, and I swung the whole weight into the air.

"But a fool of a cabman, standing outside a public house, made a sudden rush for this, and his extending fingers took me with excruciating violence under the ear. I let the whole down with a smash on the cabman, and then, with shouts and the clatter of feet about me, people coming out of shops, vehicles pulling up, I realized what I had done for myself, and cursing my folly, backed against a shop window and prepared to dodge out of the confusion. In a moment I should be wedged into a crowd and inevitably discovered. I pushed by a butcher boy, who luckily did not turn to see the nothingness that shoved him aside, and dodged behind the cab-man's four-wheeler. I do not know how they settled the business. I hurried straight across the road, which was happily clear, and hardly heeding which way I went, plunged into the afternoon throng of Oxford Street.

"I tried to get into the stream of people, but they were too thick for me, and in a moment my heels were being trodden upon. I took to the gutter, the roughness of which I found painful to my feet, and forthwith the shaft of a crawling hansom dug me forcibly under the shoulder blade, reminding me that I was already bruised severely. I staggered out of the way of the cab, avoided a perambulator by a convulsive movement, and found myself behind the hansom. A happy thought saved me, and as this drove slowly along I followed in its immediate wake, trembling and astonished at the turn of my adventure. And not only trembling, but shivering. It was a bright day in January and I was stark naked and the thin slime of mud that covered the road was freezing. Foolish as it seems to me now, I had not reckoned that, transparent or not, I was still amenable to the weather and all its consequences.

"Then suddenly a bright idea came into my head. I ran round and got into the cab. And so, shivering, scared, and sniffing with the first intimations of a cold, and with the bruises in the small of my back growing upon my attention, I drove slowly along Oxford Street and past Tottenham Court Road. My mood was as different from that in which I had sallied forth ten minutes ago as it is possible to imagine. This invisibility indeed! The one thought that possessed me was—how was I to get out of the scrape I was in.

"We crawled past Mudie's, and there a tall woman with five or six yellow-labeled books hailed my cab, and I sprang out just in time to escape her, shaving a railway van narrowly in my flight. I made off up the roadway to Bloomsbury Square, intending to strike north past the Museum and so get into the quiet district. I was now cruelly chilled, and the strangeness of my situation so unnerved me that I whimpered as I ran. At the northward corner of the Square a little white dog ran out of the Pharmaceutical Society's offices, and incontinently made for me, nose down.

"I had never realized it before, but the nose is to the mind of a dog what the eye is to the mind of a seeing man. Dogs perceive the scent of a man moving as men perceive his vision. This brute began barking and leaping, showing, as it seemed to me, only too plainly that he was aware of me. I crossed Great Russell Street, glancing over my shoulder as I did so, and went some way along Montague Street before I realized what I was running towards.

"Then I became aware of a blare of music, and looking along the street saw a number of people advancing out of Russell Square, red shirts, and the banner of the Salvation Army to the fore. Such a crowd, chanting in the roadway and scoffing on the pavement, I could not hope to penetrate, and dreading to go back and farther from home again, and deciding on the spur of the moment, I ran up the white steps of a house facing the museum railings, and stood there until the crowd should have passed. Happily the dog stopped at the noise of the band too, hesitated, and turned tail, running back to Bloomsbury Square again.

"On came the band, bawling with unconscious irony some hymn about 'When shall we see His face?' and it seemed an interminable time to me before the tide of the crowd washed along the pavement by me. Thud, thud, thud, came the drum with a vibrating resonance, and for the moment I did not notice two urchins stopping at the railings by me. 'See 'em,' said one. 'See what?' said the other. 'Why—them footmarks—bare. Like what you makes in mud.'

"I looked down and saw the youngsters had stopped and were gaping at the muddy footmarks I had left behind me up the newly whitened steps. The passing people elbowed and jostled them, but their confounded intelligence was arrested. 'Thud, thud, thud, when, thud, shall we see, thud, his face, thud, thud.' 'There's a barefoot man gone up them steps, or I don't know nothing,' said one. 'And he ain't never come down again. And his foot was a-bleeding.'

"The thick of the crowd had already passed. 'Looky there, Ted,' quoth the younger of the detectives, with the sharpness of surprise in his voice, and pointed straight to my feet. I looked down and saw at once the dim suggestion of their outline sketched in splashes of mud. For a moment I was paralyzed.

"'Why, that's rum,' said the elder. 'Dashed rum! It's just like the ghost of a foot, ain't it?' He hesitated and advanced with outstretched hand. A man pulled up short to see what he was catching, and then a girl. In another moment he would have touched me. Then I saw what to do. I made a step, the boy started back with an exclamation, and with a rapid movement I swung myself over into the portico of the next house. But the smaller boy was sharp-eyed enough to follow the movement, and before I was well down the steps and upon the pavement, he had recovered from his momentary astonishment and was shouting out that the feet had gone over the wall.

"They rushed round and saw my new footmarks flash into being on the lower step and upon the pavement. 'What's up?' asked someone. 'Feet! Look! Feet running!'

"Everybody in the road, except my three pursuers, was pouring along after the Salvation Army, and this blow not only impeded me but them. There was an eddy of surprise and interrogation. At the cost of bowling over one young fellow I got through, and in another moment I was rushing headlong round the circuit of Russell Square, with six or seven astonished people following my footmarks. There was no time for explanation, or else the whole host would have been after me.

"Twice I doubled round corners, thrice I crossed the road and came back upon my tracks, and then, as my feet grew hot and dry, the damp impressions began to fade. At last I had a breathing space and rubbed my feet clean with my hands, and so got away altogether. The last I saw of the chase was a little group of a dozen people perhaps, studying with infinite perplexity a slowly drying footprint that had resulted from a puddle in Tavistock Square, a footprint as isolated and incomprehensible to them as Crusoe's solitary discovery.

"Then came men and boys running, first one and then others, and shouting as they ran. It was a fire. They ran in the direction of my lodging, and looking back down a street I saw a mass of black smoke streaming up above the roofs and telephone wires. It was my lodging burning, my clothes, my apparatus, all my resources indeed, except my check-book and the three volumes of memoranda that awaited me in Great Portland Street, were there. Burning! I had burnt my boats—if ever a man did! The place was blazing."

The Invisible Man paused and thought. Kemp glanced nervously out of the window. "Yes?" he said. "Go on."

"So, with the beginning of a snowstorm in the air about me—and if it settled on me it would betray me!—weary, cold, painful, inexpressibly wretched, and still but half convinced of my invisible quality, I began this new life to which I am committed. I had no refuge, no appliances, no human being in the world in whom I could confide. To have told my secret would have given me away—made a mere show and rarity of me. Nevertheless, I was half-minded to accost some passer-by and throw myself upon his mercy. But I knew too clearly the terror and brutal cruelty my advances would evoke. I made no plans in the street. My sole object was to get shelter from the snow, to get myself covered and warm. Then I might hope to plan. But even to me, an Invisible Man, the rows of London houses stood latched, barred, and bolted impregnably.

"Only one thing could I see clearly before me—the cold exposure and misery of the snowstorm and the night.

"But you begin now to realize," said the Invisible Man, "the full disadvantage of my condition. I had no shelter— no covering—to get clothing was to forego all my advantage, to make myself a strange and terrible thing. I was fasting—for to eat, to fill myself with unassimilated matter, would be to become grotesquely visible again."

"I never thought of that," said Kemp.

"Nor had I. And the snow had warned me of other dangers. I could not go abroad in snow—it would settle on me and expose me. Rain, too, would make me a watery outline, a glistening surface of a man—a bubble. And fog—I should be like a fainter bubble in a fog, a surface, a greasy glimmer of humanity. Moreover, as I went abroad—in the London air—I gathered dirt about my ankles, floating smuts and dust upon my skin. I did not know how long it would be before I should become visible from that cause also. But I saw clearly it could not be for long.

"Not in London at any rate."

"I went into the slums towards Great Portland Street, and found myself at the end of the street in which I had lodged. I did not go that way, because of the crowd half-way down it opposite to the still smoking ruins of the house I had fired. My most immediate problem was to get clothing. What to do with my face puzzled me. Then I saw a dirty, fly-blown little shop in a by-way near Drury Lane, with a window full of tinsel robes, sham jewels, wigs, slippers, dominoes and theatrical photographs. I realized that problem was solved. In a flash I saw my course.

"I proposed to make my way into the establishment, watch my opportunity, and when everything was quiet, rummage out a wig, mask, spectacles, and costume, and go into the world, perhaps a grotesque but still a credible figure. And incidentally of course I could rob the place of any available money.

"The shop was old-fashioned and low and dark, and the house rose above it for four stories, dark and dismal. I peered through the window and, seeing no one within, entered. The opening of the door set a clanking bell ringing. I left it open, and walked round a bare costume stand, into a corner behind a cheval glass. For a minute or so no one came. Then I heard heavy feet striding across a room, and a man appeared down the shop.

"The man was short, slight, hunched, beetle-browed, with long arms and very short bandy legs. Apparently I had interrupted a meal. He stared about the shop with an expression of expectation. This gave way to surprise, and then to anger, as he saw the shop empty. 'Damn the boys!' he said. He went to stare up and down the street. He came in again in a minute, kicked the door to with his foot spitefully, and went muttering back to the house door.

"I began a systematic search of the place. Everything that could possibly be of service to me I collected in the clothes storeroom, and then I made a deliberate selection. I found some powder, rouge, and sticking-plaster.

"I had thought of painting and powdering my face and all that there was to show of me, in order to render myself visible, but the disadvantage of this lay in the fact that I should require turpentine and other appliances and a considerable amount of time before I could vanish again.

Finally I chose a mask of the better type, slightly grotesque but not more so than many human beings, dark glasses, greyish whiskers, and a wig. I could find no underclothing, but that I could buy subsequently, and for the time I swathed myself in calico dominoes and some white cashmere scarfs. In a desk in the shop were three sovereigns and about thirty shillings' worth of silver, and in a locked cupboard I burst in the inner room were eight pounds in gold. I could find no socks, but the hunchback's boots were rather a loose fit and sufficed. I could go forth into the world again, equipped.

"I was grotesque to the theatrical pitch, but I was certainly not a physical impossibility. I spent some minutes screwing up my courage and then unlocked the shop door and marched out into the street. In five minutes a dozen turnings intervened between me and the costumier's shop. No one appeared to notice me very pointedly. My last difficulty seemed overcome.

"I had impunity to do whatever I chose, everything—save to give away my secret. So I thought. Whatever I did, whatever the consequences might be, was nothing to me. I had merely to fling aside my garments and vanish. No person could hold me. I could take my money where I found it. I felt amazingly confident. It's not particularly pleasant recalling that I was an ass. It occurred to me that I could not eat unless I exposed my invisible face.

"I went into a place and demanded a private room. 'I am disfigured,' I said. 'Badly.' They looked at me curiously, but of course it was not their affair—and so at last I got my lunch. It was not particularly well served, but it sufficed, and when I had had it, I sat over a cigar, trying to plan my line of action. And outside a snowstorm was beginning.

"The more I thought it over, Kemp, the more I realized what a helpless absurdity an Invisible Man was—in a cold and dirty climate and a crowded civilized city. Before I made this mad experiment I had dreamt of a thousand advantages. That afternoon it seemed all disappointment. I went over the heads of the things a man reckons desirable. No doubt invisibility made it possible to get them, but it made it impossible to enjoy them when they are got. Ambition—what is the good of pride of place when you cannot appear there? What is the good of the love of woman when her name must needs be Delilah? I have no taste for politics, for the blackguardisms of fame, for philanthropy, for sport. What was I to do? And for this I had become a wrapped-up mystery, a swathed and bandaged caricature of a man!"

He paused, and his attitude suggested a roving glance at the window.

"But how did you get to Iping?" said Kemp, anxious to keep his guest busy talking.

"I went there to work. I had one hope. It was a half idea! I have it still. It is a full blown idea now. A way of getting back! Of restoring what I have done. When I choose. When I have done all I mean to do invisibly. And that is what I chiefly want to talk to you about now."

"You went straight to Iping?"

"Yes. I had simply to get my check-book and my three volumes of memoranda that awaited me in Great Portland Street, and order a quantity of chemicals to work out this idea of mine—I will show you the calculations as soon as I get my books—and then I started. Jove! I remember the snowstorm now, and the accursed bother it was to keep the snow from damping my pasteboard nose."

"At the end," said Kemp, "the day before yesterday, when they found you out, you rather—to judge by the papers—"

"I did. Rather. Did I kill that fool of a constable?"

"No," said Kemp. "He's expected to recover."

"That's his luck, then. I clean lost my temper, the fools! Why couldn't they leave me alone? And that grocer lout?"

"There are no deaths expected," said Kemp.

"I don't know about that tramp of mine," said the Invisible Man, with an unpleasant laugh.

"By Heaven, Kemp, you don't know what rage *is*! ... To have worked for years, to have planned and plotted, and then to get some fumbling purblind idiot messing across your course! ... Every conceivable sort of silly creature that has ever been created has been sent to cross me.

"If I have much more of it, I shall go wild—I shall start mowing 'em.

"As it is, they've made things a thousand times more difficult."

"No doubt it's exasperating," said Kemp, drily.

"But now," said Kemp, with a side glance out of the window, "what are we to do?"

He moved nearer his guest as he spoke in such a manner as to prevent the possibility of a sudden glimpse of the three men who were advancing up the hill road—with an intolerable slowness, as it seemed to Kemp.

"What were you planning to do when you were heading for Port Burdock? *Had* you any plan?"

"I was going to clear out of the country. But I have altered that plan rather since seeing you. I thought it would be wise, now the weather is hot and invisibility possible, to make for the South. Especially as my secret was known, and everyone would be on the lookout for a masked and muffled man."

"That's clear."

"And then the filthy brute must needs try and rob me! He *has* hidden my books, Kemp. Hidden my books! If I can lay my hands on him!"

"Best plan to get the books out of him first."

"But where is he? Do you know?"

"He's in the town police station, locked up, by his own request, in the strongest cell in the place."

"Curse!" said the Invisible Man.

"But that hangs up your plans a little."

"We must get those books—those books are vital."

"Certainly," said Kemp, a little nervously, wondering if he heard footsteps outside. "Certainly we must get those books. But that won't be difficult, if he doesn't know they're for you."

"No," said the Invisible Man, and thought.

Kemp tried to think of something to keep the talk going, but the Invisible Man resumed of his own accord.

"Blundering into your house, Kemp," he said, "changes all my plans. For you are a man that can understand. In spite of all that has happened, in spite of this publicity, of the loss of my books, of what I have suffered, there still remain great possibilities, huge possibilities—"

"You have told no one I am here?" he asked abruptly.

Kemp hesitated. "That was implied," he said.

"No one?" insisted Griffin.

"Not a soul."

"Ah! Now—" The Invisible Man stood up, and sticking his arms akimbo began to pace the study.

"I made a mistake, Kemp, a huge mistake, in carrying this thing through alone. I have wasted strength, time, opportunities. Alone—it is surprising how little a man can do alone! To rob a little, to hurt a little, and there is the end.

"What I want, Kemp, is a goal-keeper, a helper, and a hiding-place, an arrangement whereby I can sleep and eat and rest in peace, and unsuspected. I must have an ally. With an ally, with food and rest—a thousand things are possible.

"Hitherto I have gone on vague lines. We have to consider all that invisibility means, all that it does not mean. It means little advantage for eavesdropping and so forth—one makes sounds. It's of little help—a little help perhaps—in housebreaking and so forth. Once you've caught me you could easily imprison me. But on the other hand I am hard to catch. This invisibility, in fact, is only good in two cases: It's useful in getting away, it's useful in approaching. It's particularly useful, therefore, in killing. I can walk round a man, whatever weapon he has, choose my point, strike as I like. Dodge as I like. Escape as I like."

Kemp's hand went to his moustache. Was that a movement downstairs?

"And it is killing we must do, Kemp."

"It is killing we must do," repeated Kemp. "I'm listening to your plan, Griffin, but I'm not agreeing, mind. *Why* killing?"

"Not wanton killing, but a judicious slaying. The point is, they know there is an Invisible Man—as well as we know there is an Invisible Man. And that Invisible Man, Kemp, must now establish a Reign of Terror. Yes, no doubt it's startling. But I mean it. A Reign of Terror. He must take some town like your Burdock and terrify and dominate it. He must issue his orders. He can do that in a thousand ways—scraps of paper thrust under doors would suffice. And all who disobey his orders he must kill, and kill all who would defend them."

"Hmm," said Kemp, no longer listening to Griffin but to the sound of his front door opening and closing.

"It seems to me, Griffin," he said, to cover his wandering attention, "that your ally would be in a difficult position."

"No one would know he was an ally," said the Invisible Man, eagerly. And then suddenly, "Hush! What's that downstairs?"

"Nothing," said Kemp, and suddenly began to speak loud and fast. "I don't agree to this, Griffin," he said. "Understand me, I don't agree to this. Why dream of playing a game against the race? How can you hope to gain happiness? Don't be a lone wolf. Publish your results. Take the world—take the nation at least—into your confidence. Think what you might do with a million helpers—"

The Invisible Man interrupted—arm extended. "There are footsteps coming upstairs," he said in a low voice, and advanced, arm extended, to the door.

And then things happened very swiftly. Kemp hesitated for a second and then moved to intercept him. The Invisible Man started and stood still. "Traitor!" cried the Voice, and suddenly the dressing-gown opened, and sitting down the Unseen began to disrobe. Kemp made three swift steps to the door, and forthwith the Invisible Man—his legs had vanished—sprang to his feet with a shout. Kemp flung the door open.

As it opened, there came a sound of hurrying feet downstairs and voices.

With a quick movement Kemp thrust the Invisible Man back, sprang aside, and slammed the door. The key was outside and ready. In another moment Griffin would have been alone in the belvedere study, a prisoner. Save for one little thing. The key had been slipped in hastily that morning. As Kemp slammed the door it fell noisily upon the carpet.

Kemp's face became white. He tried to grip the door handle with both hands. For a moment he stood lugging. Then the door gave six inches. But he got it closed again. The second time it was jerked a foot wide, and the dressing-gown came wedging itself into the opening. His throat was gripped by invisible fingers, and he left his hold on the handle to defend himself. He was forced back, tripped and pitched heavily into the corner of the landing. The empty dressing-gown was flung on the top of him.

Halfway up the staircase was Colonel Adye, the recipient of Kemp's letter, the chief of the Burdock police. He was staring aghast at the sudden appearance of Kemp, followed by the extraordinary sight of clothing tossing empty in the air. He saw Kemp felled, and struggling to his feet. He saw him rush forward, and go down again, felled like an ox.

Then suddenly he was struck violently. By nothing! A vast weight, it seemed, leapt upon him, and he was hurled headlong down the staircase, with a grip on his throat and a knee in his groin. An invisible foot trod on his back, a ghostly patter passed downstairs, he heard the two police officers in the hall shout and run, and the front door of the house slammed violently.

He rolled over and sat up staring. He saw, staggering down the staircase, Kemp, dusty and disheveled, one side of his face white from a blow, his lip bleeding, and a pink dressing-gown and some underclothing held in his arms.

"My God!" cried Kemp, "the game's up! He's gone!"

For a space Kemp was too inarticulate to make Adye understand the swift things that had just happened. They stood on the landing, Kemp speaking swiftly, the grotesque swathings of Griffin still on his arm. But presently Adye began to grasp something of the situation.

"He is mad," said Kemp, "inhuman. He is pure selfishness. He thinks of nothing but his own advantage, his own safety. I have listened to such a story this morning of brutal self-seeking.... He has wounded men. He will kill them unless we can prevent him. He will create a panic. Nothing can stop him. He is going out now—furious!"

"He must be caught," said Adye. "That is certain."

"But how?" cried Kemp, and suddenly became full of ideas. "You must begin at once. You must set every available man to work. You must prevent his leaving this district. Once he gets away, he may go through the countryside as he wills, killing and maiming. He dreams of a reign of terror! A reign of terror, I tell you. You must set a watch on trains and roads and shipping. The garrison must help. You must wire for help. The only thing that may keep him here is the thought of recovering some books of notes he counts of value. I will tell you of that! There is a man in your police station—Marvel...."

4.

The Invisible Man had rushed out of Kemp's house in a state of blind fury. A little child playing near Kemp's gateway was violently caught up and thrown aside, so that its ankle was broken, and thereafter for some hours the Invisible Man passed out of human perceptions. No one knew where he went nor what he did. But one can imagine him hurrying through the hot June forenoon, up the hill and on to the open downland behind Port Burdock, raging and despairing at his intolerable fate, and sheltering at last, heated and weary, amid the thickets of Hintondean, to piece together again his shattered schemes against his species, and there it was he re-asserted himself in a grimly tragical manner about two in the afternoon.

In the morning he had still been simply a legend, a terror. In the afternoon, by virtue chiefly of Kemp's drily worded proclamation, he was presented as a tangible antagonist, to be wounded, captured, or overcome, and the countryside began organizing itself with inconceivable rapidity. By two o'clock even he might still have removed himself out of the district by getting aboard a train, but after two that became impossible. Every passenger train along the lines on a great parallelogram between Southampton, Manchester, Brighton and Horsham, travelled with locked doors, and the goods traffic was almost entirely suspended. And in a great circle of twenty miles round Port Burdock, men armed with guns and bludgeons were presently setting out in groups of three and four, with dogs, to beat the roads and fields.

Mounted policemen rode along the country lanes, stopping at every cottage and warning the people to lock up their houses, and keep indoors unless they were armed, and all the elementary schools had broken up by three o'clock, and the children, scared and keeping together in groups, were hurrying home. Kemp's proclamation— signed indeed by Adye—was posted over almost the whole district by four or five o'clock in the afternoon. It gave briefly but clearly all the conditions of the struggle, the necessity of keeping the Invisible Man from food and sleep, the necessity for incessant watchfulness and for a prompt attention to any evidence of his movements. And so swift and decided was the action of the authorities, so prompt and universal was the belief in this strange being, that before nightfall an area of several hundred square miles was in a stringent state of siege.

The murder of Mr. Wicksteed occurred on the edge of a gravel pit, not two hundred yards from Lord Burdock's lodge gate. Everything points to a desperate struggle—the trampled ground, the numerous wounds Mr. Wicksteed received, his splintered walking-stick. But why the attack was made, save in a murderous frenzy, it is impossible to imagine. Indeed the theory of madness is almost unavoidable. Mr. Wicksteed was a man of forty-five or forty-six, steward to Lord Burdock, of inoffensive habits and appearance, the very last person in the world to provoke such a terrible antagonist. Against him it would seem the Invisible Man used an iron rod dragged from a broken piece of fence. He stopped this quiet man, going quietly home to his midday meal, attacked him, beat down his feeble defenses, broke his arm, felled him, and smashed his head to a jelly.

Of course, he must have dragged this rod out of the fencing before he met his victim—he must have been carrying it ready in his hand. Only two details beyond what has already been stated seem to bear on the matter. One is the circumstance that the gravel pit was not in Mr. Wicksteed's direct path home, but nearly a couple of hundred yards out of his way. The other is the assertion of a little girl to the effect that, going to her afternoon school, she saw the murdered man "trotting" in a peculiar manner across a field towards the gravel pit. Her pantomime of his action suggests a man pursuing something on the ground before him and striking at it ever and again with his walking-stick. She was the last person to see him alive. He passed out of her sight to his death, the struggle being hidden from her only by a clump of beech trees and a slight depression in the ground.

Now this, to the present writer's mind at least, lifts the murder out of the realm of the absolutely wanton. We may imagine that Griffin had taken the rod as a weapon indeed, but without any deliberate intention of using it in murder. Wicksteed may then have come by and noticed this rod inexplicably moving through the air. Without any thought of the Invisible Man—for Port Burdock is ten miles away—he may have pursued it. It is quite conceivable that he may not even have heard of the Invisible Man. One can then imagine the Invisible Man making off—quietly in order to avoid discovering his presence in the neighborhood, and Wicksteed, excited and curious, pursuing this unaccountably locomotive object—finally striking at it.

No doubt the Invisible Man could easily have distanced his middle-aged pursuer under ordinary circumstances, but the position in which Wicksteed's body was found suggests that he had the ill luck to drive his quarry into a corner between a drift of stinging nettles and the gravel pit. To those who appreciate the extraordinary irascibility of the Invisible Man, the rest of the encounter will be easy to imagine.

The abandonment of the rod by Griffin, suggests that in the emotional excitement of the affair, the purpose for which he took it—if he had a purpose—was abandoned. He was certainly an intensely egotistical and unfeeling man, but the sight of his victim, his first victim, bloody and pitiful at his feet, may have released some long pent fountain of remorse which for a time may have flooded whatever scheme of action he had contrived.

There is a story of a voice heard about sunset by a couple of men in a field near Fern Bottom. It was wailing and laughing, sobbing and groaning, and ever and again it shouted. It must have been queer hearing. It drove up across the middle of a clover field and died away towards the hills.

That afternoon the Invisible Man must have learnt something of the rapid use Kemp had made of his confidences. He must have found houses locked and secured. He may have loitered about railway stations and prowled about inns, and no doubt he read the proclamations and realized something of the nature of the campaign against him. And as the evening advanced, the fields became dotted here and there with groups of three or four men, and noisy with the yelping of dogs. These men-hunters had particular instructions in the case of an encounter as to the way they should support one another. But he avoided them all. We may understand something of his exasperation, and it could have been none the less because he himself had supplied the information that was being used so remorselessly against him. For that day at least he lost heart. For nearly twenty-four hours, save when he turned on Wicksteed, he was a hunted man. In the night, he must have eaten and slept, for in the morning he was himself again, active, powerful, angry, and malignant, prepared for his last great struggle against the world.

In pencil on a greasy sheet of paper Kemp found written a strange missive, postmarked Hintondean.

"You have been amazingly energetic and clever," this letter ran, "though what you stand to gain by it I cannot imagine. You are against me. For a whole day you have chased me. You have tried to rob me of a night's rest. But

I have had food in spite of you, I have slept in spite of you, and the game is only beginning. There is nothing for it, but to start the Terror. This announces the first day of the Terror. Port Burdock is no longer under the Queen, tell your Colonel of Police, and the rest of them, it is under me—the Terror! This is day one of year one of the new epoch—the Epoch of the Invisible Man. I am Invisible Man the First. To begin with the rule will be easy. The first day there will be one execution for the sake of example—a man named Kemp. Death starts for him today. He may lock himself away, hide himself away, get guards about him, put on armor if he likes—Death, the unseen Death, is coming. Help him not, my people, lest Death fall upon you also. Today Kemp is to die."

Kemp read this letter twice, "It's no hoax," he said. "That's his voice! And he means it."

He got up slowly, leaving his lunch unfinished—the letter had come by the one o'clock post—and went into his bedroom. From a locked drawer he took a little revolver, examined it carefully, and put it into the pocket of his lounge jacket. He wrote a number of brief notes, one to Colonel Adye, gave them to his servant to take, with explicit instructions as to her way of leaving the house. "There is no danger," he said, and added a mental reser-vation, "to you."

He went up to the belvedere, carefully shutting every door after him. "It's a game," he said, "an odd game—but the chances are all for me, Mr. Griffin, in spite of your invisibility. Griffin *contra mundum* ... with a vengeance."

Something rapped smartly against the brickwork over the frame, and made him start violently back.

"I'm getting nervous," said Kemp. But it was five minutes before he went to the window again. "It must have been a sparrow," he said.

Presently he heard the front doorbell ringing, and hurried downstairs. He unbolted and unlocked the door, examined the chain, put it up, and opened cautiously without showing himself. A familiar voice hailed him. It was Adye.

"Your servant's been assaulted, Kemp," he said round the door.

"What!" exclaimed Kemp.

"Had that note of yours taken away from her. He's close about here. Let me in."

Kemp released the chain, and Adye entered through as narrow an opening as possible. He stood in the hall, looking with infinite relief at Kemp refastening the door. "Note was snatched out of her hand. Scared her horribly. She's down at the station. Hysterics. He's close here. What was it about?"

Kemp swore.

"What a fool I was," said Kemp. "I might have known. It's not an hour's walk from Hintondean. Already?"

"What's up?" said Adye.

"Look here!" said Kemp, and led the way into his study. He handed Adye the Invisible Man's letter. Adye read it and whistled softly. "And you—?" said Adye.

"Proposed a trap—like a fool," said Kemp, "and sent my proposal out by a maid servant. To him."

Adye followed Kemp's profanity.

"He'll clear out," said Adye.

"Not he," said Kemp.

A resounding smash of glass came from upstairs. Adye had a silvery glimpse of a little revolver half out of Kemp's pocket. "It's a window, upstairs!" said Kemp, and led the way up. There came a second smash while they were still on the staircase. When they reached the study they found two of the three windows smashed, half the room littered with splintered glass, and one big flint lying on the writing table. Kemp swore again, and as he did so the third window went with a snap like a pistol, hung starred for a moment, and collapsed in jagged, shivering triangles into the room.

Smash, and then whack of boards hit hard came from downstairs. "Confound him!" said Kemp. "That must be—yes—it's one of the bedrooms. He's going to do all the house. But he's a fool. The shutters are up, and the glass will fall outside. He'll cut his feet."

Another window proclaimed its destruction. The two men stood on the landing perplexed. "I have it!" said Adye. "Let me have a stick or something, and I'll go down to the station and get the bloodhounds put on. That ought to settle him! They're hard by—not ten minutes—"

Another window went the way of its fellows.

"You haven't a revolver?" asked Adye.

Kemp's hand went to his pocket. Then he hesitated. "I haven't one—at least to spare."

"I'll bring it back," said Adye, "you'll be safe here."

Kemp, ashamed of his momentary lapse from truthfulness, handed him the weapon.

"Now for the door," said Adye.

As they stood hesitating in the hall, they heard one of the first-floor bedroom windows crack and clash. Kemp went to the door and began to slip the bolts as silently as possible. His face was a little paler than usual. "You must step straight out," said Kemp. In another moment Adye was on the doorstep and the bolts were dropping back into the staples. He hesitated for a moment, feeling more comfortable with his back against the door. Then he marched, upright and square, down the steps. He crossed the lawn and approached the gate. A little breeze seemed to ripple over the grass. Something moved near him. "Stop a bit," said a Voice, and Adye stopped dead and his hand tightened on the revolver.

"Well?" said Adye, white and grim, and every nerve tense.

"Oblige me by going back to the house," said the Voice, as tense and grim as Adye's.

"Sorry," said Adye a little hoarsely, and moistened his lips with his tongue. The Voice was on his left front, he thought. Suppose he were to take his luck with a shot?

"What are you going for?" said the Voice, and there was a quick movement of the two, and a flash of sunlight from the open lip of Adye's pocket.

Adye desisted and thought. "Where I go," he said slowly, "is my own business." The words were still on his lips, when an arm came round his neck, his back felt a knee, and he was sprawling backward. He drew clumsily and fired absurdly, and in another moment he was struck in the mouth and the revolver wrested from his grip. He made a vain clutch at a slippery limb, tried to struggle up and fell back. "Damn!" said Adye. The Voice laughed. "I'd kill you now if it wasn't the waste of a bullet," it said. He saw the revolver in mid-air, six feet off, covering him.

"Well?" said Adye, sitting up.

"Get up," said the Voice.

Adye stood up.

"Attention," said the Voice, and then fiercely, "Don't try any games. Remember I can see your face if you can't see mine. You've got to go back to the house."

"He won't let me in," said Adye.

"That's a pity," said the Invisible Man. "I've got no quarrel with you."

Adye moistened his lips again. He glanced away from the barrel of the revolver and saw the sea far off very blue and dark under the midday sun, the smooth green down, the white cliff of the Head, and the multitudinous town, and suddenly he knew that life was very sweet. His eyes came back to this little metal thing hanging between heaven and earth, six yards away. "What am I to do?" he said sullenly.

"What am *I* to do?" asked the Invisible Man. "You will get help. The only thing is for you to go back."

"I will try. If he lets me in will you promise not to rush the door?"

"I've got no quarrel with you," said the Voice.

Kemp had hurried upstairs after letting Adye out, and now crouching among the broken glass and peering cautiously over the edge of the study window sill, he saw Adye stand parleying with the Unseen. "Why doesn't he fire?" whispered Kemp to himself. Then the revolver moved a little and the glint of the sunlight flashed in Kemp's eyes.

Adye turned towards the house, walking slowly with his hands behind him. Kemp watched him—puzzled. The revolver vanished, flashed again into sight, and vanished again. Adye's decision seemed suddenly made. He leapt backwards, swung around, clutched at this little object, missed it, threw up his hands and fell forward on his face, leaving a little puff of blue in the air. Kemp did not hear the sound of the shot. Adye writhed, raised himself on one arm, fell forward, and lay still.

For a space Kemp remained staring at the quiet carelessness of Adye's attitude. The afternoon was very hot and still, nothing seemed stirring in all the world save a couple of yellow butterflies chasing each other through the shrubbery between the house and the road gate. Adye lay on the lawn near the gate.

Then came a ringing and knocking at the front door, that grew at last tumultuous, but pursuant to Kemp's instructions the servants had locked themselves into their rooms. This was followed by a silence. Kemp sat listening and then began peering cautiously out of the three windows, one after another. He went to the staircase head and stood listening uneasily. He armed himself with his bedroom poker, and went to examine the interior fastenings of the ground-floor windows again. Everything was safe and quiet. He returned to the belvedere. Adye lay motionless over the edge of the gravel just as he had fallen. Coming along the road by the villas were the housemaid and two policemen.

Everything was deadly still. The three people seemed very slow in approaching. He wondered what his antagonist was doing.

He started. There was a smash from below. He hesitated and went downstairs again. Suddenly the house resounded with heavy blows and the splintering of wood. He heard a smash and the destructive clang of the iron fastenings of the shutters. He turned the key and opened the kitchen door. As he did so, the shutters, split and splintering, came flying inward. He stood aghast. The shutters had been driven in with an axe, and now the axe was descending in sweeping blows upon the window frame and the iron bars defending it. He heard Griffin shouting and laughing. Then the blows of the axe with its splitting and smashing consequences, were resumed.

Kemp stood in the passage trying to think. In a moment the Invisible Man would be in the kitchen. This door would not keep him a moment, and then—

A ringing came at the front door again. It would be the policemen. He ran into the hall, put up the chain, and drew the bolts. He made the girl speak before he dropped the chain, and the three people blundered into the house in a heap, and Kemp slammed the door again.

"The Invisible Man!" said Kemp. "He has a revolver, with two shots—left. He's killed Adye.

Suddenly the house was full of the Invisible Man's resounding blows and they heard the kitchen door give.

"This way," said Kemp, starting into activity, and bundled the policemen into the dining-room doorway.

"Poker," said Kemp, and rushed to the fender. He handed the poker he had carried to the policeman and the dining-room one to the other. He suddenly flung himself backward.

"Whup!" said one policeman, ducked, and caught the axe on his poker. The pistol snapped its penultimate shot and ripped a valuable Sidney Cooper. The second policeman brought his poker down on the little weapon, as one might knock down a wasp, and sent it rattling to the floor.

At the first clash the girl screamed, stood screaming for a moment by the fireplace, and then ran to open the shutters—possibly with an idea of escaping by the shattered window.

The axe receded into the passage, and fell to a position about two feet from the ground. They could hear the Invisible Man breathing. "Stand away, you two," he said. "I want that man Kemp."

"We want you," said the first policeman, making a quick step forward and wiping with his poker at the Voice.

The Invisible Man must have started back, and he blundered into the umbrella stand.

Then, as the policeman staggered with the swing of the blow he had aimed, the Invisible Man countered with the axe, the helmet crumpled like paper, and the blow sent the man spinning to the floor at the head of the kitchen stairs. But the second policeman, aiming behind the axe with his poker, hit something soft that snapped. There was a sharp exclamation of pain and then the axe fell to the ground. The policeman wiped again at vacancy and hit nothing. He put his foot on the axe, and struck again. Then he stood, poker raised, listening intent for the slightest movement.

"Where is he?" asked the man on the floor. blood running down between his eye and ear.

"Don't know. I've hit him. He's standing somewhere in the hall. Unless he's slipped past you."

The dining-room window was wide open, and neither housemaid nor Kemp was to be seen.

Mr. Heelas, Mr. Kemp's nearest neighbor was one of the sturdy minority who refused to believe "in all this nonsense" about an Invisible Man.

He was taking and afternoon nap in the parlor in accordance with the custom of years, when he woke up suddenly with a curious persuasion of something wrong. Raising his head, he looked across at Kemp's house, rubbed his eyes and looked again. Then he put his feet to the floor, and sat listening. He said he was damned, but the house looked as though it had been deserted for weeks—after a violent riot. Every window was broken, and every window, save those of the belvedere study, was blinded by the internal shutters.

"I could have sworn it was all right"—he looked at his watch—"twenty minutes ago."

He became aware of a measured concussion and the clash of glass, far away in the distance. And then, as he sat open-mouthed, came a still more wonderful thing. The shutters of the drawing-room window were flung open violently, and the housemaid in her outdoor hat and garments was struggling out. She pitched forward and vanished among the shrubs. Mr. Heelas stood up, exclaiming vaguely, and saw Kemp stand on the sill, spring from the window, and reappear almost instantaneously running along a path in the shrubbery and stooping as he ran, like a man who evades observation. He vanished behind a laburnum, and appeared again clambering over a fence that abutted on the open down.

"Lord!" cried Mr. Heelas, struck with an idea, "it's that Invisible Man brute! It's right, after all!"

There was a slamming of doors, a ringing of bells, and the voice of Mr. Heelas bellowing like a bull. "Shut the doors, shut the windows, shut everything!—the Invisible Man is coming!" Instantly the house was full of screams and directions, and scurrying feet. He ran himself to shut the French windows that opened on the veranda. As he did so Kemp's head and shoulders and knee appeared over the edge of the garden fence. In another moment Kemp had ploughed through the asparagus, and was running across the tennis lawn to the house.

"You can't come in," said Mr. Heelas, shutting the bolts. "I'm very sorry if he's after you, but you can't come in!"

Kemp appeared with a face of terror close to the glass, rapping and then shaking frantically at the French window. Then, seeing his efforts were useless, he ran along the veranda, vaulted the end, and went round by the side gate to the front of the house, and so into the hill-road. And Mr.

Heelas staring from his window—a face of horror—had scarcely witnessed Kemp vanish, ere the asparagus was being trampled this way and that by feet unseen. At that Mr. Heelas fled precipitately upstairs, and the rest of the chase is beyond his purview. But as he passed the staircase window, he heard the side gate slam.

Emerging into the hill-road, Kemp naturally took the downward direction, and so it was he came to run in his own person the very race he had watched with such a critical eye from the belvedere study only four days ago. He ran it well, for a man out of training, and though his face was white and wet, his wits were cool to the last. He ran with wide strides, and wherever a patch of rough ground intervened, wherever there came a patch of raw flints, or a bit of broken glass shone dazzling, he crossed it and left the bare invisible feet that followed to take what line they would.

For the first time in his life Kemp discovered that the hill-road was indescribably vast and desolate, and that the beginnings of the town far below at the hill foot were strangely remote. Never had there been a slower or more painful method of progression than running. Was that footsteps he heard behind him? Spurt.

His breath was beginning to saw in his throat. The tram was quite near now, and the "Jolly Cricketers" was noisily barring its doors. Beyond the tram were posts and heaps of gravel—the drainage works. Further on the astonished features of the workmen appeared above the mounds of gravel.

His pace broke a little, and then he heard the swift pad of his pursuer, and leapt forward again. "The Invisible Man!" he cried to the workers, with a vague indicative gesture, and by an inspiration leapt the excavation and placed a burly group between him and the chase.

He became aware of a tumultuous vociferation and running people. He glanced up the street towards the hill. Hardly a dozen yards off ran a huge laborer, cursing in fragments and slashing viciously with a spade, and hard behind him came the tram conductor with his fists clenched. Up the street others followed these two, striking and shouting. Down towards the town, men and women were running, and he noticed clearly one man coming out of a shop-door with a stick in his hand. "Spread out! Spread out!" cried someone. Kemp suddenly grasped the altered condition of the chase. He stopped, and looked round, panting. "He's close here!" he cried. "Form a line across—"

He was hit hard under the ear, and went reeling, trying to face round towards his unseen antagonist. He just managed to keep his feet, and he struck a vain counter in the air. Then he was hit again under the jaw, and sprawled headlong on the ground. In another moment a knee compressed his diaphragm, and a couple of eager hands gripped his throat, but the grip of one was weaker than the other. He grasped the wrists, heard a cry of pain from his assailant, and then the spade of the workman came whirling through the air above him, and struck something with a dull thud. He felt a drop of moisture on his face. The grip at his throat suddenly relaxed, and with a convulsive effort, Kemp loosed himself, grasped a limp shoulder, and rolled uppermost. He gripped the unseen elbows near the ground. "I've got him!" screamed Kemp. "Help! Help—hold! He's down! Hold his feet!"

In another second there was a simultaneous rush upon the struggle, and a stranger coming into the road suddenly might have thought an exceptionally savage game of Rugby football was in progress. And there was no shouting after Kemp's cry—only a sound of blows and feet and heavy breathing.

Then came a mighty effort, and the Invisible Man threw off a couple of his antagonists and rose to his knees. Kemp clung to him in front like a hound to a stag, and a dozen hands gripped, clutched, and tore at the Unseen. The tram conductor suddenly got the neck and shoulders and lugged him back.

Down went the heap of struggling men again and rolled over. There was, I am afraid, some savage kicking. Then suddenly a wild scream of "Mercy! Mercy!" that died down swiftly to a sound like choking.

"Get back, you fools!" cried the muffled voice of Kemp, and there was a vigorous shoving back of stalwart forms. "He's hurt, I tell you. Stand back!"

There was a brief struggle to clear a space, and then the circle of eager faces saw the doctor kneeling, as it seemed, fifteen inches in the air, and holding invisible arms to the ground. Behind him a constable gripped invisible ankles.

"Don't you leave go of en," cried the big workman, holding a blood-stained spade, "he's shamming."

"He's not shamming," said the doctor, cautiously raising his knee. His face was bruised and already going red. He spoke thickly because of a bleeding lip.

He stood up abruptly and then knelt down on the ground by the side of the thing unseen. There was a pushing and shuffling, a sound of heavy feet as fresh people turned up to increase the pressure of the crowd. People now were coming out of the houses. The doors of the "Jolly Cricketers" stood suddenly wide open. Very little was said.

Kemp felt about, his hand seeming to pass through empty air. "He's not breathing," he said, and then, "I can't feel his heart. His side—ugh!"

Suddenly an old woman, peering under the arm of the big laborer, screamed sharply. "Looky there!" she said, and thrust out a wrinkled finger.

And looking where she pointed, everyone saw, faint and transparent as though it was made of glass, so that veins and arteries and bones and nerves could be distinguished, the outline of a hand, a hand limp and prone. It grew clouded and opaque even as they stared.

"Hullo!" cried the constable. "Here's his feet a-showing!"

And so, slowly, beginning at his hands and feet and creeping along his limbs to the vital centers of his body, that strange change continued. It was like the slow spreading of a poison. First came the little white nerves, a hazy grey sketch of a limb, then the glassy bones and intricate arteries, then the flesh and skin, first a faint fogginess, and then growing rapidly dense and opaque. Presently they could see his crushed chest and his shoulders, and the dim outline of his drawn and battered features.

When at last the crowd made way for Kemp to stand erect, there lay, naked and pitiful on the ground, the bruised and broken body of a young man about thirty. His hair and brow were white—not grey with age, but white with the whiteness of albinism—and his eyes were like garnets. His hands were clenched, his eyes wide open, and his expression was one of anger and dismay.

"Cover his face!" said a man. "For Gawd's sake, cover that face!" and three little children, pushing forward through the crowd, were suddenly twisted round and sent packing off again.

Someone brought a sheet from the "Jolly Cricketers," and having covered him, they carried him into that house. And there it was, on a shabby bed in a tawdry, ill-lighted bedroom, surrounded by a crowd of ignorant and excited people, broken and wounded, betrayed and unpitied, that Griffin, the first of all men to make himself invisible, Griffin, the most gifted physicist the world has ever seen, ended in infinite disaster his strange and terrible career.

So ends the story of the strange and evil experiments of the Invisible Man. And if you would learn more of him you must go to a little inn near Port Stowe and seek out the landlord, a short and corpulent little man with a nose of cylindrical proportions, wiry hair, and a sporadic rosiness of visage.

He is a bachelor man—his tastes were ever bachelor, and there are no women folk in the house. Outwardly he buttons—it is expected of him—but in his more vital privacies, in the matter of braces for example, he still turns to string. He conducts his house without enterprise, but with eminent decorum. His movements are slow, and he is a great thinker. But he has a reputation for wisdom and for a respectable parsimony in the village, and his knowledge of the roads of the South of England would beat Cobbett.

And on Sunday mornings, every Sunday morning, all the year round, while he is closed to the outer world, and every night after ten, he goes into his bar parlor, bearing a glass of gin faintly tinged with water, and having placed this down, he locks the door and examines the blinds, and even looks under the table. And then, being satisfied of his solitude, he unlocks the cupboard and a box in the cupboard and a drawer in that box, and produces three volumes bound in brown leather, and places them solemnly in the middle of the table. The covers are weather-worn and tinged with an algal green—for once they sojourned in a ditch and some of the pages have been washed blank by dirty water. The landlord sits down in an armchair, fills a long clay pipe slowly—gloating over the books the while. Then he pulls one towards him and opens it, and begins to study it—turning over the leaves backwards and forwards.

His brows are knit and his lips move painfully. "Hex, little two up in the air, cross and a fiddle-de-dee. Lord! what a one he was for intellect!"

Presently he relaxes and leans back, and blinks through his smoke across the room at things invisible to other eyes. "Full of secrets," he says. "Wonderful secrets!"

"Once I get the haul of them—*Lord*!"

"I wouldn't do what *he* did. I'd just—well!" He pulls at his pipe.

THE END

Made in the USA
San Bernardino, CA
27 July 2014